NAKED DEATH

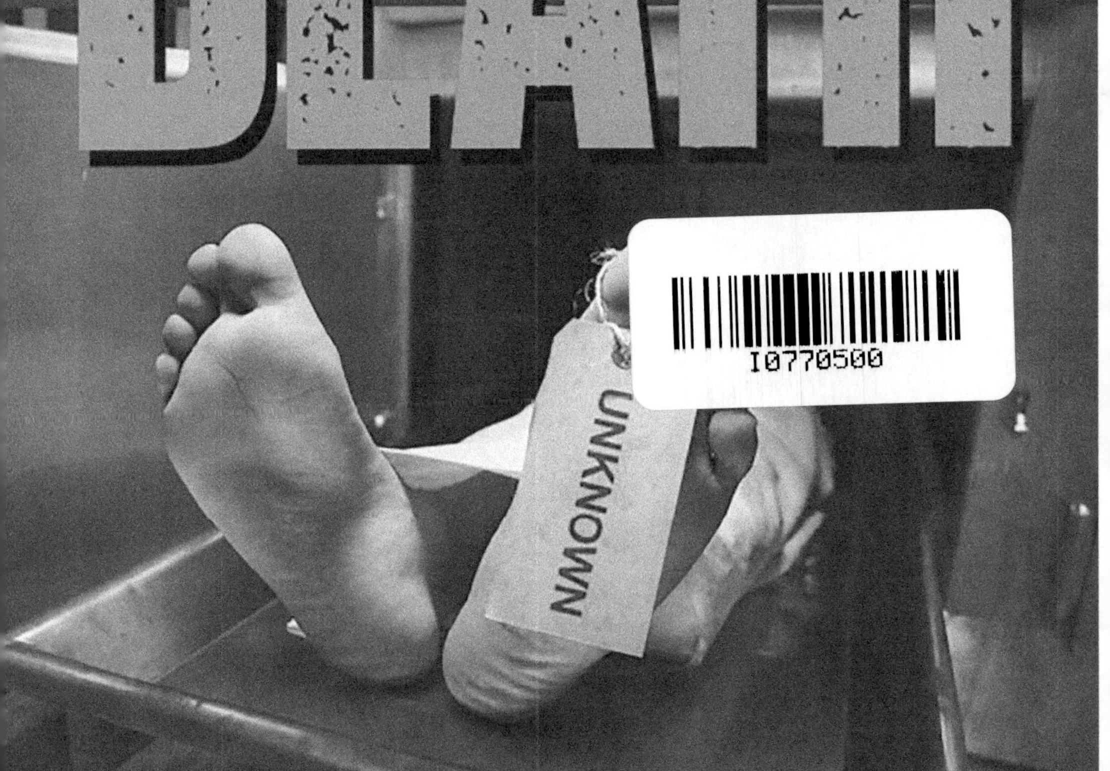

G.L. BARBOUR

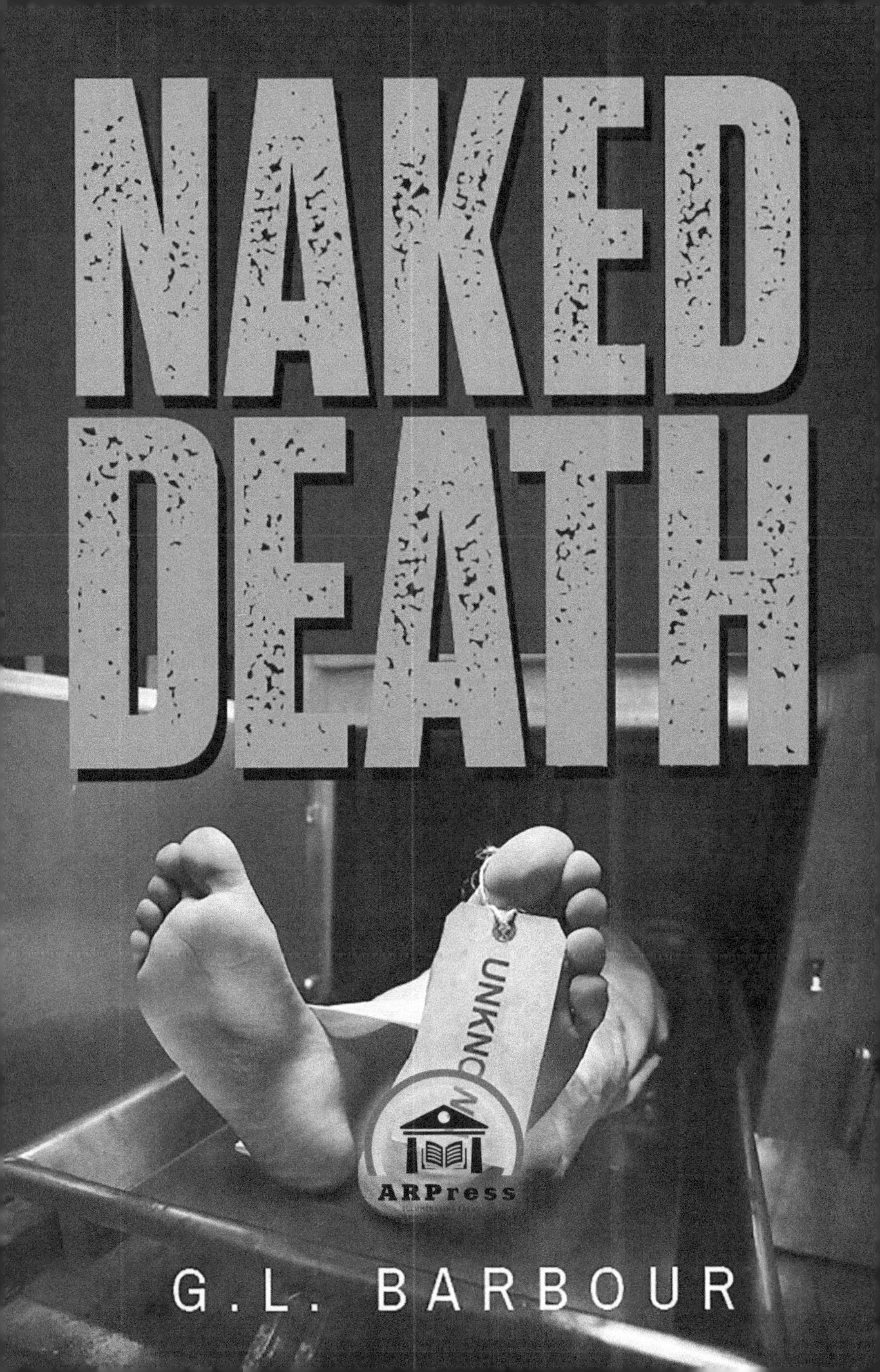

NAKED DEATH

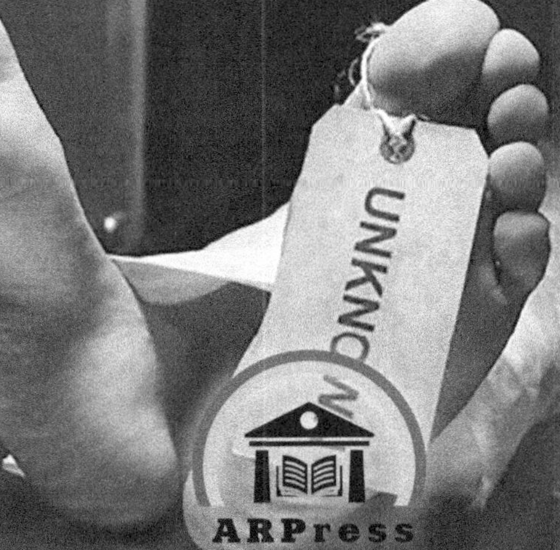

G.L. BARBOUR

Copyright © 2023 by G.L. Barbour

All rights reserved. No part of this publication may be reproduced, distributed, or transmitted in any form or by any means, including photocopying, recording, or other electronic or mechanical methods, without the prior written permission of the copyright owner and the publisher, except in the case of brief quotations embodied in critical reviews and certain other noncommercial uses permitted by copyright law. For permission requests, write to the publisher, addressed "Attention: Permissions Coordinator," at the address below.

ARPress LLC
45 Dan Road Suite 5
Canton MA 02021
Hotline: 1(888) 821-0229
Fax: 1(508) 545-7580

Ordering Information:
Quantity sales. Special discounts are available on quantity purchases by corporations, associations, and others. For details, contact the publisher at the address above.

Printed in the United States of America.

ISBN-13:   Softcover   979-8-89356-524-9
           Hardcover   979-8-89356-525-6
           eBook   979-8-89356-526-3

Library of Congress Control Number: 2024902494

Other Books by G. L. Barbour

Academic

Quality in the Veterans Health Administration

Redefining a Public Health System

Fiction

The Ron Looney Series 

Death Unexpected

One, Two, Three Times a Murder

A Twisted Death

A Researched Death

Alibi for Death

Other

Montana in the Rearview Mirror

Contents

PROLOGUE

As usual, this soon after quitting time, the bar was not yet full. Two of the customers were at the bar when the man entered, and they paid him little attention. They were sitting two stools apart, socially distanced and occupied with their own thoughts; one reading the sports page, the other looking at his phone. At the rear, on the right, a gray haired couple sat in a booth across from each other. One of the pool tables was occupied; a pair of roughnecks in checkered flannel shirts was playing for money. The juke box was playing softly and the only person to notice the man's entrance was the barmaid.

He was dressed differently from the bar's usual patrons. They wore denim pants with flannel shirts; he was wearing a suit. Most of them were hefty men, and he was thin. He seemed clearly out of his element in the bar and stood just inside the door and looked around uncertainly before cautiously moving to the bar. He was reminded of the protagonist's entrance in the Shooting of Dan McGrew "fresh from the creeks and loaded for bear'. Except that he didn't feel 'loaded for bear'.

The woman behind the bar glanced up and smiled, "Whatcha have, honey?"

"Uh, maybe a beer?"

"Draft or bottle?"

"Draft, I guess."

"Good call," she said and reached for a mug. The man in the suit looked around the bar noting empty booths and stools and smiled nervously at her.

"You looking for somebody, honey?" she asked while pulling his beer.

"Ah, yes. To meet here. I, ah, appear to be early."

"Well, take your beer and go sit in that booth right there," she said motioning to the left side of the establishment. "You can see anybody who comes in."

"Thanks," he said, carefully picking up the filled mug and carrying it with both hands like it might contain explosives. He looked at the booth and placed himself in the back corner where he could watch the door. He found a coaster that read, "Friends don't let Friends go Thirsty" in a small stand at the back of the booth. He put his beer on the coaster and rubbed his hands on his pants. The barmaid went back to her work.

The man sat in the booth and looked at the mug in front of him for a few minutes. He looked up every time the door opened with fading hope in his eyes. At last, he lifted the mug with both hands and took a deep sip of the golden liquid. As he sat the mug down, he realized he had gotten suds on his nose and began searching his pockets for his handkerchief. He found it, wiped his nose, and then decided to clean his glasses as well.

A moment later, he looked up to find a man standing beside the booth holding a mug of beer. This man was of a size like others in the bar. He wore heavy khaki pants, work boots, and a long-sleeve denim shirt.

"Oh, hey," the man in the booth said. "I didn't see you …"

"No names, okay?" the other man said, as he sat down across from the man in the suit. "Never know who might be listening. No proper nouns."

The man in the suit thought for a brief second and then nodded his agreement. "Are we in trouble?"

"I don't think so, but let's not start anything. You can never tell who is listening to a conversation in a bar."

"All right." He took another two-handed sip of beer, this time avoiding the foam on the nose.

"I just think we should agree on what we have found so far," said the newcomer, sipping from his drink as well.

"Okay."

"I told you that number you gave me didn't work and there's no website either."

"Yes, I remember. I checked the number against the invoice. It's accurate. But I also found there's no street address on the invoice either."

"Now that's really strange, right?" The larger man lifted his mug and drank. "You said you found something else that's odd?"

"Well, I also found some additional invoices from, ah, that company for some other jobs, too."

"What do you mean, 'other jobs'?"

"Other than the one we were initially talking about."

"So, this isn't the only time!"

"It seems so. There were several other jobs. Over several years. And that's not the only odd thing about it."

"Really? This is getting deep."

The man in the suit seemed uneasy about that remark and looked over his shoulder and around the bar before adding, "All the invoices are for the exact same dollar amount. Every time, every month, no matter what the job."

"All right, now. That is very suspicious. Who are these guys?"

The man in the suit eyed the surroundings again and leaned across the table to whisper, " I think I know."

"Tell me."

"I looked the company up in Zippia to see …"

"What's that?"

"A listing of jobs. Anyway, the company is listed but without contact information. And they aren't advertising for workers, either. So, I called a friend at Dun and Bradstreet. There is no listing for that company!"

"And that's important, why?"

"If a company isn't listed with Dun and Bradstreet, it means it doesn't really do business and has no credit history."

"Wait a minute. You're saying these guys aren't even real? If that's true you have turned over a big rock."

The man in the suit sat up a little straighter and said, "That's not all. It would be hard for them to operate here in Ohio without some cover. So, I called the Secretary of State in Columbus."

"Should I know what that was about?"

"I don't know. The reason I called was to determine whether the …uh, company, was operating legally."

"Okay, then. What did you find?"

"I got the incorporation information."

The larger man said, "I wouldn't have thought of that. What'd those documents show?"

The man sat up straighter in his seat, leaned forward and spoke softly, "Three incorporators. A lawyer, now retired, a woman, and a man.

"Okay. I don't know what that means."

"Well, the man turns out to be her son."

"Tight group."

"Yeah. Wait till you hear who her husband is."

CHAPTER 1

THURSDAY, APRIL 1

The ambulance lights and siren were going full blast as it pulled up to the scene of the accident. The two EMTs leaped out of the vehicle and quickly ran to the hit-and-run victim on the sidewalk. Their quick assessment indicated that his injuries were not life-threatening, so they slowed into their assessment of damage and shifted to preparation for transport.

The lead EMT spoke to the man lying on the sidewalk, "Sir, can you tell me your name?"

"Yeah. It's Harry," he muttered through clenched teeth.

"All right, Harry. We're going to check you over and get you to the hospital right away."

"No, no. I think I'm okay. He didn't really hit me."

"What do you mean?"

"I mean that SOB turned the corner and came directly at me. I had just stepped off the curb, and I jumped back. I think I landed on that spare tire thing." He pointed at the CRV parked at the curb near where he was lying.

"Okay, but I still want to check you out."

"Not necessary, really. I'll be fine."

"Sir. Just let us do our job. Are you hurt? Do you have pain anywhere?"

"Kinda, over here," he indicated his lower rib cage on the right.

The EMT insisted he remain lying down and checked his blood pressure and listened to his lungs. "Good breath sounds," he said to his partner. "Pressure is a little high."

"Better than low," was the response.

"Is this tender, sir?" the EMT asked as he pressed on the rib cage.

"UHmmph," Harry grimaced and pulled away.

"I'll take that as a Yes. I think you have some broken ribs in there. You need to get that checked out at the hospital."

Harry briefly nodded.

The two EMTs finished their assessment and pulled out the gurney to transfer the man to the ambulance.

"Hey, I can walk," Harry protested.

"Sir, we want you to lie down. We will get you to the hospital. You probably have a broken rib, and we don't want you moving around if you don't have to. That's dangerous with a broken rib."

Harry tried to sit up, and the effort caused him to wince and stop his movement. The EMT looked at him and extended a hand to help.

"Yeah, okay," he agreed as they helped him to move over and then lie down on the gurney. The EMTs elevated the carrier and rolled him to the rear of the ambulance. They opened the doors and slid the collapsing legs into the back of the vehicle, causing another wince from Harry. The junior EMT climbed in and was about to close the door when a uniformed policeman stopped him and asked, "Can I get a quick picture of what happened?"

"Ah, sure. He's stable. We can take a minute."

The officer stepped up on the back bumper so he could see Harry, "Sir, I'm officer Noble. What's your name?"

"Harry," said the man on the stretcher as he faced the ceiling of the vehicle.

"Harry what, sir?"

"Just Harry. Okay?'

"Can you tell me what happened here?"

"Sure. I was walking and started to cross the street, but I saw this car start to turn the corner behind me. I stopped to let the car pass, but I was already in the street a couple of feet. I think the driver cut sharply in his turn and almost hit me."

"You were not hit?"

"Maybe he brushed me. No, he didn't get me. I jumped out of the way and landed on the spare tire holder of that car." He pointed to the CRV at the intersection.

The policeman looked at the EMT, who said, "Best we can tell, he broke some ribs and got a nasty abrasion on his left elbow. Pressure is fine, and we don't suspect internal injuries."

"Sir, can you describe the car?"

"I only got a glimpse. Dark color. Sedan, I think."

"Did you see the driver?"

"No. I was paying more attention to getting out of the way."

"Very reasonable, sir." He turned to the EMT and said, "Thanks."

As the policeman backed away, the EMT closed the door, and the ambulance pulled away and headed for the emergency entrance of New City Hospital.

The officer turned to his partner and said, "It's almost two in the morning. Nobody else on the street. No horn or crash sound to make anyone look out a window. We've got no witnesses and a description that fits almost every other car in Cincinnati."

His partner nodded and said, "Let's write up what we got and let it go. We didn't get here for maybe ten minutes after the accident, and we'll never find that car."

"Agreed."

They went back to their patrol car and got in.

The ambulance turned into the drive leading to the emergency entrance at New City without lights or siren. The driver had radioed ahead with their arrival time and information about their patient, so they were expected. As the vehicle came to a complete stop, the emergency area doors opened, and two orderlies and a nurse came out to meet them.

The EMTs dismounted and pulled their gurney from the rear of the ambulance. The orderlies assisted in opening the doors ahead of the movement of the gurney into the Emergency Department. The nurse walked beside the senior EMT while he gave her brief medical information. After passing through the entryway doors, the EMTs turned the gurney to the right and quickly wheeled it down a short hallway lined with examination rooms. When they arrived at the designated room, they wheeled their gurney in parallel to the bed in the room. Then the orderlies and the EMTs shifted Harry to the bed in the room and quickly disappeared, taking the Ambulance gurney with them. The nurse remained in the room and started her assessment.

"And what's your name?"

"Harry."

"Hello, Harry. I'm Annie. I'll be taking care of you while you're here. Can you tell me what happened?"

"Yeah. I almost got hit by a car. I jumped outta the way and landed on one of those spare tire cases on the back of an SUV. Those ambulance guys think I broke a rib."

"I see. They are often right about things like that. Where does that hurt?"

"Down here," again he indicated his lower rib cage on the right.

She put her hand on the area and gently pressed. Harry jerked away and said, "Hey!"

"I'm sorry," she said. "I agree. That's tender enough to suggest that you do have a fracture. The doctor will probably order some x-rays. How about the rest of you? Are you hurt anywhere else?" Her calm voice, the apology, and her concern calmed Harry.

"Uh, yeah, I think I scraped my elbow here," he said, pulling up his sleeve and showing her a deep abrasion on the left forearm and elbow. The shirt sleeve was torn and bloodied and spotted with road surfacing material.

"That's pretty nasty. Just a minute and I'll get that cleaned up for you. Can you move your arm?"

Harry responded to the question by flexing and rotating his forearm.

'Uh-huh," she said, pressing on various parts of his arm. "Well, we will x-ray that, too. Just to make sure there's no break in there. Anything else?'

"No. I guess I was lucky."

"I guess so, too. How were you able to get out of the way?"

"Reflex, I guess. I don't even remember seeing the car. I guess I just sensed it and reacted by turning and jumping back out of the way."

The nurse nodded and said, "Let's get you out of those clothes and into one of these beautiful hospital gowns."

"Do I have to?"

"Yes. We will want to check you over completely and you can't wear those clothes into radiology, anyway." Annie then helped him undress and get into a hospital gown as she took additional history. "Do you take any medications?"

"Not prescription ones. I take some Tylenol for aches and pains."

"Do you have any chronic illness?"

"Nope. Pretty healthy." He struggled to get the gown closed in the back, and she stepped behind him to tie it closed. She raised the head of the bed and helped him get his feet up on the bed. Then she placed a blood pressure cuff on his right arm and measured his pressure. She smiled at the completion and made a notation in the electronic medical record beside the bed. She put a clip on his right index fingertip and pushed a button on it.

"What's that thing? Harry asked.

"That is a pulse oximeter. It monitors the amount of oxygen in your blood." She looked at the digital readout, "And yours is perfectly fine."

She looked at him and smiled, "Are you comfortable? Would you like a warm blanket?"

Harry looked at his knees sticking out of the gown and said, "A warm blanket sounds right."

"I'll be right back," she said and disappeared out the door. She was back in less than a minute with a warm, fluffy blanket which she spread over Harry from the armpits down. "There," she said, "the doctor will be in a few minutes. Is there anything else you need before I leave?"

"I don't suppose I could get a cup of coffee," Harry asked dryly.

"I can get you some juice or a bottle of water," was the response.

Harry shook his head and lay back on the pillow.

"I'll be back to check on you in a few minutes, then," she said. I put the call button there by your hand. If you need anything, you just push the button, Okay?

Harry nodded and said, Okay."

"The doctor will be by shortly. I'm sure he will want to order some x-rays." She parted the curtains at the door and disappeared

"Thanks," Harry said. He welcomed the quiet after the nurse had left. He began to think how he was going to respond when they insisted on knowing his last name..

CHAPTER 2

FRIDAY, APRIL 2

Sam Mastone was the hospital director at New City. Part of his routine was the Morning Meeting at eight A.M. every weekday. Most hospital administrators have a similar meeting to be aware of whether significant events had occurred in the preceding 24 hours. Since becoming director of the hospital, he insisted that key players attend along with their executive assistants. Sam, a former personnel officer, tried to use the meeting to better understand the clinical aspects of hospital care. Unfortunately, Sam tended to do little learning during any discussion, often jumping to his conclusion early and then falling into his familiar pattern of micromanagement. This became a frequent happening since, like most major hospitals, the people at the morning meeting heard about few problems or issues of consequence. That left Sam feeling a need to discuss issues more than they required, or to bring up issues of his own.

Sam was renowned for his tendency to see all problems in black and white. There were very few gray areas in Human Resources; in his view, every problem should have a clear-cut response and solution. And, of course, Sam was not shy about outlining that solution in some depth. Unfortunately, however, the specific person he thought appropriate to address the problem was usually not at the table. And that was a recurring disappointment for Sam. That absence required him to give explicit directions to those present to ensure that the solution followed his prescription.

Tom Bolling was the chief of staff at New City and had been so for over five years. He was a retired brigadier general and orthopedic surgeon from the U.S. Air Force. He had been recruited specifically to New City Hospital to oversee and improve the academic affiliation with the South West Ohio Medical School also in Cincinnati. New City had a long presence in Cincinnati, beginning as the Railway Hospital and morphing into a for-profit healthcare deliverer in the Regents Health System over a space of several decades. The hospital was an amalgam – part reaching back to The War and part gleaming newness pushing patient care towers upward in the western sun. The original building, near the railroad, was red brick and narrow, only fifty feet wide. At five stories it was, in 1947, one of the tallest buildings in that part of the city. Located on a rail spur in the western part of town, it originally had been The Railway Hospital, and it provided inpatient care for railroad workers and their families. When the new University Hospital was completed in 1947, that modern building – one of the earliest to have air conditioning – was seen as the contemporary way to train medical students and residents. For several obvious reasons, the University Hospital became an immediate attraction for patients. Even though the recognized cure rate for most diseases was abysmally low, the national exuberance with the 'science' that ended the war began to be an attraction for patients. For some time, hospitals had been the place to go to die – primarily if you had no other place. But after 1945, that attitude began slowly to change. First, there was the 'marriage' between medical academia and the Veterans Administration that brought medical students and medical faculty into the nation's largest hospital system. Shortly after that, recognition of a shortage of hospital beds led to the construction of shiny new buildings with previously unattainable amenities. As a result of such changes in Cincinnati, the Railway Hospital census began steadily to fall as its intended pool of patients increasingly chose to go elsewhere for their care, and it looked for a time like the facility would have to close its doors.

The city decided to use available federal funds to upgrade the facility in the early 1950s with new construction and greater inpatient care capability. But the new attached building was flat and dull in appearance and did not attract either physicians or patients. Further, a comparison of their quality care with the University Hospital and the Veterans Administration hospital left Railway in a distant third place. Cash flow was a problem, and the city considered the sale of the property and closure of the facility to give more support to the University.

Then, in 1955, a local group, Regents Incorporated, offered to buy the facility from the city; the group successfully lobbied for the continuation of the Certificate of Need, renovated some of the buildings and opened a nearby lot for parking and thus was born the New City Hospital, as a for-profit venture. Not immediately attractive to locals, New City marketed its services and capital city location to the outlying areas where small hospitals were having financial difficulties. Within just a few years, the foresight of the Regents Group was rewarded as their outreach began to show some success. Building on the steadily increasing load of patient referrals from surrounding counties, the for-profit business began to operate in the black.

Real change began after the passage of Medicare in 1965. With the tension about 'socialized medicine' in the physician referral base especially in the city limits, New City Hospital became one of the first hospitals nationally to develop a program for recruiting Medicare patients and ensuring the full collection of engendered fees. Three years later the system was financially strong and had developed a new reputation within the community as a progressive medical care institution. As the medical profession developed additional technical skills, techniques, and technology, New City Hospital built a new medical tower and opened the city's first open-heart surgery program. The University hospital also started a cardiac surgery program, and the two programs functioned cooperatively and collaboratively for education and training issues. New City soon became a major teaching hospital for the University.

Throughout the 1970s and 80s, New City stayed on the cutting edge. A new neurosurgical program was opened, then a Neonatal

Wing on the Research Tower. Further, New City kept adding staff physicians recruited from major medical schools and increasing their local reputation and expertise. Five years ago the Board completed the amalgam stretching from the New Emergency Department sprouting from the Railway building across two city blocks and up into the flaring top of the Medical Tower. New City was visually arresting and visible from Interstate 75 by commuters going north and south. Further, the State Forensic Laboratory opened a branch toxicology and microbiology center in the old Railway building laboratory space. New City was many things, but especially it was New.

New City was an academic partner of the medical school with the Cincinnati Veterans Affairs Medical Center for most of the past decade. That affiliation was a source of clinical and administrative friction for most of that time. Initially, private practice physicians viewed the addition of interns, residents, and medical students into the hospital as an influx of workers to assist them in their care of patients and to allow them more time in their offices. A previous chief of staff was run out of the job after insisting the physicians spend some of their time teaching. His successor was a bright woman who foundered on a different reef. Sam Mastone and the administrative staff did not see their way to financially supporting the students and residents beyond providing their salary to the medical school. The complaints about sleeping quarters, nighttime support personnel, and other issues led her to quit the job after only one year.

When Tom Bolling applied for the position, Sam was certain he was the right person and told him so. His presentation of how he, Sam Mastone, saw the friction between academia and daily practice was quite definitive. So was his brief comment on how Tom, as the new chief of staff, should address the problem. Sam had been completely taken aback when Tom told him that his ideas were wrong-headed and would quickly lead to the loss of the affiliation. That frank exchange should have ended Tom's candidacy. But the Board of Directors was impressed and insisted Tom be offered the job, so Sam had several additional meetings with Tom to discuss the future. In the end, Tom only agreed to take the position with the clear understanding that he would make decisions about the clinical activities and personnel, not Sam. Grudgingly, Sam had agreed.

Their five-year association was steadily improving in both men's eyes. Tom did not shirk difficult decisions and earned Sam's respect. He convinced the practicing physicians that spending time teaching would make the residents more amenable to caring for their patients. Several years ago, Tom persuaded Sam to yield a few salaried positions for full-time medical teachers. He also convinced leaders of profit centers in the labs and radiology and the anatomical pathology department to accept major roles in the resident education program. Slowly, the rotations at New City were seen as desirable by the residents. Several of the hospital's practitioners were awarded Golden Apples for teaching excellence by the medical students.

Tom had other problems in adjusting to a non-military organization other than Sam Mastone's micromanagement. He also had to find a way to work effectively with the Nursing Service leadership. Roslyn Burke, the Chief Nurse, firmly believed that all physicians looked down their noses at nurses and were prone to treat them as handmaidens. She made this clear to Tom in their first meeting and brought out the argument anytime there was a difference of opinion about an issue, no matter how small. Roslyn herself was tall, nearly five foot ten inches, and tended to look down her nose at all others. She was approaching sixty years of age, White and squarely built with perfectly coiffed hair that never seemed to have one hair out of place. Her executive officer, Alena Preston RN, Ph.D., was, by contrast, Black and thin as a rail. Her opinions always tracked perfectly with those of her boss.

Allen Defarge MHA was the assistant hospital director. His background included rising through the ranks in the Regents Health System as an engineer. Sam would usually assign Allen the responsibility to fix broken pipes, stuck windows, or slippery floors. Tom often wondered what else the assistant hospital director was responsible for. Holly Ellington, a recent graduate from a local MHA program was Sam Mastone's executive assistant. Tom wondered what she did much of the time, also. It seemed her tasks were primarily to deliver Sam's instructions to others.

On Tom's side, however, was Beverly Hancock, his executive assistant, and right arm. She was about fifty, short at five foot four inches, and had the value of having spent most of her working life in various departments in the hospital. Beverly had an important insight into the history of New City. She also understood workflow processes in most of the administrative and several clinical departments. Her knowledge was invaluable and provided Tom with wisdom and sagacity concerning issues that made his decisions more timely and more often correct.

The seating arrangement at the table in the Director's Conference Room for Morning Meetings was also uncomfortable for Tom. Sam would sit at the head of the table with Holly Ellington sitting slightly behind him, Tom and Beverly sat on the side to Sam's right, and Roslyn and Alena sat directly across. Tom thought the arrangement was almost adversarial by nature, but efforts to change the seating pattern had been fruitless.

Tom's experience with the military included many similar meetings, all of which ran very differently. In the Air Force, no one raised an issue at the morning meeting if it fell in their area of responsibility unless they needed assistance in resolving the matter. In Mastone's meeting, people brought up issues, in Tom's opinion, just so they could talk. Problems that cut across disciplines were usually talked about a great deal before someone-very often not in the room-was identified as the individual to resolve the issue. Then everyone listened while Sam gave indirect guidance on how the problem should be addressed.

This morning's meeting was much like many others; there were petty concerns, complaints of minimal import, and notifications of occurrences of little impact. Sam paid rapt attention and propounded detailed solutions to these minimal issues. There was no mention of Harry's admission. Then the meeting dissolved, and the workday began.

CHAPTER 3

FRIDAY, APRIL 2

Anton Greene, USMC Col. ret., cut an imposing figure. He didn't tower over others, being five foot, eleven inches, but his bearing made others feel small in his presence. He walked and stood ramrod straight, and looked directly at others with dark brown eyes. His facial features were reminiscent of the face of a hawk or eagle, and predatory. His nose was sharp, the brows heavy and close and the slightly receding chin emphasizing the eyes and nose. Greene was somewhat ashamed of the chin and had long worn a Van Dyke to conceal it. He had a habit of caressing the beard and mustache by running his fingers over the mustache, circling the chin hair, and ending by twirling the growth at the tip of the chin. He thought this gave the impression of deep thought. Others thought of Snidely Whiplash if they were old enough.

Greene had served in the Marine Corps as both a combat commander and in the Judge Advocate Division. He retired with a full pension after 22 years and being passed over twice for promotion to general officer. He had a post-service law practice in Cincinnati for the past decade and was recognized for civic activities. Six years ago, Greene had decided to run for City Council and was elected easily. He continued his practice at half-speed and was always present at every council meeting. He also gave frequent press interviews; his baritone intonation and lawyerly style of presentation were well known in the city.

Greene maintained two offices, one for his law practice and the other in City Hall for councilman duties. Wherever he was, however, two men of his employ always accompanied him. These two knew him from his days as combat commander; both had served with him in their younger days. No one questioned Greene about his need for a personal protection detail, mostly because it was considered impolite. These men usually sat in the office of Sam's executive assistant, Conor MacCarter, when Sam was in the law office. At the City Councilman's office, they sat in the waiting room with Greene's secretary.

Greene was in his law office, and his protection detail was getting cross-examined.

"Well, what the hell went wrong?" he barked at them.

"He jumped right before we hit him." The speaker was a tall, thin man of dark complexion and oiled black hair combed straight back. His Spanish descent was obvious in his complexion, hair, and eyes, black and sharp. His name was Nestor Aramano. He was the driver of the attempted hit-and-run and was trying to explain his failure. "I still think I hit him. He bounced off a parked car and didn't move after he landed on the pavement."

"And yet he was sitting up a couple of minutes later and got on the ambulance stretcher without help."

"Yes, sir. But there were too many people around to try to get to him then."

"So you waited until now to bring this up?"

"Sir, you were in the council meeting all morning."

"I have my phone."

"You told us not to leave any trace."

"Well, yes, I did. Where is he now?"

"He was admitted to the hospital and put in isolation."

"Isolation? What for?"

"I don't know. We overheard the nurses in the emergency room talking about him. He didn't give his real name so we can't call to ask where he is. The nurses kept referring to him as 'the guy in Room 32', not by name."

"The hospital is not that big. Find him. And take care of the issue."

The second bodyguard spoke, "What do you expect us to do, walk around asking where this guy is?" The speaker was Jorge Quiles, the shorter of the two, but he had more heft. Jorge was about five foot six inches tall and weighed slightly more than 200 pounds. Like Nestor, his Spanish and Mesoamerican Indian heritage was evident in his wide cheekbones and sharp nose, as well as the tobacco-stain coloring of his skin. Jorge was a body-builder and a trained martial arts fighter. He did not talk as much as Nestor, but his comments usually were direct and on point.

"No," said Greene, "I expect you to do something clever that won't call attention to you. But I expect that you will find him. And he better not get out of that hospital." The two men stood and touched their forehead in a semblance of a salute and said, "Sir. Yes, Sir," and they headed for the door. As the door closed behind them, Conor MacCarter entered the office from his adjoining room. From his name, one would expect Conor to be an Irishman, but he looked more like a *consigliere*. He was about forty years old, thin, five foot ten inches, and only 165 pounds. His coloring was the warm end of olive; his hair was jet black, as were his eyes. A patrician nose separated them over small, tight lips and mouth. Clean-shaven, he was dressed, as usual, in a form-fitting Italian suit and black, glossy finish oxfords. The expression on his face varied little from time to time between neutral and vaguely disinterested.

"Sir? Is there something I need to be involved in here?" he asked.

Greene looked at his executive assistant before shrugging and moving to sit behind his desk. He stared at Conor for several moments before taking a deep breath and answering. "I guess you do have the right to know."

He leaned back in the chair. Conor remained standing in front of the desk with hands clasped behind his back. Greene scratched his head, grimaced, and said, "You remember a couple of days ago when I asked you to get them to ask around the yard to see who was snooping for information about Dahgs?"

Conor nodded. They had gone to the construction site for the new bus station in Cincinnati, contracted to the ABConstruction company, and done what Greene asked, and Conor had ordered. In less than an hour, the two security men had an answer. They had learned that Harry Wilton, a demolition expert with ABC, had asked about the contractor for waste hauling at the site. The report to Conor indicated that Wilton's question originally was, "Who does our waste and rubbish hauling?". A day or so later, Wilton asked, "Have you ever heard of J.Y.Dahgs?" Several workers mentioned that they knew nothing about Dahgs, and others said they told Wilton the waste hauler for ABC was Debree BeGon.

Conor said, "Yes, sir. I remember that conversation."

Greene smiled a tight little smile and went on, "Well, I told the guys to see that he had a bad accident."

"I see," Conor said with the slightest question on his face.

"Do you? I should not have bypassed you and given them such a direct order myself. I know that. But I was more than a little distracted by that telegram."

"Yes, sir. I remember you asking me who sends telegrams today.

"And I didn't tell you. It really shook me up."

"Can you tell me what was in the telegram?"

"Oh, yeah. I have it memorized. It said, 'Have confirmation Dahgs is sham. Call today.' And there was a local number. So, I called it.

"And …?"

"I got an answering machine, a recording, a disguised voice that said he wanted $1 million or he would send information to the newspapers exposing Dahgs, and me."

"Sir, you should have allowed me to deal with the matter."

"Yes, probably so. But I was so upset I simply wanted to find out who was doing this. "I figured whoever it was must have been asking around on the construction site, and I did ask you to find that out."

"Yes, sir. And I did. The men were able to find out about Wilton quite soon. They were back the next day with that answer. But I did not know why you had asked for that name."

"No. I should have told you, but I thought I could take care of it, and I moved on it right away."

"If I may ask, sir, what did you do?"

"I asked Nestor to do a hit-and-run on this Wilton guy."

"I presume he missed. That would explain the meeting I just witnessed."

"Yes. Nestor missed him. Well, now he says he may have hit him somewhat. But the man was sitting up on the sidewalk later and was taken off to the hospital. Obviously not dead."

"That's distressing."

"Certainly. Now Wilton will be on the lookout. The guys went to the hospital, but they couldn't find him. They said he didn't use his name, but they did figure out that he was in isolation for some reason. They said they looked all over the hospital and couldn't find an Isolation ward. I just sent them back and told them Wilton better not get out of that hospital."

"This is quite serious, sir."

"Of course it is. Dahgs is the side action keeping us all in the game." Greene paused a moment, then looked directly at Conor. "Look, I'm sorry I didn't get you involved sooner. Help me get this cleaned up, will you?

"Certainly, sir."

CHAPTER 4

FRIDAY, APRIL 2

Harry awoke shortly after ten that morning. Initially, he was puzzled about his whereabouts. He was in a single bed with side rails in a room with gray painted walls and no pictures. His head hurt, and he was stiff from the accident. He winced as he tried to sit up and remembered something about two fractured ribs on his right side. As he reached his left hand over to touch his right side he noted an intravenous line attached to his arm. He shook his head to try to clear his thoughts and realized he was in a hospital bed. He looked around and noticed an overbed table next to the bed. On that table sat what appeared to be his breakfast tray.

Harry determined he would sit up. He held his breath, gritted his teeth, and lurched himself into a sitting position on the side of the bed. He cautiously leaned over, picked up the cold cup of coffee on the breakfast tray, and sipped it. He looked around the room for his clothes but didn't see anything to wear. There was a bedside table, the overbed table, and an uncomfortable-looking stackable patio chair in addition to his bed in the room. He still wore the skimpy gown he had put on in the emergency area the night before. The gown was untied and tended to slip off his shoulder but lifting his right arm caused pain in the ribs, and he decided to leave the gown untied. So, he sat on the edge of the bed with his gown slipped off his shoulders, and down to his elbows, sipping a cup of cold coffee, awaiting whatever would happen next.

A nurse, wearing a set of blue scrubs, entered the room a few minutes later and said, "Oh, look who has rejoined the ranks of the living!" She smiled at him and came up to where he was sitting.

Harry replied, "Living? Not so sure about that. But I am awake enough to know this coffee is cold, and it doesn't taste all that good, anyway. Where're my clothes?"

"We have them safe in the locker room. How are you feeling this morning? Besides grouchy about the coffee."

"Things hurt."

"I'm sure you do. The doctor ordered some pain medication, and I'll get that for you as soon as I get your vitals." She pulled a blood pressure monitor to the bedside and started wrapping a cuff around his left arm.

"I need to get my clothes and get out of here," Harry tried to sound rational and persuasive.

The nurse called his attention to the bandage on his left arm at the elbow. "You know you have a serious infection in that abrasion. We're giving you some antibiotics to treat that for the next few days."

"Days? Wait a minute. I can't stay here for days. I mean, ah, I have a job and things I have to get done."

"Don't you worry. We will notify your boss about your condition, and once we get your infection under control, you can leave." She shushed him as she put the stethoscope in her ears and measured his pressure.

Her statement caused more anxiety.

The nurse looked up and said, "Pressure is a little high. Let's try it again. You try to relax. Take a few deep breaths before I do it again."

She smiled after the second attempt and commented, "There, now. You must feel better. Your pressure is down to only a little bit high."

Harry thought about how he didn't want his boss to know where he was. "That sounds good and all that, but I have to get out of here," he said.

"Your blood pressure is a little high right now. I'm sure you're concerned and anxious. I'll get you that pain medication now." She patted him on the leg reassuringly and left the room.

Harry thought, 'If he finds out where I am, he'll be coming here to get me. I gotta get out of here.'

A few minutes later, the nurse returned with a syringe and a small paper cup containing two white pills. "I've got your pain medicine here," she said, handing him the pills, "and I will give you your next antibiotic treatment in that i.v. line."

Harry took the pain pills and watched as she carefully cleaned the rubber nub of the i.v. line at his arm and slowly injected the syringe contents while pinching the plastic line with her fingers. After the injection, she opened the i.v. line and ran in several spurts of fluid before adjusting the speed back down to a drop every few seconds.

"What's all that for?" Harry wanted to know.

"It's an antibiotic for your infection."

"Why can't I just take a pill?"

"This is a very serious infection and is best treated with these shots."

"Why is this so serious? My arm doesn't really hurt all that much." He said this as he flexed his left arm to show her.

"Oh, this is more about the bug that's in your wound. Not really about the wound."

"Why's that?"

"Well, you've gotten infected with a superbug. It's called MRSA."

"What's that mean?"

"That's a bacteria that is resistant to common antibiotics, particularly ones you could take by mouth. You can probably imagine the danger of spreading that kind of infection around and having lots of people with an infection that was resistant to most antibiotics. And if you left the hospital before we get it under control, you could easily spread that around, and that would be bad for other people. That's why we want you to stay in your room."

Harry realized he didn't care about those other people,; he needed to get out of the hospital before he was discovered. "How much treatment? And for how long?"

"A few days at least. The doctor can tell you more about that when he comes."

"When is that gonna be?"

"He's usually here right after lunch."

"Huh. Hey, will you tie this stupid gown? It keeps sliding down."

"Sure thing. Turn around."

The attending physician on that ward was Andrew Luckett. He arrived on the ward at 12:40 that afternoon, or right after lunch, as predicted. Andy was one of the hospital staff physicians and he had spent his morning on teaching rounds with students and residents. He had a 3x5 card with Harry's name and room number on it and he went there directly. When he did not find Harry in his room, Lockett inquired at the nurses' station.

"Where's the man in Room 314?"

One of the nurses looked up and replied, "He's wandering around the ward area. But he does want to see you about getting discharged."

"I'm going to be keeping him for another day, at least. Did you tell him about the Isolation Order?"

"I'm not his nurse; I'm not sure what he was told. But I know he wants to go home. He's nervous about being in the hospital for some reason."

"Whatever. I'll talk to him about it if I can find him. By the way, I've asked Dr. Merrill to see him about the MRSA. If she clears him for outpatient treatment, I can probably let him go. Oh, did he get that repeat chest x-ray?"

"I'm not sure, but I doubt it. He hasn't been around. Radiology called for him an hour ago and we couldn't find him then. I just got back to the station, though and he may have gone down since then."

"Well, he isn't going anywhere until I'm sure he didn't poke a hole in his lung with those broken ribs. I'm going on to see some other patients. And I'll cruise past Radiology in case he got there. Could you buzz me if he shows up here?'

"Of course, doctor."

"Thank you."

CHAPTER 5

FRIDAY, APRIL 2

Just past four that afternoon, Dr. Merrill arrived on Ward 3C for her consultation regarding Harry's infection. Walking briskly so that her long white coat blew out behind her, she stopped briefly at the nurses' station and then went to his room. She was taken aback that his bed was empty and he was not in the room. She quickly checked the bathroom and looked up and down the hallway before returning to the nurses' station to inquire, "What's happened to the MRSA guy in 414?"

The nurse behind the desk at the moment looked up and said, "You mean Mr. Smith?"

"Yes, that's right, Smith," Merrill said, checking her consult sheet. " I received an infectious disease consult to see him about a superficial MRSA infection. I've already checked in the microbiology lab to confirm the MRSA diagnosis. I notice you have all the isolation signs up in his room. Why is he not confined?"

Dr. Merrill was concerned about finding this patient with a potentially serious infection and great potential for spread throughout the hospital had eloped from his confinement.

"Ah, I really don't know, doctor. His day nurse said he just ignores the sign and wanders around."

"Has he been informed about the seriousness of this infection?"

"All we heard at report was that he was here and all the steps for confinement and sanitation are in place."

"You are aware that none of that is of any value if you let the infected man go walking all over the hospital, right?" Merrill was getting more exercised by the minute. "When was he last checked on?"

"I'm not on that side of the ward, Dr. Merrill. Let me see if I can find out who saw him last." She left the station and hurried down the hallway, looking in each room for other nurses.

Merrill thought about calling Tom Bolling to notify him of the breach of infection control on 4C but decided she would work the issue herself before involving the chief of staff.

The nurse returned a few minutes later and said, "Nancy said she saw him an hour or so ago. He wasn't in his room for lunch when the trays came, and he came back and ate it later."

"Did she, or anyone, tell him we would lock the door to his room if he leaves again?"

"Uh, I'm pretty sure no one said anything like that to him."

"Who is the attending?" Merrill asked as she pulled the consult sheet out of her coat pocket. Before the nurse could obtain the same information from the automated medical record, Merrill said, "It's Andy Luckett. He's the attending for Smith, isn't he? What did he tell him?"

"Dr. Merrill, I don't know what anyone else has said to him. I've never actually seen the man. I do know that Dr. Luckett couldn't find him when he made his rounds at noon."

"For crying out loud! Andy knew a MRSA patient was wandering around?" Merrill shook her head in dismay. Then, remembering that Andy Luckett was a sharp physician and not prone to stupid mistakes, she asked, "What is wrong with this guy? Smith, I mean."

"He was in a hit-and-run accident last night. Broke a couple of ribs and Dr. Luckett is worried about a punctured lung."

"Where is this MRSA infection?"

"I think it's on his arm. Like from a scrape in the accident. At report, we heard it's all dressed and treated."

"With what?"

The nurse turned to the electronic record and typed in a few commands. Seconds later, Harry's chart opened, and Dr. Merrill went behind the station desk to view it with the nurse. They went directly to the pharmacy page and reviewed the medications.

"It looks like Dr. Lockett started him on Vancomycin last night, and he's had two doses," the nurse noted

"He also started him on some oral Bactrim. That's good. If this infection isn't deep or abscessed, we can probably treat him at home. This is beginning to sound like maybe he was colonized and he doesn't have some deep wound."

"He is really unhappy here and wants to go home." The nurse shrugged her shoulders. "That's all I know. He hasn't been around since we came on."

"Great. A MRSA spreader wandering the halls."

"His wound is completely bandaged and covered."

"And how do you know that if you haven't seen him?"

"That's what we heard in report. Susan said he scraped his arm in the accident. She said she cleaned it and changed the bandaging this morning."

"Are you sure he didn't bolt? You said he wanted to go home." Merrill asked as she made a quick note on the consult sheet about the absence of the patient from his room.

The nurse smiled and chuckled a little. "He won't be going anywhere dressed in his little gown and showing his butt around. We have his clothes locked up in the locker room."

"Well, he's certainly not here now. I hope you're right about that bandage. When he comes back, tell him to stay in that room until I personally permit him to leave. Call me, and if I'm still here, I'll come right away."

"Okay, Dr. Merrill."

As Merrill left the ward to check on another patient before going home, she thought about the situation. Although the microbiology technicians could confirm the MRSA strain, she would need to determine the extent of the wound involved. What she was hearing, coupled with Luckett's actions, made her think this probably wasn't a big deal, and she was glad she hadn't called the chief of staff. A minor abrasion with colonized MRSA picked up on rapid ID testing, and the guy is already getting systemic treatment with two drugs. She wasn't going to hang around for hours waiting for this guy to return for a late supper.

CHAPTER 6

FRIDAY, APRIL 2

Thomas Pritchard was nervous. He knew he had to make this short trip but thinking about it made his hands sweat and gave him a headache. Nervousness was not a common condition for Thomas because he didn't often get out of his lane in life. Thomas was a 37-year-old bachelor of medium height and below medium build, which contributed to his lack of athletic experience. But that didn't mean he wasn't competitive. Thomas had dreams about the big house and the nice car and the good life, as he imagined it.

When he was hired as a mid-level accounts manager for ABConstruction a few years previously, he saw the opportunity for growth and career development within the company. He already had one promotion and was generally seen as competent and capable of more than his present position. A hard worker, he was rightly respected by his coworkers and well thought of by his superiors. His life was quiet, predictable, and not a cause for nervousness. In fact, other than rooting for the Cincinnati Bengals and worrying every time they got behind, serious concern was not a part of Thomas' life. Until he took that phone call from Harry Wilton.

Thomas was filling in for someone in Contracting who was out on maternity leave when the call came. He did not even know the person he was filling in for, and he definitely had not requested to provide the cross-cover. His supervisor had called him into the office one afternoon and broached the subject. He remembered that his supervisor had recommended him as the temporary fill-in because "you're smart enough to pick up the job and not let anything slide." Besides, Thomas knew that getting experience in other areas would help him when the time came for another promotion. So he was sitting at Cindy's desk when Harry called.

"Contracting, Pritchard," he answered.

"Uh, say, yes, this is Harry Wilton. I'm in charge of the demolition here for the new bus station, and I need some information."

"How can I help you, Mr. Wilton?"

"I'm looking to schedule some demo soon, and I want to coordinate the clean-up with the company that's going to haul off the rubbish."

"Right,"

"But I don't know who that is. Can you tell me the company name and contact info?"

"Possibly. I'm actually just filling in for someone who would probably know the answer right away. May I look into that and call you back?"

They exchanged cell phone numbers.

Later that day, Thomas finished the necessary work and started looking for information to answer Harry's question. After going through a couple of filing cabinet drawers, he found a hanging file labeled "Waste/Haul". Inside that file were several folders dating back some years, each marked with the name of the construction job handled by ABC Construction. For a brief moment Thomas considered asking the supervisor in the area why these files were not digitized. He let the thought slide and sifted through the contents of the folder.

Inside each file, Pritchard found invoices from the company Junk Yard Dahgs. The invoices were nearly identical, each submitted requesting payment for "removal of waste, trash and rubbish from the construction site". It seemed reasonable to Pritchard that this company, which sent invoices under the title of J.Y. Dahgs, was the company that Harry Wilton was seeking. He found the folder for the current bus station construction project, and he copied down the telephone number and closed the drawer.

When he returned to his desk, he called Harry. The information seemed to be what Harry needed, a local phone number where Harry could speak to the contractor.

Harry said something like, "Thanks, man, I owe you a beer."

Pritchard, who was not much of a beer drinker, said, "Whatever. You're welcome." He hung up and put the incident out of his mind.

Later, when Harry called back and said the number did not answer, Thomas said he had no further suggestions. And any concern he might have had just slipped into the rearview mirror and then out of sight.

That is, it was out of sight and out of mind until Thomas went back to his regular job, and within a matter of weeks found himself responsible for issuing a check to J.Y. Dahgs as a result of an invoice. He stared at the invoice and recalled that the wording, " removal of waste, trash, and rubbish from the construction site", was identical to the ones he had seen previously. Further, the amount billed was identical to that on the previous invoices. Then, it occurred to him that Harry had implied that no hauling had yet been done at the bus station site when he had called.

Later that day, after everyone had left in Contracting, he slipped into Cindy's desk and opened her computer. After a short pause, he went over the accounts from the months he was in contracting and found a monthly invoice from Dahgs for the same amount as all the others. His targeted search was quickly accomplished, revealing the monthly payment from ABC Construction to J.Y. Dahgs for "removal services". The billing and payment existed on every ABC construction site for several years.

Everything about the relationship between ABC and JY Dahgs appeared out of order to Thomas. So, he called Harry; they agreed to meet at a small Irish pub away from the job site after work.

But, before that meeting occurred, Thomas made some other inquiries including calling in a favor from a friend in New York and finally calling the Ohio Department of State. He then tried a Google search because he thought the incorporators sounded vaguely familiar. His discovery created both excitement and a nebulous feeling of discomfort. When he explained the connections to Harry, they quickly put together how the kickback system was operating. They also agreed it was completely wrong, and who at ABC likely was probably involved. They had talked about the situation a good deal. Pritchard remembered that both he and Harry had strong feelings about the immorality and the illegality and how someone should do something. But he did not remember who first mentioned blackmail. As soon as they made that decision, however, Thomas started feeling nervous.

The nervousness grew when they made the demand and it all spiraled out of control when Harry was involved in the automobile hit-and-run. Harry called Thomas from the hospital and warned him to watch his back. Both men knew Harry's mishap was no accident.

Since then, Thomas had been afraid to go to work and scared to stay home. Despite his increasing apprehension and anxiety, he knew he had to keep this next appointment. His life and his future depended upon a proper outcome from this meeting. He steeled himself to make the trip and planned for it to be short. He thought perhaps he could leave town for a while after this meeting. He took a deep breath, turned off his lights, and stepped out into the hallway. He was going to do it.

But Thomas Pritchard was very nervous.

CHAPTER 7

SATURDAY, APRIL 3

The room was dark, and the man had experienced some difficulty finding it. It was 3:10 in the morning; the sky was pitch black and the hallways used only dim lights along the footboards. He entered the room slowly as if expecting someone to ask why he was there. The lights were off; he could see some furniture pieces and other objects, but the center of the room was open. He was only five foot seven, and he felt small in the large, darkened room. He wondered where his partner was.

After waiting a few minutes, the man became anxious and concerned that he might be in the wrong place. He went to the door to check the room number. His eyes began to adapt to the darkness, and he noticed a bed. He decided to sit on the bed to wait.

He had barely sat down when another man entered. This man was larger, but he moved uneasily, wincing somewhat as he closed the door and turned around.

"Man," the first figure said, "I thought you weren't coming."

"Anybody see you?"

"No. But I gotta tell you. I'm scared. I think we should back off."

"You do, huh? Think we should back off? Do you have any idea why I'm here? He already knows. Backing off now puts us on defense."

The smaller man shook all over and replied, "Look, I'm scared. I mean if he can do this . . ." he motioned at the larger man.

"Obviously, he can. We can't sit back now. We have to push on. Move the date up. Take the offensive."

"I don't know." As he said this, the first man looked as if he became physically smaller. He wrapped his arms around his body and bowed his head. "I don't think I can go on."

"What do you mean, can't go on?"

"I mean I have to get out. I'm afraid. I know he will be coming after me. I can't stand the pressure. I have to get out of this."

"And I'm telling you that I can't stop. He knows who I am and will not stop coming for me."

The first man nodded jerkily, indicating only that he heard and understood, not that he agreed.

"Where is all the proof?" the second man asked.

"I hid it."

"Good. Where?"

"I put it where no one will ever look."

"I'm encouraged by your assurance. Where exactly did you put it?"

"Why do you want to know?"

"We are in this together and he's coming after me. No reason for him to even know about you. Let me take the proof and disappear. It will be my insurance."

For a brief moment, the idea sounded good to the little man. He would no longer have any connection to either the data or the blackmail operation. But, as he thought more deeply, he discovered a hitch in that solution.

"What if he finds out about me?" he asked.

"Maybe you should disappear, too."

"No. I don't want to run. I want to keep my job and keep my head down."

"That's up to you. But I need to have access to that proof."

"I think we can destroy it, and he'll never find out."

"Are you nuts? I told you, he already knows about me, and destroying the proof will take all pressure off him."

The smaller man was silent for a moment and then edged toward the door. "I'm getting out," he said.

"You're not listening. The cat is out of the bag. If we don't finish this, it will finish us."

"I don't care. I'm quitting," he said, turning for the door.

The larger man slid his left arm around the smaller man's neck and lifted him off the floor, using his hip as a fulcrum. The smaller man struggled and began kicking and clawing at the arm that was closing off his throat.

"Be still, and I'll let you down," the larger man said. "I just want to talk to you about this decision." Instead, the smaller man got his hand inside his coat and brought out a mechanical pencil. Using his right hand he stabbed the larger man in the right leg. That caused the larger man to jerk his grip tighter on the throat. He also wrestled the pencil out of the smaller man's hand.

The man struggled more against the arm and tried to make noise. He pulled against the arm that was choking him with both hands.

"Stop it! I said I'd put you down if you stop fighting."

When the struggling became more frantic, the larger man stuck the mechanical pencil in the smaller man's right ear and shoved it in causing more agitation and wriggling. He hammered the pencil into the ear canal with the heel of his hand.

The smaller man jerked convulsively twice, and then all muscle activity ceased.

CHAPTER 8

SATURDAY, APRIL 3

Harry Wilton did not have the taxi driver take him to his house. He asked to be let out two blocks away and waited to move until the taxi had turned the corner. Then, he walked carefully to the corner and slipped into the rear yards of his neighborhood. He approached his house in the dark and moved carefully to look in several windows to assure himself no one was waiting inside.

He found the extra key hidden in the flowerbed and entered through the rear door. He stood silently there in the kitchen for more than three minutes before finally relocking the door and moving about the house. Harry did not turn on any lights. He used the light from the streetlights through the windows to find his way through the house.

First, he found the small flashlight in the kitchen drawer and used its limited illumination to help him locate the basement stairs. He shielded the light carefully and descended the stairs. In his workshop, he found his lockbox and took out his handgun, a year-old Glock-19. He took a moment to savor handling the weapon again. Just under two pounds, the 9mm gun immediately felt warm to his touch. He checked the slide, confirmed the absence of a bullet in the chamber, and laid it aside. He found his two magazines and ensured they were each full before placing the gun and the clips in a small zippered carrying case. He opened one of the drawers in the worktable and grabbed his monocular surveying telescope.

Again shielding the flashlight, Harry went back upstairs to the kitchen. He looked at the kitchen table and remembered sitting there reading the newspaper while Carole cooked. Memories of Henry raiding the refrigerator after practice and later eating a full meal came to him. He had a strong urge to move over to the corner cabinet where the Keurig machine was and make a cup of coffee. He resisted only taking a deep breath and feeling the sharp pain from his broken ribs. The men responsible for the rib fractures had even worse ideas in mind. He continued through the kitchen and dining room and into the hall.

He quietly moved up the stairs to his bedroom. After his wife died, he had decided to sleep in the guest bedroom, even after cleaning out her clothes from the master bedroom. In his room, using the light from outside, he found a couple of changes of underwear, three T-shirts, several pairs of heavy socks, and two polo shirts. He pulled an old black Subzero backpack out of the closet and carefully packed the clothes in it. He pulled two pairs of khaki pants from the closet and added them and an Ohio State sweatshirt to the overnight bag with the cases from the workshop.

Harry sat on the edge of the bed. He struck him that leaving this house, he would be leaving behind all the life he had in Cincinnati. Harry wasn't much attached to the house since his wife died, but he did have memories of his son, Henry, growing up and finishing high school while the family was in the home. A moment of grief washed over him, and he suddenly felt alone and bereft of support. He got off the bed and wandered down the hall to Henry's old room, uncertain at first, why he went there. He stood in the doorway and looked around the room. Posters of bands he couldn't remember hearing covered the walls, and all the flat surfaces had pictures of Henry, Little League, lacrosse uniform, graduation, with friends. Harry decided to take a picture of his son with him. With little hesitation, he found what he wanted: a photograph of Henry in his lacrosse uniform. Then Harry collected the overnight bag from his bedroom and went in the bathroom to grab some mouthwash and a toothbrush before heading back downstairs.

Harry rummaged through the front hall closet, pulled out his military raincoat, and a weathered old knit cap in a smudged navy blue color. He put them in the bag and reached back in to grab his work boots. They were classic tank boots, high anklet, dark brown, and heavily worn and scuffed. Exactly what he wanted, so he sat on the bottom step, took off the shoes he was wearing, and laced the work boots tightly over heavy wool socks. Last he went back to the front hall closet and took out the Cabella Mountain Trapper sleeping bag tightly secured with three web straps. Then he located the survivor torch on the upper shelf. He checked and made sure he had grabbed a couple of charger cords.

Then Harry went back into the kitchen. He found his thermos and the pack of burner phones he had purchased earlier. He laid those items on the counter and opened the refrigerator to extract two 12 ounce water bottles. They easily fit in the outside pockets of the backpack. Harry knew his appearance would have to match a homeless person to avoid suspicion while carrying the backpack and the bedroll.

He decided he needed a pair of gloves and went back to the front hall closet. He took down the wicker basket his wife Carole had used to store all the various gloves over the years. Rummaging through the stock, Harry had memories of snowball fights, sledding, and shoveling sidewalks with Henry. He shoved those memories to the back of his attention and selected a pair of dark leather gloves with woolen lining. However, as Harry put them on, he realized those gloves did not fit with the picture of homelessness. He took them off and shoved them in an outside pocket on the backpack, and decided to go gloveless for the moment.

At the back door, Harry turned to look at the interior of his home for the last time. Then, as his gaze fell once again on the refrigerator, he realized he was hungry and put everything down to go back to the refrigerator. Harry was a bachelor since Henry went off to college and his refrigerator held mostly cheese, some fruit cups, and water bottles. Harry regretted that he had fallen into the trap of mostly eating fast food or frozen dinners. He opened the cheese drawer, grabbed a handful of string cheese chunks, and stuffed them in his pocket. He unsuccessfully looked in the nearby cabinets, hoping to find some crackers or cookies.

Harry had his head in the pantry when he heard a sound outside. It might have been the sound of a car door closing, and he finally decided the time to leave had come. He had only been in the house for 40 minutes, and it was still dark outside. He needed to hurry before anyone was around to see him. Leaving, he retraced his steps out the rear door, locking it behind him. Then he quietly moved to the side of the house with the driveway.

His car was in the driveway, and he slipped in quickly after placing his carrying bags in the trunk. He started the car and backed into the street before slowly accelerating, hoping not to attract attention. He had a plan, but he couldn't call ahead at this time of night. He decided to drive to a nearby apartment house and park among the cars in their large lot until dawn. Once there, Harry thought, he would eat some cheese and drink some water and maybe get a little nap.

CHAPTER 9

SATURDAY, APRIL 3

Ward 3C in New City hospital at six o'clock in the morning was, like other wards in other hospitals, a study in contrasts. The lights were off in rooms and the hallways, imbuing the area with a feeling of stillness and rest. At the same time, the outgoing shift of nursing staff was bustling about closing out charts, finishing their notes, and setting up for recording the first vital signs of the day in preparation for report. As they moved about, their rubber-soled shoes made faint squeaking sounds. In dark hallways, the night nurses dark uniforms moving quickly about to the tune of eerie squeaking sounds was reminiscent of a haunted house in a Halloween movie. Most of the patients were unaware of the dichotomy occurring just outside their rooms.

One of the nurses' aides on Ward 3C came out of room 314 with a puzzled look on her face. She went to the nurses' station and asked the nurse behind the desk, "Was 314 discharged?"

"I don't think so, honey. We haven't had a discharge since yesterday morning. Why?"

"He's not in his room for his vitals check."

"Oh. You know, Susan told me he wandered around all day yesterday. Not even here for his meals. Maybe he's up early."

"You sure he wasn't discharged?"

"Yes. Pretty sure. There was nothing about it in report. You were there."

"Well, his bed is all made up, and there's nothing in the bedside table."

"Let me see what you're talking about," the nurse said and quickly walked into 314. The infection control and quarantine signs were still in place, but the room otherwise appeared unused. The bed was made and, as the aide had said, the bedside table contained no personal items. The room appeared ready for its next occupant.

The nurse went back to the station and contacted the charge nurse. She, too, examined the room and then started the 'missing patient' protocol. All staff immediately checked the ward and waiting rooms for the missing person. The charge nurse called other wards and asked for information about him. She told nurses on the other wards he was a low-risk patient as far as she knew; she was referring to his mental stability and not to the diagnosis of MRSA.

When all reports back to her quickly confirmed 'Mr. Smith' was nowhere about, she called the night nursing supervisor.

"I think we have a patient on 3C that's gone AWOL."

"I'll be right up." The supervisor hurried up to 3C and repeated the examination of Room 314, again noting its emptiness. She then called all personnel to the nurses' station. So, at six-thirty in the morning, the nursing executive, ward nurses, and the charge nurse on 3C gathered to determine what to do about the man who should be in room 314.

"When was he last seen?" asked the supervisor.

"Sometime yesterday," answered the nurse on the ward. "He was wandering around most of the day. He missed meals and then would show up hours later and eat what was on the tray."

"What is his diagnosis?"

"He was in a hit and run accident and has a couple of broken ribs."

"But he can get up and walk around? His room is labeled Isolation."

"Yes. But he was pushing us to let him go home. He said being in the hospital was a big mistake."

"Why was he here? And what was the reason for him to be in Isolation?"

Another nurse spoke up. "Dr. Luckett was concerned he might have a punctured lung from the fracture. He wanted a 24-hour follow-up x-ray."

The executive nodded, "And did he say the man could leave if the x-ray was clear?"

"Well, he said that to me. I don't know if he explained that to Mr. Smith."

"Is that this man's name?"

"Yes. Smith. Harry Smith."

"And we are all certain there's no discharge order in his chart?"

The charge nurse spoke up, saying, "M'am, we checked his chart. No one has seen him since he ate his meal last night at nine o'clock. We have checked all the bathrooms and sitting areas on the ward. He is definitely not here."

"Well, that qualifies him as 'missing', for certain. I will alert security to check the rest of the hospital before we declare him AWOL," said the executive.

Security was notified; guards mobilized, and security camera recordings scrutinized. Within twenty minutes after they began to look for Mr. Smith, the security guard at the Emergency entrance reported that a review of the video recording showed someone who looked the description of 'Mr. Smith', leaving the hospital out the Emergency doors around four o'clock in the morning.

The search was called off: nursing personnel made their report up the chain of command. The reporting tree ended with a call to Alena Preston at home.

Alena heard the telephoned report and very professionally asked a few questions about the patient, his diagnosis, and whether anyone had a home address. She thanked the supervisor and asked that someone bring the paper report to her before the morning meeting on Monday. She also asked several questions about the search process but was satisfied when told that the man was seen leaving the hospital. Alena's initial worry involved concern that the patient was lost in the building. However, knowing that the individual was safe, and importantly no longer the responsibility of New City, her concern lessened. All that helped her decide to wait till Monday morning to report the incident.

On Monday morning, Alena took the full report and walked across the office space to Roslyn Burke's office, and tapped quietly on the door.

"You won't believe what happened yesterday," she said. "We'll have to talk about it at the Morning Meeting, of course. But it appears, the man left on his own. No foul, no worries, right?"

CHAPTER 10

SATURDAY, APRIL 3

Quiles and Aramano huddled outside the door to Green's office, waiting for him to have time to talk with them. They had just returned from a thorough walk-through at New City without any hint of the whereabouts of Harry Wilton. Nestor Aramano had inquired at the information desk but found no patient admission for the name Wilton. He tried to charm the lady at the desk to tell him the names of all people admitted through the emergency area, but she became suspicious and asked him to leave. The two men then went 'visiting' on every medical and surgical ward, peeking into each room.

Nursing personnel on the wards often stopped them to inquire what they were doing. They used this opportunity for interchange and tried to learn if their 'friend' had been admitted from emergency, but consistently got no useful information. Nurses went into considerable detail to explain such information was not available because of privacy laws.

After searching fruitlessly for several hours, they met in the lobby and decided they should let Greene know their findings. The drive back to his office was not a quiet one.

"You know he's gonna be mad," Jorge said. "He wants this guy out of the picture."

"Of course I know that," Nestor replied. "He's already got it in for me 'cause I missed him with the car."

"Well, he said that this guy better not get out of the hospital, and now he's out. How're we gonna explain that?"

"We don't know he's out," Nestor frowned at his partner. "We can't cover every door in and out of that place. You know that."

"Does the Colonel know that?"

"Probably. But I bet he doesn't care. That sounds like an excuse. You remember what he always says about 'excuses'."

'Yeah, they're just bad reasons why someone failed to get their job done."

"And now we're those guys."

Greene's secretary motioned to them. She indicated that the Commissioner was able to see them, and they moved slowly to the doorway.

Greene looked up from his desk and the papers he was working on and met their eyes. "Well? Did you take care of it?"

"Not exactly, sir," Nestor said.

"What does that mean? This is a black and white situation. Either you have taken care of it for me, or you haven't. Which is it?"

"Uh, we can't find him in the hospital, Colonel. We went all over the place. Looked for an Isolation ward, but there's not one. The nurses keep quoting a privacy law to not tell us where emergency admissions are, and he's not listed under his own name."

Greene looked at them steadily as his gaze darkened. "So, you can't hit him when he's in front of you, and now you can't find him when he's crippled, and in the hospital? Is that what I'm hearing?"

Both men stood still in front of the desk and looked at their shoes. There was a brief pause, and then Greene asked, "Did you consider that he may have left the hospital?"

They quickly looked at each other and took deep breaths. Clearly, that idea had not occurred to either of them. Nestor sheepishly shook his head, "Uh, no, sir. We figured that after a car accident and him being in isolation he would be there a couple of days."

"And, of course, he may still be. But you can't prove that. But maybe he left. People do that, you know. They leave the hospital and go home." Greene's voice was getting louder. He realized he was about to shout at his men and stopped himself from speaking. He got up from behind his desk and walked to confront them.

"Look, if he's still in the hospital, he will leave at some time and go home. And if he has already left the hospital, he may now be at his home." Greene's voice was controlled and not loud but still forceful. "And either way, somebody should check his home, don't you think?"

Both men nodded and remained silent.

"Should I find someone else to go to his house and see if he's there?"

"No, sir," both spoke simultaneously.

"Are you sure you can take care of this?"

"Yes, sir," again both spoke at once and unconsciously braced their backs.

"Then get it done!"

The men turned without speaking and headed for the door, but before they opened it, Greene spoke again, "I don't want any more excuses either."

The chorus of "No, sir" hung in the air for a brief moment as they scurried out the door.

CHAPTER 11

MONDAY, APRIL 5

The discussion in the morning meeting was substantive for a change. Roslyn Burke announced the finding that a patient on 3C had gone missing sometime during the night during the weekend, but, before she could finish her reporting of the facts known to nursing and security, Sam Mastone began peppering her with questions.

"Did the nurses search the ward?"

"Yes, sir. Of course, they did."

"Right. But did they look on other wards, as well?"

"Of course. They followed our protocol for determining a missing patient."

"Was security notified? You know, sometimes if a patient goes wandering, the security officer might see them somewhere."

"Security was involved in determining that the patient left the hospital."

"He left? Then he's not 'missing' technically, right Tom?" The Director turned to Tom Bolling for support. "That would make him AMA, wouldn't it?"

Tom shook his head slightly before answering, "Not really, Sam. AMA means 'against medical advice', and that usually requires us to formally notify the patient in writing that leaving the hospital is not in their best interests. Our lawyers say we need to have the patient sign a statement indicating that he or she knows what they intend to do is contrary to medical advice. It appears this guy just up and walked out. Is that right, Roslyn?

Roslyn nodded quickly in Tom's direction, glad to have the conversation back somewhat in her control. "He was known to be out of his room a lot and just walked out, yes."

Tom interrupted before Sam could ask another question. "Why was he in the hospital?"

"He had been in a car accident and had broken ribs."

"Punctured lung or injured spleen?"

"No. He was scheduled for a follow-up x-ray this morning but left before that."

"Was he going to be discharged today?"

"Probably. If his x-ray was clear, then Dr. Luckett was going to let him go home. If Dr. Merrill cleared him."

Tom sat up even more straight. "Merrill? What's she got to do with this patient?"

Roslyn paused and looked uncomfortable. When she answered, she did so with less volume than before. "He also had a diagnosis of a MRSA infection, and she was going to determine whether he could be treated as an outpatient."

Tom looked at the ceiling. "An MVA patient with MRSA and he was 'wandering around' in the hospital? What were the folks on the ward thinking?"

Sam said, "Perhaps we should call him AWOL, then. He's certainly absent, and he definitely didn't get permission to leave."

Tom spoke to Sam without taking his eyes off Roslyn, "AWOL concerns patients who don't come back from a permitted leave. This guy was not on leave. He's missing as far as I'm concerned. And that's a big problem for us since he's walking around with a potentially dangerous infection."

Roslyn again tried to control her part of the discussion, saying, "The nurses and Dr. Merrill think his positive culture may have been from colonization rather than an infection, and he received treatment with both Vancomycin and Bactrim."

"So Merrill was going to approve his discharge, then?" Tom asked.

'Uh, she had not actually seen the patient yet. He was off the ward when she came to see him yesterday. She only reviewed his record."

Tom's eyes went to the ceiling again. "Does your report contain the information for tracking him down?"

"Yes. I have the patient's name and home address right here." Roslyn handed the folder containing the nursing report across the table. Tom took it and turned to Beverly. "Get a phone number for this guy and ask Dr. Merrill to come to the office." He handed her the report, and she excused herself from the table and left the room.

Sam returned to the issue of what to call the event. "What are we going to say about this, then? You don't like AWOL, and AMA won't pass a smell test with the lawyers."

Tom said, "Look, Sam, what we call this is not as important as ensuring that we haven't let someone leave who still needs medical care. He's missing and known to not be on the premises."

"What're you gonna do?"

"I will get Dr. Merrill to discuss the issues, and then we will send somebody to his house and get some answers. I don't know if he has a serious infection or not. Apparently, we also don't know for certain that his rib fractures are stable. I can tell you what I'm going to do after I find out the answers to some important questions."

Sam nodded sagely as if he had just had the same idea. He turned to Roslyn and said, "Roslyn, we will need a full report of this."

She looked at him steadily for a moment and then replied, "I just gave it to Dr. Bolling."

"Right. Good. All right, then. Let's go to work."

CHAPTER 12

TUESDAY, APRIL 6

Sam Mastone and Tom Bolling met on Ward 4C shortly after seven o'clock the next morning, well before the scheduled morning meeting. The night nursing supervisor had notified them of the problem and asked them to come. Tom had held the elevator for Sam in the lobby and they rode up together, When they entered the storage room at the end of the hall, they found the chief of anatomic pathology, Dr. Monique Song, already there. She was examining a body lying on one of the beds in the room. The body was mostly covered by a sheet, and the doctor was paying most of her attention to the head. Monique nodded her recognition of their arrival but continued her examination without comment.

Dr. Song's short stature, five foot four inches, was somewhat obscured as she leaned over the body on the bed. She was dressed for work in surgical scrubs, her hair was pulled into a tight bun at the back of her head. Strikingly visible were her trademark bright orange knee-high socks and the dark blue gel-fit Asics.

After a few minutes, Monique turned her face toward the new arrivals and smiled a tight grin. Her round face reflected her Philipino background. She said, "Morning, gentlemen. Just a second, and I'll tell you what I know."

As she turned back to examining the head of the man in the bed, the nurse standing at the foot of the bed spoke to Tom. "We don't know who he is, sir. He's not a patient on 4C."

"Who found him?" Tom asked.

"Johnny. Our aide. I sent him to get a wide transport chair for one of our patients. He said he thought the man was sleeping until he touched him and found he was cold."

"Where's Johnny now?"

"He's sitting in the break room. Do you want me to get him?" she asked as she made a move toward the doorway.

"Not right now." Tom noticed that Monique had stood up and was brushing her coat. "What's the story, doctor?"

Monique Song, a ten-year veteran of New City, was a former Medical Examiner in Cuyahoga County, and she ran her Pathology Department like it was another medical examiner office. Monique was a very confident lady, without being abrasive, she gave the immediate impression that she probably was the smartest person in the room, any room, any time.

She nodded at the Director and said, "Forty-something man found dead in the bed about an hour ago. Time of death was at least twenty-four hours ago; rigor has come and gone, and the smell is starting to be noticeable."

"Who is he?" asked Sam.

Monique answered simply, "I don't know. He was completely naked and without any identification. Nurses say he is not one of our patients."

"At least not on this ward," Tom said.

"Without an identification bracelet, I will wager he's not from any of our wards," Monique said, cocking her head slightly.

"Why would he come here to die?" Sam wanted to know.

"I don't think that was his intent," Monique said, looking at the Director.

'Why do you say that, Dr.? Is there something else you haven't said?"

Tom looked at Monique, and she nodded and stepped back to the bedside to indicate her finding. Tom stepped to the other side of the bed, and Sam moved to the foot. The man's body was lying on his back, the sheet covering his nakedness up to mid-chest. Monique carefully turned the man's head to the left, exposing the right side of the face, and indicated the mechanical pencil extending from the right ear orifice.

"Oh, my God," Sam said, swallowing heavily and backing away from the bed.

Tom looked at the pencil, and then at Monique. "So, murder, then?"

"Oh, definitely. He didn't go anywhere after that pencil went in, so there's no chance he was wandering around."

Sam was shocked, "Murder?"

Monique nodded solemnly, "Oh, yes. Murder in a dark and empty room at the end of a long hallway distant from the nurses' station. With no clue as to who the victim is or why he is here in the hospital."

Sam turned to Tom, "You're going to take care of this, right?"

"Certainly, Sam. I will call Detective Looney. He knows the hospital fairly well by now."

"Do we have to tell the Joint Commission?"

"Probably. I'll check on that and let you know. The first thing is to get started on finding out who this guy is and what happened to him."

"Right, Okay. I'm going back to the office. You let me know, okay?"

"Sure, Sam. I will."

The Director left, and everyone in the room began to feel a little more comfortable. Tom asked Monique, "Are you all right with taking him to the lab?"

"Yes, but I think I should call Dr. Darringer. This is really more her bailiwick than mine. It's not a patient death."

"Your call, Monique. But this is going to be known as a death in New City. I want us in control of facts and reportage."

"Well, you're going to call Ron Looney, aren't you? That should keep us in the loop."

'We'll see. Ron will have to get some kind of clearance to take this case. But, assuming he's in charge, I think we will know what's going on."

Tom nodded at the pathologist and left for his office. Monique asked the nurses to get a gurney and help transport the body to the morgue.

CHAPTER 13

TUESDAY, APRIL 6

Detective Ron Looney of the Cincinnati Homicide Division was sitting at his desk when Tom Bolling called. The two men had been friends for many years with a shared service in the U.S. Air Force. Early in his career, Major Tom Bolling was stationed at Sheppard Air Force Base, Wichita Falls, Texas. One day he was assigned to visit the stockade to care for a prisoner, and he expected no difficulties. He was met at the door by Master Sergeant Looney and escorted in.

When the Master Sergeant opened the door, someone shouted, "Officer on the ward!" and everyone –guards and prisoners alike – snapped to attention. The Major had no inkling what this meant, and he froze. Looney, standing nearby, whispered to him, 'as you were' and, after a momentary pause, Major Bolling repeated that phrase out loud. Everyone relaxed, and the medical visit went as planned. The NCOIC later introduced himself to Bolling, and they recognized in each other's accent a familiar twang of Arkansas.

Later, Looney invited the young Major to a pickup basketball game, and they shared a beer afterward. Then their wives met and formed a friendship, too. That close relationship lasted only a few months. Bolling was promoted to LT. Colonel and shipped to Balad. A year or two later, Looney retired from the Air Force, and moved to Cincinnati, his wife's family home.

Ron Looney was not a complicated man. And he had never been a complicated child. He was one of four Looney offspring on a small farm in southeast Arkansas. All the children had daily chores by the time they started school. There were no after-school activities for Looney children; they had chores. Not difficult chores, but time-consuming ones: feeding the hogs and the chickens and occasionally mucking out the barn and, in the fall, chopping some firewood every day. Ron's chores were routine and regular. That predictability produced a man with a commitment to regularity and routine.

Ron was known to be reliable and trustworthy. His word was a fungible commodity: no one doubted him or his ability or his work ethic. Although he didn't play any school sports, he was active in hunting and fishing with his father and brothers. Before he graduated he had walked every road and streamside in the county. He liked walking.

After high school, Ron enlisted in the Air Force. The draft had ended two years before, but he was registered with the Selective Service, and decided to go see the world. He gravitated to Security Police and moved up quickly in the ranks. He was a rising star in the Law Enforcement Branch until he was promoted to supervisor. Ron Looney didn't see the sense in having to tell others what their duties were, or how and when to do them. As far as he was concerned everyone should do as his father had told him, "If you work for the man, work for the man!"

His superiors quickly realized they got better results with Ron in the field and changed his responsibilities to fit his personality. He went on to enroll in distance learning courses and to earn a degree in Criminal Justice. At that point, a Colonel in the command approached Technical Sergeant Looney about moving into the officer corps. Ron explained he preferred to do his job as a noncom, and things were left alone.

After retirement, however, his degree helped him get a job in the Cincinnati police department. The strong recommendation from his brother-in-law, Paul Andicott, undoubtedly had a positive effect also. Ron's early years on patrol were marked by his proclivity to walk his beat rather than cruise in a patrol car. Ron Looney had grown up on a farm in southeast Arkansas and had walked the county with his father and brother, hunting and fishing when the chores were completed. He felt closer to his work when he was on foot, and his appreciation of geography in his territory became well known. In less than a year on the force, Ron Looney became known as "Walker". After making detective, 'Walker' Looney was the partner everyone wanted to have with them out in the field.

Tom Bolling's interest in the chief of staff position at New City Hospital was an occasion for the two couples to reconnect, and the friendship picked up as if never interrupted. Tom and Ron met outside of work several times a year at a sports bar to cheer the Razorbacks. Ron and Meg were co-hosts for Tom's Christmas Party for the medical staff at New City, and Tom and Sandra helped the Looney's handle the police party at their home on the fourth of July. The two men were very comfortable with each other despite the usual distance between their professional spheres. In the past few years, however, they had several occasions to work together. These occasions fostered a comfortable rapport beyond the Arkansas link.

",Walker," Looney said as he answered the phone.

"Hey, Razorback, I've got something you might be interested in."

"Well, General, If it's got anything to do with Sandra's pecan pie, I'm your man."

"This one is not about food, Ron. Believe it or not, it's another murder."

"At New City?"

"Yes."

"What kind of place are you running over there, General?"

"Don't give me that 'General' stuff. You only do that when you want a favor."

"Well, I don't have a case on my desk right now, so maybe I am looking for a favor."

"Ron, I called you, remember?"

"Yes. What can I do for you, Doctor? And will it involve me coming to New City and meeting with your personal barista?"

"If you can take the lead on this, you will certainly have to visit New City, and I'm sure Nick would be happy to serve you with your usual coffee."

"Will that include Gene?"

"Absolutely."

"I think you've got a deal, then. We're about up in the rotation. Just last week, Gene asked if we couldn't just drop in to see Nick and say hello. What's going on? You don't sound like it's the end of the world."

"Actually, I don't know what's going on, and this is very different from our previous cases."

"Want to tell me enough to sell Thor on our assignment?" Ron asked, referring to his Captain, Arne Thorason.

"One of our nursing aides found a naked man dead in a storage area this morning. Been dead at least a day according to Monique."

"Patient of yours?"

"No. We don't know his identity."

"So, not employee, either?"

"Nope. No clue. Just the way you like 'em, right? A blank sheet of paper."

"Anything else? How was he killed?"

"Mechanical pencil in the ear. Pushed into the brain."

"Ouch. I thought that was only a movie trick."

"Monique says that the cause of death."

"That's one smart lady. I won't argue. Let me get Gene and talk to Thor. I'll call you if we can't cover. Otherwise, we'll probably be over there to see you in an hour or so. You can keep all the personnel available for an interview?"

"Certainly. I'll tell Nick to be expecting you."

CHAPTER 14

TUESDAY, APRIL 6

Looney pulled out his phone and sent a text to his partner, Gene Novalchek. Gene was down in the ballistics section checking on findings concerning another case the two were working on. His message was simple; "Got new case at New City. Meet me at the car in 15 minutes." Then he grabbed his coat and weapon and walked over to the corner of the area where the Homicide detectives worked and knocked on the open door of the Captain's office.

Looney's office was on the fourth floor of the Cincinnati Police Department Building. The Homicide Detective Bureau operated out of the southwest corner of the building using their slightly less than a quarter of the floor to house a large open space with desks pushed face-to-face for partners. One corner was dedicated to printers and copiers with a large table for spreading out work, and another corner accommodated an enclosed, locked room containing active and inactive files. The main doorway entering the "Dick Pen", as it was known, was near the center of the floor; on either side was a short wall with coat hooks where personnel left their heavy coats during the winter. Otherwise, coats and sweaters and caps took up residence on desks and backs of chairs when the wearers were 'at work'.

The corner outside office was the Captain's. Located adjacent to a stairwell, the office was enclosed with walls of thin plaster up to waist height, topped by frosted glass up to the ceiling. The door also had frosted glass on which was lettered "Arne Thorason, Captain, Chief of Detectives" in bold Copperplate font. The door to the office was almost always open.

Captain Arne Thorason, or 'Thor', as he was known behind his back, was a 23 year veteran of the Cincinnati police department and, perhaps more importantly, a former college linebacker. Still built like he could plug holes in a defensive line, he was just short of six feet tall and was a solid 265 pounds with only a slight waistline bulge. Thorason liked wearing three-piece suits but always left the coat in his office while he was in the building. Overall, he resembled an old-time newspaper editor in a jacket-less three-piece suit with collar and tie loosened and sleeves rolled up. But his bulky appearance, squarish head, and bushy eyebrows were clear reminders of his former occupation. The eyes were the most important. When Thor squared up his body, tucked his head ever so slightly, and fixed you with his solemn, wide-eyed stare you felt like a freshman running back about to hit the turf on your back. 'The Look' was known throughout the department, and probably accounted for a major part of the work ethic in the detective division. No one wanted to explain their failure to meet the boss's standard.

Thor had an outstanding career in Homicide and was the natural choice for Captain when that position became available. Truth was, Arne Thorason was more than a little uncomfortable telling seasoned men and women the components of their job or how to do them. Nonetheless, he had accepted the job almost two decades previously and had then undertaken a slow and steady replacement of detectives to get precisely the ones he wanted working with him in the Dick Pen.

Part of Thor's career development strategy was "The Look". When a particular detective found that his work product or the effort he was expending was found lacking in Thor's eyes, he or she shortly came to suffer The Look. Whenever Thor squared up, and opened that wide-eyed stare, anyone who could get out of the way would promptly leave the vicinity. After only a few months of this strategy, several individuals requested a transfer out of Homicide, creating openings within the division.

Arne Thorason personally interviewed anyone wanting to transfer in and was shortly able to fill available posts in the division with individuals who met his standard. That standard was never expressly stated, but everyone understood it was 'start fast and speed up'. Plus, the underlying tenants were also assumed to be, 'don't ask me how to do your job' and 'be successful'. Anyone who could stick to those basic principles would have a fruitful career in Homicide. The standard came with a package of trust from Thor, a willingness to allow his detectives fairly broad lanes of scrutiny. He trusted his officers and let them use their intuition and 'gut' feelings rather than expecting strict by-the-book investigation.

A characteristic of the Captain's reluctance to tell detectives their job was his conversational reticence. Detectives would brief him on their progress at their discretion unless he specifically asked for a briefing. Most of Thor's responses to briefing material were transmitted as the monosyllabic, "Huh." Thor was prone to the use of that word to express a question, surprise, growing disinterest, or dismissal. His meaning was all in the inflection, and that was exceptionally subtle. There were those in the Dick Pen who believed there was no variation in inflection and that Thor was always basically disinterested unless the conversation involved an arrest.

Thor ran a good ship; the Homicide Division under his leadership was responsible for obtaining 60% closure of their cases with an arrest. Ron Looney had found that his style of working meshed very well with Thor's leadership style. Over the years, Ron had few instances where he had been the recipient of the famous 'Look' from Thor. Ron was also considered a leading interpreter of the Captain's single-word comments.

"Cap'n," Looney said.

Arne Thorason looked up from his desk. "Walker," he noted, using the appellation Looney had earned in the department.

"I got a call from my buddy over at New City. He has a DB," Looney said.

"Huh."

"Not a patient. Not an employee. They don't know the person, and he called to see if I could take the case."

Thor did not hesitate, He nodded quickly and went back to his desk work.

Looney spoke to the top of Thor's head, "I'll get Gene and we'll let you know." He turned and headed down the nearby staircase to the parking garage.

CHAPTER 15

TUESDAY, APRIL 6

Harry made a few calls from his burner phones. First, he called his supervisory associate at ABC, Morgan Riley.

"Riley here."

"Hey, Morgan, it's Harry. I'm not gonna be in today."

"Yeah, man. I heard about the car accident and all. Are you okay? I mean, we weren't expecting you back for a few days anyway."

"Oh. Okay, then. I didn't know. I'm getting out of the hospital later and just wanted you to know I wouldn't be there today."

"Not a problem. We've got your back. Take your time. I'm pretty sure this bus station will still be needing your touch whenever you get back."

"Okay, man. Thanks."

Harry hung up and thought, 'So, everybody thinks it was an accident, huh?'

His next call was to someone less familiar to him.

"Hello, this is Jess."

"Coach Tatterhorn?"

"Yes?"

"This is Harry Wilton. Henry's father."

"Yes. Of course, Mr. Wilton. How is Henry doing?"

"He's fine. That's not why I called. I need a favor and I thought you might be able to help me out of a jam."

"If I can, I'd be happy to do so. What do you need?"

"The pest control company is fumigating my house, and I can't stay there for a couple of days. I remember you mentioning that you have a spare room where some of the guys came and spent the night with you before games."

"That's right, I do have a room. And you are welcome to use it. When do you want to come over?"

"Well, I'm already out of the house so . . ."

"Okay. Look, I'm already at the high school. Do you have the address?"

"Yes."

"There's a spare key in the hollow of the maple tree to the right of the door. There's some cereal and milk, so make yourself at home."

"Thanks so much. Tell you what, I'm buying dinner tonight."

"Whatever. See you then, Mr. Wilton."

"Harry, please."

"Okay, Harry. See you tonight."

Harry felt better now that he had a roof over his head for the night. He had a fallback plan, in case Coach Tatterhorn's room was not available, but a real bed, warm food, plus hot and cold running water was preferable. He drove out of the parking lot and found a nearby

ATM. He was careful not to allow the camera to get a clear view of his face or any of his clothing that could identify him. He withdrew the maximum amount of money allowed and drove away. Rather than heading straight to the coach's house, however, he drove around to where Pritchard lived. He thought he might go in the apartment and find where the blackmail material was hidden. But when he got there the front door was so open and visible from the street he decided not to try it. So he slowly proceeded to Tatterhorn's neighborhood.

He circled the address a few times looking for somewhere to park his car and keep it hidden. He found a place two blocks away next to a fallen tree limb. Harry parked close to the downed limb and went to the trunk to repack some of his belongings. He left the Glock, the magazines, the sleeping bag, the telescope and the torch in the rear of the car. He removed some of the clothes from the backpack to lighten it. He had a cheap canvas car cover in the trunk that he spread quickly over his vehicle. Then he hoisted the backpack in place and walked to Tatterhorn's. The key was easily found and Harry went in.

He laid the key on the small side table beside the door, and looked around. Tatterhorn had a nice place. It had two bedrooms but only one bathroom. He went in the bathroom and rummaged through drawers until he found some Advil, took two, and went into the back bedroom. The room was warm and inviting but had the feel of being uninhabited. He tossed the backpack by the bed and laid down. After only a few minutes, however, he sat up again. He had made a decision. A question had been nagging him ever since the 'accident'. He knew it was deliberate, and he knew it was because of his initial telegram. Somehow Greene had figured out the telegram came from him. And now he, Harry Wilton, was a marked man. He had hoped to take the payoff and put it in the bank for Henry's college fund and keep on working. That plan was out of the question now.

He had worried about what to do, but now he had decided. He was going to up the ante and see how Greene responded. If Greene had someway of finding the blackmail information, he would never negotiate. Harry was still smarting from the attempt on his life and remembered that the attempt was made when it was almost certain that Greene did not have access to Pritchard's cache. Harry wanted

Greene to pay for that attempt, and for Pritchard, too. He decided to double the blackmail request, and then run with the money. He pulled out one of the burner phones and sent a second telegram. Then he changed the greeting message on the referenced phone and lay back down. This time he was able to sleep.

CHAPTER 16

TUESDAY, APRIL 6

Gene Novalchek slid into the passenger's seat and fastened his seatbelt. At six feet tall and 190 pounds Gene had more DNA from his Swedish mother than his Polish father. He had a narrow but attractive face, topped by light brown hair with a widow's peak on the forehead. His nose turned up slightly at the end giving plenty of room to his broad, usually smiling mouth. His smile revealed even, white teeth that sometimes appeared too large for his mouth. His face was expressive and generally smiling because he had a positive attitude about life in general. Gene had been a cruiserweight boxer in college and knew what it felt like to be knocked down; he preferred to remain standing.

Gene and Ron had a good partnership. Gene met Ron's standard of not requiring instruction and Ron met Gene's standard of a positive outlook on life, even in the midst of homicide cases. They each respected the other's instincts and the lack of running around wearing a hard pucker all the time. Gene was also the best dressed man in the Homicide squad room, an area referred to as the 'Dick Pen'. He seemed to have a new suit every few months and every day wore an attractive tie that no one could remember having seen before.

In spite of all the positivity in the partnership, Gene constantly chipped away at his partner's decision to take his personal car on assignments.

"Is this seat still broken?" he asked as he clipped the seat belt.

"Never has been broken." Ron replied, not looking at him.

"It fells like there's a metal bar or something running through it."

"Probably is. Part of the construction."

"But it's uncomfortable. I think there's something broken."

"It's not the seat. It may be your skinny ass that doesn't have enough padding."

"Hardly a family-oriented selling point for . . . what is this car again?"

"It's a Nissan Sentra."

"Oh yeah, I remember. The one that used to be Datsun."

Ron gave his partner an eye-roll as he pulled out of the parking deck and headed for New City Hospital.

The hospital, located to the west of downtown, near the rail yards had originally been the Railway Hospital for railroad workers and their families. After World War II a building boom in hospitals brought a new University Hospital, with air conditioning, to Cincinnati. When the University partnered with the Veterans Administration to provide care at the VA facility, Railway began to lose attraction. The facility changed hands, was bought by the city and tried to keep up with the times over the next decade. Finally, it was purchased by Regents Incorporated and fashioned into a for-profit hospital named New City.

Regents played the long game and initially spent effort attracting patients from the surrounding towns and cities. In 1965, the organization embraced the Medicare program more quickly and fully than other city facilities. With three years, New City Hospital was financially strong. As the medical profession and technology developed better treatments and higher cure rates, New City became a local leader in innovation and opening programs such as the heart surgery program, the neonatal specialty wing, and the recently opened women's program. Construction added to the original Railway building and the 'new' New City on Front Street included the new hospital building, a research wing and a special cardiac tower.

The old building became a medical office building with upmarket private practice office space for outpatient care directly tied to the hospital. The State Forensic Laboratory opened a branch toxicology and microbiology center in the building. The recent affiliation between the hospital and the Southwest Ohio Medical School in town completed the functional transformation of Railway to cutting edge medicine in New City. The functional upgrade was also a visible one as the new two-block structure and flaring tower were visible from I-75 for miles.

Gene changed the subject as Ron drove. "It's been a while since we were out here. I hope Nick hasn't forgotten us."

"I gather that Nick never forgets a 'usual'. Tom says he's convinced they would lose85 business in the hospital if Nick ever left."

They were discussing the barista in the Green Bean kiosk in the New City lobby. Nick was a former Air Force member with incredible skills with an espresso machine. Further, he seemed to remember the favorite drink of everyone who frequented the kiosk. On a recent case at New City, Nick had decided that both Ron and Gene should have a 'usual' drink, a Red-Eye. An Americano with a shot of espresso. The detectives became quite fond of the drink and of Nick.

"Let's be sure we stop at the Green Bean before going to Tom's office."

"Really? You think I need to be reminded to do that?"

They walked into the lobby in mid-morning and the line at the kiosk was short. The detectives took their place in the line and when Nick looked up from his work and saw them, he grinned and asked, "The usual, guys?"

They both nodded agreement and headed for the cashier. Nick brought their drinks over and said, "I haven't seen you for months. Everything okay?"

"Well," Ron said, "we're here on business so, not completely."

Gene quickly added, "But our day is so much better now since we have your coffee."

"Glad to be of service," Nick said, giving a semblance of a salute and returning to his machine.

The detectives moved across the lobby to the door leading into the executive suite. Inside, they found their way to Tom's office area and were greeted by his secretary, Mary Brighthouse.

"Gentlemen," she said rising from her desk. "Let me see if he's ready for you." She tapped on Tom's office door and cracked it open. "The detectives are here."

Receiving some signal from inside, she opened the door and indicated that Ron and Gene should enter.

They found Tom sitting at his desk with his executive assistant, Beverly Hancock and the pathologist, Monique Song also in the room.

Ron nodded to the women and said to Tom. "Looks like we're getting the band back together." They had a short period of hand-shaking and reminiscing and then everyone sat down and turned to business.

Tom started the discussion. "I've given you a brief picture over the phone. Let me give you the story as we know it right now."

Ron interrupted, "Crime scene?"

Tom nodded, "In time. The body is not there but it is closed off for your investigation. Ron and Gene shrugged and indicated agreement. Tom continued, "Early this morning, one of our nursing aides went into a room used mostly for storage of items like beds and wheelchairs. He found a naked man in one of the beds. When he realized the man was dead he called the nurses and they notified me and Sam."

At the mention of the director's name, Ron cocked his head and raised his eyebrows. Tom inserted, "He's stepped back and told me to run this."

Then he went on, " We are now certain that the man was not a patient in the hospital, now or ever. He is not an employee and we are reasonably certain he is not a relative of an employee."

"So, no identification," Gene's comment was declarative, not a question.

"Agreed." Monique examined him and determined the cause of death was a mechanical pencil jammed into his right ear and into the brain."

Gene whistled.

"Further, Monique says he died about twenty-four hours before he was found."

The detectives looked at Monique. She nodded and they turned back to Tom. He went on, "Monique felt this was a city issue and she called your medical examiner. She has the body downtown already."

Ron again asked, "Crime scene?"

Tom nodded and said, "Obviously, no one had gone in there until the body was discovered. Since then the only people in that room are the aide, the charge nurse, the night nurse supervisor, Monique, me, Sam and Dr. Darringer and her team."

Monique spoke up, "I did examine the body but I also took some pictures with my phone before touching anything."

"That's great, doc. You're right on top of things, just like always."

Beverly said, "We have all the people gathered upstairs in a conference room for you to interview. They are night shift and would like to get home soon."

Ron nodded, "Got it. I guess we can start there and then look at the scene. Gene?"

"Totally backwards but probably okay in this instance. Let's go."

Coffee cups were dispatched into the wastebasket beside Tom's desk and the detectives followed Beverly out the door.

CHAPTER 17

TUESDAY, APRIL 6

The pattern of crime scene inspection by Ron and Gene involved each of them circling the scene individually. They did this from different directions, one clockwise the other in the opposite. Only after they had individually observed the scene would they put their heads together and settle on what facts were clear.

They circled the empty bed as best they could in the crowded room where the bed was headed up against the wall. Every few steps, one or the other would stoop low and use their flashlight to closely examine the floor or the area immediately under the bed. They took their time because no one was waiting for them to clear the scene for body removal. But, they were satisfied with their examination of the bed and surroundings in less than fifteen minutes.

They met at the foot of the bed, and Ron spoke first, "I don't see any marks on the floor."

"Nope, me either."

"Dr. Song's pictures indicate he was lying on his right side as if he was asleep."

"No cover, though. The bed has no sheets."

"That's right. Someone put a sheet over him later. That's evident in her later pictures."

"So, no drag marks means someone carried him to the bed."

"I think that's right. Meaning the killer is strong."

"How big is our guy?"

"He doesn't look very big in the pictures. The doc will have a weight for us."

"I'm good with that. But why take his clothes?"

"Mess with the identification maybe?"

"Do you have to undress a body to take his billfold?"

"No. You don't. But you would if you needed the clothes for some reason."

"I can imagine somebody wanting my clothes," Gene said with a smile. "But I don't see changing clothes with a dead guy helping anybody."

"Maybe the killer was wearing something distinctive like a Reds jacket and needed to blend in better. Be less noticeable."

"That's an idea. So he gets our guy in here and kills him and then changes clothes and leaves the body behind … and, what? Gene reacted to his partner shaking his head.

"So, where are the other clothes? The ones he took off?" Ron asked.

"Well, he couldn't leave them, could he? If they were distinctive that would pin this killing on him. So, he took them and threw them away somewhere."

Tom, Beverly, and Monique had been standing to one side watching the detectives do their job. Ron now turned to Tom and said, "Could you get someone to look in all the trash containers between here and the exit? It's possible the killer changed clothes with this guy so he wouldn't be recognized."

Tom looked at Beverly and she left the room, pulling her cellphone out of her pocket.

Gene said, "I'm pretty much done here. I want to go see the body."

Ron asked Tom, "How long to finish that search?"

Tom shrugged, "Couple of hours I expect."

"Okay. We'll be back to follow up on that. Gene's right we need to see the body and see what Darringer can tell us." He turned to Monique and handed her back her phone. "Those pictures were very helpful, doc. Thanks again for thinking of that."

In the car on the way to the city morgue, Gene asked, "What do you think about killing someone with a pencil in the ear?"

"I don't know. Seems like that would be hard to do. The bones around the ear are thick as I recall."

"Yeah, that's true but the earhole does run all the way in."

"That would take some skill."

"And probably need to have the guy with the ear hold still for it."

"You think he was already dead?"

"I'm just saying, it would be hard to hit that little hole with a guy dancing around. I read something a few years ago about a guy in prison killing his cellmate by driving a pencil into his ear."

"I thought that was just for fight scenes in the movies."

"Well, in this instance, the cellmate was asleep. That would give you time to line things up, I guess."

"Still have to be lucky."

"Or skilled."

"You mean like the Special Operators we've dealt with before?"

"Maybe. Could be. We oughta check. Maybe the dead guy was a visitor and the killer was in some special uniform with medals and braids and stuff. He needed to get out of the hospital without being recognized, so he kills somebody his size and changes clothes."

'Hmmm."

"You don't sound like you agree."

"Couple of things about that bother me. First, If the killer picks somebody the same size, how does he kill him and handle everything without leaving a mark? No, I think our killer is a big guy. Bigger than the dead guy.

"Second?"

"Well, a guy in uniform with ribbons and all would certainly be noticeable, right? We could ask and see if anybody saw anyone like that around. But a guy with that uniform and medals wouldn't throw that stuff away. He would find a way to carry it out."

"You mean like in a clothes bag?"

"Something like that. And if that's true, then we are not going to find any clothes left behind to help us track down the killer."

"Okay, then. I'm sorry I thought of it."

"Maybe we can keep pieces of your theory."

"Like what?"

"Like maybe the guy is one of the Special Operators. But we don't have to dress him up in uniform with medals and ribbons."

"Okay. What do we dress him in?"

CHAPTER 18

TUESDAY, APRIL 6

"Greene," he answered using his cell phone.

"Colonel, it's Nestor."

"What did you find?"

"Nothing. He's not here."

"Been there?"

"Probably. The car is gone."

"Was it there before?"

"Can't be sure. He didn't have it at the hospital."

"Why was he out walking that night?"

"He had been at a restaurant."

"Maybe he drove, and his car is in some parking lot down there."

"You want us to ask the neighbors?"

"No. Don't be seen around there. Why do you think he's been there already?"

"Well, I was guessing because of the car being gone and all."

"All what?"

"Nothing, really. The place looks all buttoned up."

"What about mail?"

"There's some on the floor in the front hall."

"Are you in the house?"

"Yes, sir. We came in the back way. Picked the kitchen door lock. A piece of cake."

Greene's voice became harsh. "You better not leave any fingerprints or other evidence in there."

"We won't, Colonel. We're wearing gloves."

"When is the mail dated?"

"Last three days."

"So, even if he did come back to the house, he didn't mess with the mail. Why do you think he's been there?"

Nestor thought about that for a moment. "Uh, I guess just the car."

"Any clothes missing?"

"Can't really tell. Lots of stuff hanging in every closet. No real gaps in the arrangement."

Greene was quiet, thinking. He did not want his men spotted or to leave any trace at Harry's house. If this guy, Wilton, turned up dead somewhere and the cops decide to look at his house …, well, that shouldn't happen. Greene took a breath and made a decision. "I'm betting his car is in some downtown parking lot. If he got out of the hospital, he would have gone right there and then run out of town."

"You said he might still be in the hospital."

"I said he might still be there. We don't know where he is, do we?"

"No, sir."

"Can you put a watch on the house?"

"Sure, but we're likely to be noticed. It's a small street, and the houses are close."

"Open at both ends?"

"Yes, sir."

"Then drive by frequently in different cars. See if his car shows up or the lights go on at night or something. And get some other guys to go look in all the parking decks near where he was eating at that restaurant. Give them the description of the car and see if they can find it."

"Yes, sir."

"And don't be seen getting out of there."

"Roger that."

Greene leaned back in his chair and considered the possibilities. First, Wilton may now be gone, scared for his life, and willing to run and hide to stay safe. That would be the best option, as far as Greene was concerned. But somehow, deep inside, he did not believe Wilton had run for his life. So he considered the second possibility: that Wilton was alive and in hiding but intended to keep up the blackmail. This possibility was unsettling for Greene since it probably meant that Wilton had moved his operation to someplace other than his home. Such a move would make Wilton hard to find. Unless ..., Greene smiled to himself as he came across an idea to use Wilton's carefulness against him.

Greene smiled at his own clearness. Now, all it would take is for Wilton to try to continue the blackmail scheme.

CHAPTER 19

TUESDAY, APRIL 6

Kathryn Darringer looked more like someone's grandmother than the Cincinnati City Medical Examiner. She was five foot eight inches and solidly built with a broad face and expressive blue eyes. Her hair was light brown and streaked with gray but always neat and kept out of her face. Her wide mouth was commonly slanted in a wry grin as if she had just discovered something inappropriately humorous. When she put on her apron for a post-mortem and her wire-framed glasses, she mostly resembled a grandmother busily working in her kitchen. But when she went to work and engaged the police in discussions about her work, she was anything but grandmotherly. Her insightful comments and occasionally stinging remarks often provided a highlight for Ron's day.

Gene, however, was often the butt of Darringer's comments and was somewhat less comfortable in her 'laboratory'. She was aware of Gene's interest in food; she aimed several of her humorous comments at that target. Dr. Darringer's 'laboratory' looked almost exactly like every other city morgue. Gray painted concrete flooring slanted into a large, centrally placed drain, walls of puke colored ceramic tile on the bottom half, industrial gray paint on the top. One side of the large room had a series of refrigerated mortuary cabinets, three high and eight in width. Between the drain and the wall on each side was a metal non-vented autopsy table with over-hanging operating room lights, each affixed with a hanging microphone operated by a foot pedal. No casual observer would ever confuse this room with anything other than a morgue.

Darringer, however, always referred to the room as her 'laboratory'. Her approach to the work in the morgue had always been that of scientific examination. She considered nothing, and no body, as run-of-the-mill; everyone was unique and deserved her utmost care and attention; in current parlance, everybody matters. Kathryn Darringer considered herself, first and foremost, a scientist, and she correctly viewed the morgue as her area for conducting a scientific inquiry. She was most comfortable asking hard questions, putting findings to rigorous analysis, and seeking the best answers. In short, as far as she was concerned, she worked in a scientific laboratory. And she told everyone that, and she expected the same attitude from everyone else.

"Good morning," she said to the detectives as they entered.

"Morning, doc," Ron said, noting that Darringer had the man from the hospital on her table, and was about to make a "Y" incision. "Anything on external examination?"

"There was the obvious metal pencil in his right ear. It wouldn't come out easily, so I left it in until I open the skull." She paused in her approach to answer Ron.

"No identifying marks?"

"No. You can see the x-rays on the box over there. No implants or anything to track."

"I see you already got the fingerprints," Gene said, pointing at the inked fingers.

"Oh, yes. I sent those over first. That seemed like our best shot at an identification." Another aspect of Darringer's approach that Ron appreciated was her attitude that she was part of a team investigating deaths, not a technical gatherer of tissue. Her use of the plural in seeking identification was another indicator of her deep involvement.

Responding to that opening, Ron commented, "We don't have any additional information from the hospital and the crime scene. We thought the killer must have lifted this guy and put him on the bed. How much does he weigh?"

Darringer nodded toward the whiteboard on the wall where the diener had posted vital information during the autopsy. "He was five foot seven and weighed 158 pounds."

"So, if we're right about the movement of the body, the killer must be closer to six feet tall and have some significant upper body strength."

"Maybe I did see something that you want to know about," Darringer said. She laid her knife down and stepped to the head of the body. She rotated the head to the left, commenting, "There's the cause of death," pointing at the mechanical pencil protruding a couple of inches from the man's ear. She went on, "I noticed this but wasn't sure what it meant." She then raised the man's chin and showed the mild reddish-purple bruising on each side of the neck. "Your idea about moving the body may fit with this."

"A chokehold?"

"Yes, exactly. And a hold that would allow a taller man to lift this man off his feet ..."

"By leveraging him on his hip," Ron finished for her.

"I believe so," she said, pleased that they saw things in the same way.

Gene said, "If the killer had him in a chokehold with his left arm like this," and he mimicked such a position, "then his right hand would be free to insert the pencil."

"That's good, detective," Darringer said approvingly. "That means the killer is likely right-handed."

"Nice work, you two," Ron said sarcastically. "Now we've successfully narrowed our suspect pool down to 85% of the population."

"Every little bit helps," Darringer said and picked up her knife.

Gene wrinkled his nose at what would happen next. "Hey, I think I'll just go check on those fingerprints, okay?"

Darringer looked at him from under her eyebrows as she bent over the body. "Why don't you get something to eat while you're at it, detective?"

"I think I'll wait to eat lunch somewhere else, but thanks for the thought, doc." He pushed through the swinging doors.

Twenty minutes later, with the chest cavity and abdomen open, Darringer looked up at Ron and said, "I don't think there's going to be anything in here to help. The stomach was empty, and there's no obvious finding that will help identify this man. I'll get portions for the microscope, of course, and I'll section the brain this afternoon."

Ron nodded.

Darringer said, "After that, I will have the instrument of death available for you to examine."

"All right, then. Thanks, doc. Call us when you do, and we'll keep you posted." Ron said, emphasizing his recognition of the team effort, too. Then he went looking for Gene.

CHAPTER 20

TUESDAY, APRIL 6

Greene looked at the second telegram and ground his teeth. He was in his law office when the telegram was delivered, reading a brief on a small settlement case. When the deliveryman handed him the envelope, Greene knew it contained a message he would not like. After reading the short note, he crumpled it and threw it against the wall.

"Conor," he yelled.

A muffled "Coming" came from the outside office.

Conor MacCarter came in quickly to see what his boss wanted.

"Yes, Colonel?" he asked as he entered and closed the door behind him.

"This damn guy is at it again," Greene said, pointing at the crumpled paper on the floor.

Without speaking, Conor picked up the telegram, opened it, and read. He looked at Greene with no comment other than a raised eyebrow. The message was:

STOP LOOKING. YOUR ACTION DOUBLED

OUR REASONS. ALL DATA RETURNED

WITH PAYMENT.

"Double! Now he wants double!" Greene spit the words at his executive assistant.

"And that is still something we can do if that's what you want," Conor said with a flat affect. He maintained his eye contact with Greene until the Colonel huffed and returned to his seat behind the large mahogany desk.

"Yes," he said, "I know we can manage that amount. But if the man is going to jack us up now, I think we can be certain this is not the end."

"You did try to have him killed, sir."

Greene stared at Conor and squared his shoulders, not denying the accusation. His unspoken attitude was 'so what?' and seemed to indicate he was waiting for a response to an implicit 'what shall we do?'

Conor re-read the telegram, then asked, "What about the differences between this message and the first?"

"What do you mean? He's asking for $2 million this time."

"There are some other differences, too. Maybe important ones."

"What differences?"

"If I remember correctly, the first message said, 'The fake is known.' And we took that to mean he knew about JY Dahgs as a front."

"Right. So? There's nothing about that in this message."

"I agree. The first message read: For a million reasons, I won't tell, right?"

"Yes."

"And by 'tell' he meant he would reveal 'facts' to the newspapers."

"We've gone over this before. That's what he said, and that's what we understood. What's your point?"

"Well, I think our previous discussions centered on finding out who he was, rather than what information he had to give to the newspapers. I assumed he intended to tip them off and let them dig out the facts for themselves."

"I remember all that. Again, what's your point?"

"Well, this message says he will 'return all data with payment.' I think that means he has documentation. Probably copies of fake invoices and payment checks."

"How did he get those?"

"That's my point, boss. The other difference in this message is a clear indication that there are at least two individuals involved in this blackmail operation. The message says 'your action doubled our reasons'. I take that to mean that the attempted hit-and-run increased the price for 'them'. That means at least one other person."

"Who?"

"Again, you asked the key question before. You said, how would 'he' get documentation. Initially, we thought this was the action of a single person, a guy out on the worksite with ABC who had stumbled on the Dahgs fiction."

"But now . . ."

"But now," Conor said with a tight little grin, "We know he didn't stumble on this information at the worksite. He got the information from someone in Accounts or Contracting."

"How will we find that person?"

"That won't be easy. I will have to find a reason to go to ABC to talk to people in those areas. Maybe you can think of a legal issue with some case you have."

"Or I can start an investigation for the Council."

"Let's not do that just yet. I would rather keep your name and the council out of any inquiry. That might happen if I get recognized asking about things in there."

"Right. Good idea."

"I know a woman who has a friend at ABC who recently had a baby. She works in Contracting, and maybe I can talk with her for some reason. Let me think about it, boss."

"I've got Nestor and Jorge out looking for Wilton. He seems to have slipped out of the hospital and gone into hiding if he feels safe enough to send a second telegram."

"Maybe when we find the second person, we can root out his hiding place." Conor took the telegram and left, again closing the door behind him.

Greene leaned back in his chair and thought for a moment about what he would do when he caught Wilton. It would have to look like an accident, of course. But, then there's the 'accident' that didn't kill him. Maybe someone would think too hard about a second 'accident'. No, it would be better if Wilton, and whoever his accomplice or partner turns out to be, would disappear. Disappearance is much harder to figure out.

As long as no one ever finds the body. That's the tricky part. Bodies thrown in the lake will sometimes float. Animals open up graves in the woods. Too bad we can't put them in a rocket and shoot them to the moon.

Greene shook his head and opened the bottom right-hand drawer of his desk and took out a bottle of single malt Scotch whiskey, and poured himself a generous drink. He sipped at the whiskey, hoping it would help him develop a way to handle the situation. He leaned back in his chair and closed his eyes to visualize the problem and immediately realized he had the answer right in front of him. ABC was doing a major construction project. His men could take the bodies into the worksite and put them into the forms where ABC was pouring the footers for the bus station. No one would ever find those bodies. Not in this century, at least.

Delighted with himself for a plan that would solve all his problems, Greene opened the drawer again, refreshed his drink, and picked up the folder on the case he had been studying.

CHAPTER 21

TUESDAY, APRIL 6

Ron and Gene slid into their usual booth. Ron spent his initial moments wondering what the previous occupant had spilled on the seat. Gene was looking to the rear of the café for Sandy.

They had been coming to this café for over two years. One reason was the nearness to headquarters, another was the food. American-style sandwiches, French fries, and onion rings were the staples of the menu. But the overriding reason for their continued patronage was the main waitress, Sandy, a tall, red-haired, shapely lass who took to calling Gene 'honey' on their third visit. Gene had been only slightly embarrassed by her action.

That familiarity progressed. Soon each detective had a 'usual' sandwich. Ron had broken the mold and changed his order once, and Gene was concerned this might break their bond with Sandy. Four months after their initial visit, Ron started heckling 'honey' Gene about how he stared at Sandy and pushed him to ask her on a date. Gene was usually not shy around women but he seemed reluctant to approach Sandy at first. Ron pointed out two important facts to sway his partner's decision: first, Sandy had made the first move with the whole 'honey' thing. Second, there were many other places they could go for lunch. He pressed Gene to ask Sandy out on a date.

Gene had done so, with more than a little trepidation, and took Sandy to an upscale restaurant for dinner. The evening was a success. And, of course, the relationship did not stop there. Now the cop and the waitress were a pair, expected at any social gathering, and Gene seemed a more content policeman than he had been for months. And they made plans to have lunch in this café every day.

Sandy saw them and made a small wave while continuing to take other patrons' orders. Gene realized she would be a few minutes before getting to them. The detectives no longer needed to look at the menu, so Gene started reviewing the case by asking, "Where do we go next?"

"What do we know?" Ron asked. He liked being the one who wrote down their lists and his interview notes in a small pocket notebook. He now regularly used the Parker T-ball Jotter that his children gave him for Christmas. Previously he had been the epitome of an old-fashioned detective, taking his notes with a stubby pencil. He pulled out the notebook and found a blank page.

Gene pondered a moment and said, "Not much, really. I guess we can say we know the cause of death and the approximate time of death, but that's about all."

"Well, we know the place, too."

"Okay, yeah. We know that."

"That's a short list."

"And we have none of the important ones, like victim's identity or a motive."

"Or why he was left naked."

"I think naked should be one of the Knowns …"

Sandy appeared at the table at that moment and asked, "Why do you want gnomes to be naked, Gene? That sounds a little kinky."

Even though he knew she was kidding, Gene blushed and tried to explain, "We're making our list of Knowns. That's all."

She winked at Ron and asked, very businesslike, "Are you having the usual today?"

Gene said, "Yes, please."

Ron shook his head and indicated he wanted the hot pastrami sandwich with onion rings and no fries.

Sandy took their orders for drinks and walked back to the kitchen. Both detectives silently watched her walk until she left their sight.

Ron took a deep breath and said, "I agree, naked is a definite Known."

They discussed the total lack of help from the fingerprints. There was no match for the man's fingerprints in any criminal database and, on first look, he had no military experience, either. They discussed other known fingerprint databases and weighed the possible value of trying those for a match.

"We don't have any reason to think this guy would be in the Interpol file, do we?" Gene wanted to know.

Ron said, "I don't think so, but our lack of a reason doesn't mean that there is no reason." That philosophical insight pushed them into quiet reflection until Sandy showed up with their orders.

While eating their sandwiches, they continued to discuss what they did know. Gene, eating his patty melt, suggested they spend more thought figuring out why the dead man was naked.

"Your comment does remind me of something," Ron said.

"What's that?"

"An old Arkansas saying. If you're nude, you simply don't have any clothes on, but if you're naked, then you have no clothes on, and you're up to something!"

"Spot on, partner. This guy was definitely up to something, and it got him killed."

Ron tried to start at a beginning point, "So, if we agree that he did not walk into the hospital naked, then we have a series of questions: Did the killer take the clothes, and if so, why?"

"And where are the killer's clothes? What did the killer do with them?"

I see only three possibilities. One, he discarded them somewhere in the hospital. Two, he took them with him and discarded them elsewhere. Or three, he wore them."

"Wait, you mean he took the dead guy's clothes and put them on over his own?"

"Well, I see that as a possibility."

"Why would he do that?"

"I don't know. To change his appearance I guess. We're talking in circles here."

"People are looking for some discarded clothes in and around the hospital. If they find them, then we have something to go on. If not, we may be closer to number three."

"Of course, if we get to number three, we still have to determine what the killer may have done with his own clothes."

"All the same questions."

When they had finished eating, Ron gave some bills to Gene and went to collect the car. This was part of their routine. Gene would pay the bill and have some time to chat with Sandy. Ron slowly walked up the block to the car and even sat in the driver's seat for a minute or two before starting the engine. There was an odd thought running through his head about the last item he and Gene discussed. Something about the killer doing something with his own clothes.

The thought didn't crystallize, so Ron started the car and drove to the front of the café to pick up Gene.

Later that afternoon, Greene's cell phone buzzed.

"Greene"

"Boss, it's Conor. I've been over to ABC. There's a guy in Accounting named Thomas Pritchard who helped out for a short time in Contracting a while back. He would have had all the access to get to that information on Dahgs."

"Get him over here."

"That's just it. No one has seen him for the last two days."

"Find him and bring him in here!"

"Yes, sir."

CHAPTER 22

TUESDAY, APRIL 6

Anton Green was shuffling through some papers in his Councilman's office. He did not have his mind fully engaged with the issues on his desk at the moment. His secretary buzzed on the intercom and notified him that Mr. Aramano would like to speak to him. It further irritated him that Nestor would call him when he was in the city office.

"Yes?" Greene's voice was clipped.

"Sir, we were not able to find that ah, particular article you asked for."

"Why not?"

"We checked the one store where we thought it might be. There's nothing on the shelf."

"Did you ask around?"

"Yes, sir. We asked the owner of the store. He said he was not aware that he was out, and didn't have a notion where else we could maybe find one."

"How about delivery vehicles?"

"None here, of course."

"You should probably trace that delivery vehicle. If you can locate it, you can ask the driver, right?"

"Absolutely. We will get right on that, sir." The line went dead.

Greene sat back in his chair. Things were not going well right now. For some reason, Nestor had chosen to call him at City Hall, necessitating a need for talking in code. He understood Nestor's code. Aramano said he and Jorge had located Thomas Pritchard's apartment, but the man was not there. Further, the landlord had no idea he was gone and no idea about where he might be.

And Pritchard's car was not around, either. Greene considered possibilities and decided that meant Pritchard is probably running. And he, Greene, had no idea when Pritchard might have started running. Further, there's no telling which way he may have gone or how far he may have gotten by now. Green wanted to slam his hand on the desk but refrained. Why does everything have to be so hard?

Greene knew that Nestor had some inside method to track automobile traffic, probably from a cop he knows. If they get any information to indicate that Pritchard has left the city, we probably will have to let him go. But if he's still here in Cincinnati, Greene had to hope his guys would find him. They have to. And they have to find that Wilton guy, too. Or the whole plan could collapse in on itself.

CHAPTER 23

TUESDAY, APRIL 6

Harry was good for his word about buying dinner that night. After the coach, Jess Tatterhorn, came home from school, Harry suggested Chinese food for dinner. Jess thought that sounded good so Harry called a take-out he knew and had the food delivered. The two men fussed about in the small kitchen a bit, finding plates and silverware before Harry and Jess sat at the dinner table and ate. Tatterhorn made hot tea, and Harry said that was all right even though he would have preferred a beer. Hot tea with a meal of Chinese food seemed historically correct.

Harry tended to eat from the carton using chopsticks, but Tatterhorn put his food on a plate and ate with a fork. Harry hesitated but, since they were sharing the courses, he also forked out a measure of the shrimp in lobster sauce on a plate for himself, leaving plenty for his host. He did use the included chopsticks, however. To each his own. After they finished with the entrees, Jess heated up the teapot, and Harry cracked open the order of Chinese doughnuts.

"That was very good, Harry. I've never had anything like the Green Jade scallops. They were very delicious. Thank you for suggesting Chinese," Jess said, taking a doughnut.

"The least I could do for someone sheltering me. Henry and I had Chinese about once a week and we tried the whole menu at that place at one time or another."

Jess nodded as he said, "Well, you certainly picked two spectacular dishes. And we didn't come close to eating it all."

Harry chuckled, "That's because Henry wasn't here. That kid put away more calories in a day than I do in a week."

"Yeah, that's one of the attributes of that age," Jess agreed. Both took bites of donuts, and Jess changed the subject, "How long will you be out of the house?"

"Not completely sure. A day or two, probably. If I'm in the way here, just let me know, I'll move right away."

"Oh no, you're fine. I wasn't suggesting anything. I'm just curious. What are they fumigating for?"

"Apparently, a whole spectrum of bugs." Harry had searched the Internet for services provided by fumigators so he could back up his excuse. "They go in and check on the results after 48 hours."

"Was it termites?"

"Yes, predominantly. I let the protection plan lapse after Carole died, and noticed some activity a couple of weeks ago. The inspector said it's too advanced for spraying."

"Nasty business."

"You're not kidding. First, I had to get all the plants over to neighbors. Then, I needed to specially pack all the food in the refrigerator and the freezer. Might have been easier to burn it down and take the insurance money."

Jess looked surprised at this comment until he realized Harry was joking. "Yeah, that's what some people say about moving."

"That may be even worse."

They moved their tea and last doughnuts into the living room. Harry was hoping they wouldn't be watching the television news. He was relieved when Jess made no motion to turn on the television. Instead, he asked Harry, "How is Henry doing?"

"Oh, you know. First year away from home. Everything looks bright and shiny."

"Classes okay?"

"Well, you know he wasn't in competition for valedictorian in high school. But he seems to be doing all right. He has a solid 3.0 GPA from the first semester."

"Does he have a major, yet?"

"I don't think so, but he is taking courses in the Econ track."

"And his lacrosse?"

"He says they practice all the time. He has gained about twelve pounds, and he says it is all muscle. He's eating in the athletes' dining hall and loves that."

"Is he getting much playing time?"

"Not much yet. I'm sure you know, the team has budding All-Americans at attack and on long-pole, and Henry may not get in much this year."

"He knew about that long-pole boy when he agreed to go there. Said it was an attraction," Jess said with a wry smile. "It always looks better in theory."

"I guess that's true about lots of areas."

"You're in construction, aren't you?"

"Yes. That's right. We're working on the new bus station."

"Are you going to clean it up or take it down?"

"Oh, it's coming down. That's my part of the job. I'm the demolition guy."

"Oh, wow! That sounds like a lot of fun. Blowing stuff up."

"Again, better in theory than in practice."

"How did you get into that line of work?"

"A natural progression, I guess. I was in the Army and applied for Ranger training. I did well enough to get into the company, and everybody on the team has a specialty. I got the explosives. You, know, blow open doors, close off tunnels, things like that."

"So what happened?"

"I got hurt jumping off a building. That did a number on my knee. Three surgeries and a year of physical therapy, and I still couldn't run up a flight of stairs."

"Meaning?"

"Meaning I was no longer fit for duty as a Ranger. So I transferred into the Engineering Brigade, and they made me the demolition expert."

Jess shook his head and commented, "I guess everyone has a story about how they got to their destination, right?"

"Probably. How about you?"

"Nothing exciting. I got a degree in Education while playing D-III lacrosse. Started at the school here right out of college. Was the assistant coach for three years and stayed when the other guy moved on."

"What do you teach, other than coaching?"

"Mathematics. Speaking of which, I have to grade some papers before tomorrow. Then I'm gonna hit the shower and go to bed.

Chinese food always makes me sleepy." He picked up the cups and took them into the kitchen. Harry joined him and helped with the minimal cleanup after dinner.

Jess smiled and said, "Thanks again for dinner. I think we may have enough leftovers for tomorrow."

"I like leftovers."

"Okay, then. If you want to watch TV, the remote is on the side table."

"Ah, no thanks. I believe I'll just go to bed early, too."

"I'll be up and out of here by six-thirty in the morning. Are you going to work?"

"Uh, not for a day or so. Nothing for me to blow up just yet."

"Well, sleep in or whatever, then. I'll see you tomorrow night."

"Right. Good night."

CHAPTER 24

WEDNESDAY, APRIL 7

Tom and Beverly were the first to arrive at the morning meeting. They took their usual seats to wait for the other to arrive. Beverly had already briefed Tom on the Gains and Losses sheet from the previous twenty-four hours, so they sat and sipped their coffee. Tom looked at his phone and said, "Why do they do stuff like that?"

"What are you talking about?"

"My phone did an automatic update this morning, and that rearranged all my icons."

"That's what the programmers do. They make things 'easier' for you."

"I know your son is working for those devils, but that's no excuse for you to try to explain this kind of negative improvement."

"Negative improvement, is it?"

"Yes. Once I get things the way I want them, I want everything to stay the same unless I decide to make a change."

"Aren't you the famous 'Change Agent' of the Air Force?"

"I didn't change the furniture when people were sleeping. I led people to decide what changes they wanted to make."

Sam entered in the middle of that statement by Tom. He said, "I don't want the furniture moved. It's right where I want it."

"Morning, Sam."

"What are you discussing?"

Beverly explained, "Dr. Bolling is unhappy because his phone has new capabilities."

Tom waved that away, "Not what I am unhappy about. Sam, the latest upgrade 'adjusted' my phone and rearranged all the little icons I use to do business."

"Oh, I hate that, too," he said, looking up and smiling as Roslyn and Alena came into the room.

As the nurses took their seats across the table, Tom noted Roslyn was carrying a cup declaring her 'The World's Greatest Nurse'. He was certain that she bought that cup for herself, although Alena might have done so.

Sam went through his usual re-review of the G&L sheet and commented, "No trouble of any kind last night, I see."

Terse nods from the others at the table met this pronouncement, and he went on, "Tom, do we have any progress on identifying that man found on the ward?"

"No, sir. I am in touch with the detectives, and they are pursuing several avenues, but there's no success yet."

"Very strange to have him show up like that."

Roslyn joined, "The nurses are uncomfortable with the circumstances, too. Something should be done."

"Uncomfortable? About the identification?" Tom asked.

"No," she said in a clipped voice. "They are uncomfortable that a murder occurred on an active ward during the night shift. They are concerned for their own and their patients' safety."

"Of course," Tom said, trying to soothe feathers that lately seemed to have grown perpetually ruffled. "I understand how they would feel. The detectives seem certain that the murderer has left the hospital, however."

"That still leaves a murder on the ward and a killer on the loose."

Sam said, "We can increase our security presence on the wards during that shift. I'm sure the chief of security would be able to do that until the police have solved this case."

Roslyn nodded, and Sam sniffed, "We will take care of that right away."

Sam looked at Holly and approved of her writing a note to that effect. Then he turned to Tom again and asked, "Did you find anything like the discarded clothing the detective asked about?"

"Well, the search isn't over yet, but no, we have found nothing to suggest the killer left his clothes in the hospital."

Roslyn pointed out, "The nurses are also concerned that security may have allowed a naked man to enter the hospital and prowl around."

Tom and Beverly looked at each other with raised eyebrows. He asked, "Did someone see a naked man in the hospital?"

"No. But if you haven't found his discarded clothes, he must have been."

"I'm not sure that conclusion is warranted," Tom said. Roslyn stiffened as if preparing to fight the accusation.

Sam interrupted, "Tom, you will let us all know whenever the police have come to some conclusion about this, won't you?"

"Of course."

Roslyn spoke again, "The nurse practitioners in the specialty clinics aren't getting the support they need."

Tom said, "That's the first I've heard of that. The doctors down there tell me that the NPs are doing good work."

"They certainly are. And doing so despite not having adequate support."

"Tell me what they are experiencing, please."

"Since you have insisted that all their orders have to be co-signed by a physician . . ."

"Roslyn, you agreed that during the probationary period, all nursing orders would require co-signature by a physician."

"That isn't necessary elsewhere in the state."

"We both know what the state requirements are. Yes, nurse practitioners can have a standard scope of practice and operate without daily oversight or even co-signature. But you agreed months ago that we would move toward that level of practice slowly and develop each nurse practitioner's scope individually."

"Well, in the meantime, the nurses are standing around waiting for their orders to be 'approved' before their patient can check out."

"Why?"

"Because the doctors don't want to be disturbed."

"You mean because they are also seeing patients, don't you?"

"I suppose so."

"I spoke with Dick Abert last week, and he said the doctors in those clinics are happy about the nurses' work and glad we made the change."

"Well, the nurses aren't happy," Roslyn said, while raising her nose.

Tom studied Roslyn's posture and defensiveness before asking, "Are you asking me to address this and make it better?"

"I am," she replied after a brief pause.

"Okay. Tell your nurses that I will be meeting with them about their concerns."

"I just told you their concerns."

"If I'm going to look into this, I will need to hear directly from the people who are primarily involved."

"Will that include the doctors?"

"Absolutely."

"Well, we'll see." Roslyn was not satisfied with Tom deciding what needed to change, but she felt she had somehow been backed into a corner. Her closing comment intended to make her skepticism apparent.

The meeting ended, and everyone went back to their own offices.

CHAPTER 25

WEDNESDAY, APRIL 7

Later that morning, Ron and Gene made another trip to New City. They had a deep discussion before leaving the office the night before, and Ron suggested they had not done due diligence at the actual crime scene because the body had already been moved. Gene asked for specifics, and Ron's answer was, "Interviews. We only talked to people who were in that room."

"They were the ones that were at the murder site."

"And not all of them. Did you talk to . . . ?

"Yes, but there are many other people in the hospital we could interview."

"And who would those be?"

"To start with, we need to pick Tom's brain a little more about how someone gets in the hospital naked."

"Then?

"I want to talk to some of the nurses on that ward. We may have to come back after midnight to catch the ones that were on then."

"You know I have a date tomorrow night."

"I didn't, but it doesn't surprise me. I thought we talked about you asking that girl to marry you. Then you don't have to be so touchy about your dates. She would be at home every night."

"I remember you talking. I don't recall listening."

"Well, there's another area for improvement."

The drive from headquarters to New City involved another set of Gene's complaints. He continued to be critical of the passenger seat in Ron's car.

"This seat won't adjust."

"Sure it will. Pull up on that lever under the seat and push back."

"I tried that, and it doesn't work. Who sat in this seat, a pygmy?"

"Next time, try making the seat adjustment before we start down the street."

"Why? Does the seat only unlock for comfort when the car is at a standstill?"

"I was hoping to get your complaints and carping out of the way before I started the car. That's all."

"Yeah, that's not likely to work. Unless you bought a new car. Like a Mercedes with the electric seat adjustments and seat warmers."

"Dream on, partner."

In the lobby, they went immediately to the Green Bean kiosk, where Nick recognized them. Only a few other customers were there, and he had their drinks shortly and brought them to the cashier's stand.

"Back again? Or still?"

Gene saluted him with his cup as Ron said, "Still, I'm afraid."

"Dead guy on 4C?"

"Nothing gets past you, does it?"

"Well, if I ran a bar, people would be talking to their bartender, right?"

"Except you don't have any stools for them to sit and tell you their tales."

"But I can listen to all the chatter this way."

"Can you help us find the guy responsible?"

"Nope. But if you need rumors to follow up, I am your man."

"All right, then. And we know right where you are."

They waved to each other, and the detectives moved toward Tom's office.

Before they started talking, Tom asked Beverly to join them. Ron's first question was the logical starting place, "How did this unknown man show up naked in the ward?"

"Tom answered, "I've been thinking about that, too. I'm sure he didn't waltz in here in the middle of the night naked. I think he obviously came in wearing clothes."

"We agree on that," Gene said, sipping his Redeye.

"Which brings all of us to the next apparent conclusion. Whoever killed him, stripped off his clothes. So, the question is, what then happened to the clothes?'

"We did not run across them in any of the waste containers in or around the hospital," Tom noted. "So they must have left the premises"

"And that brings us to why take the clothes?"

Tom suggested, "Maybe he needed them."

"The killer, you mean?"

"Yes."

"Again, why?"

The group all shrugged their shoulders and looked at each other. After a moment, Beverly said, "Maybe the killer needed the clothes because he didn't have any."

Gene sniffed, "That just moves the question to why is there a naked killer walking the halls?"

Tom looked at Beverly and said, "What are you thinking?"

"Remember the AMA incident?"

"That was days before, wasn't it?"

"Let me get my notes," Beverly said as she exited the office.

Ron sat his coffee down and held up his hand. "Hold on Razordoc, what's an AMA?"

"She means someone left the hospital Against Medical Advice."

"Can you do that?" asked Gene.

"Certainly. It's not recommended, of course."

Beverly returned carrying her notebook and noting, "The AMA was reported on Tuesday morning."

Tom interjected, "And the body was found Wednesday morning."

Ron sat up and stuck in, "The medical examiner determined that the naked guy was dead for twenty-four hours when he was found."

Tom said, "That's right. Monique said the same thing. I missed the connection."

Ron returned to the earlier conversation, "So, one of your patients, may have killed this man and taken his clothes."

Tom nodded, "It's the best explanation at the moment."

Ron stood and tossed his cup into Tom's wastebasket. "Where was this guy who disappeared? I want to talk to the folks on that ward."

Tom looked at Beverly, who quickly consulted her notes.

"4C," she said, turning and heading out.

They all followed her to the door.

CHAPTER 26

WEDNESDAY, APRIL 7

On Ward 4C Tom introduced the detectives to the charge nurse.

Ron asked, "Do you remember this Harry Smith?"

"Of course, detective. He was quite memorable."

"In what way?"

"He was never in his room. He was supposed to be on isolation, and we told him that, Dr. Bolling," she said, turning to the chief of staff. "We told him we would lock the door if he didn't behave."

Tom nodded but did not comment.

Gene asked, "And you took his clothes?"

"Yes," the nurse replied, "patients' are usually allowed to keep their clothes in their room, but we thought he would elope if we allowed him to have his clothes."

"And where did you put his clothes?"

"We put them in the nurses' locker room."

"And where are those clothes, now?

"In the same place. No one has moved them."

"May we see them, please?"

"Certainly," the charge nurse said and led them to the door of the locker room.

She rapped on the door loudly and opened it slightly. "Anyone in the locker room? Gentlemen coming in!"

When there was no response, she opened the door and preceded them into the room, leading them to a closed locker at the end of a row. She opened the locker door and indicated that the clothes inside were what the detectives were seeking.

Ron reached in and pulled out the trousers, shirt, and light jacket from the hanging hook and turned around looking for a place to set them down for examination.

Tom indicated he could use the small table in the room. Meanwhile, Gene grabbed the underwear from a shelf inside the locker and then picked up the man's shoes and socks from the floor. Both detectives took their bundles to the small table and began their inspection. Ron took the shirt and jacket, and Gene picked the pants; each went at their business for a few quiet minutes as the nurse and Tom watched.

The Locker room door opened, and two nurses came in chatting about their plans for the evening. They stopped dead and froze in position when they caught sight of the detectives. The charge nurse stepped out and asked about their business in the room. They had come to collect their purses to go to lunch, and were allowed to do so, quickly and without comment.

As they were leaving, Gene held up a wallet. He opened it and called out to the group, "Not Smith. Wilton. Harry Wilton."

Tom said, to no one in particular, "I think we all thought the 'Smith' was not real, anyway."

Gene went on to list an address from Harry's driver's license; pull out three credit cards and a membership card to AMC theatres. He also found three $1 bills and a $5 bill. Ron's inventory of the shirt and jacket yielded some old movie theatre ticket stubs, a receipt from a downtown restaurant dated the night he was brought to the hospital, and a set of keys.

Ron looked at the size twelve shoes and the forty-inch waist on the trousers and opined, "This is a pretty big man."

The charge nurse agreed, "He was too big for the nurses to herd him back into his room."

"Was he threatening to them in any way?" Gene asked.

"No, not really. He was anxious and very insistent that he didn't need to be in the hospital."

Ron was surprised at this comment. "What's that? He gets slammed in a hit-and-run and comes out with broken ribs and says he doesn't need to be in the hospital?"

"That's what he kept saying to the nurses."

"Did he have somewhere he needed to be?"

"I don't know about that. He said he shouldn't be here in the hospital and that he needed to go home."

Gene said, "Maybe there was something very important at his house, then."

The charge nurse cocked her head to one side before commenting, "I don't think that was the issue, even if he kept saying so."

"Why do you think that?"

"Well, he didn't ask to call anyone to go check on things and he only mentioned going home a couple of times. What he really wanted was out of the hospital."

Ron offered, "There are many people afraid of the hospital."

She countered, "This wasn't fear of the hospital. He kept looking around and watching the elevator door closely. I think he was afraid someone would find out he was here."

"Huh," said Gene, immediately sharing a look with Ron. "What do we know about this hit-and-run?"

"Just what's in the chart. No accident report. Just the medical stuff about his ribs and the scrape on his arm," Tom said. "I've had a look at the chart because he went missing."

Ron looked at Tom for a brief moment and then asked, "Can we talk to anyone else here that talked to him before he got to the ward?"

"Sure," Tom said. "Let's go to the Emergency area and see who that was."

In Emergency, they found that all personnel who had talked with Harry or seen him were on shifts later in the day, with one exception. The radiology technician who made the x-ray of his chest was now on days.

When they had located her, Tom explained the reason for the detectives' interest in the case to her, and she said, "I do remember that man. Evenings and nights down here, we see a fair number of auto accidents, but he didn't seem like that."

"What do you mean?" Ron asked.

"Usually, someone in an accident like that, they are all shook up about events, you know. I mean, we sometimes have to tell them three or four times what we're doing. It's like most of them are in a fog and can't remember what happened. But this guy, he wasn't like that at all. I mean, you know, he was hurt and all, but he was mad more than anything."

"Mad? You mean he was angry about being run down?"

"No, sir. He was angry because the police were calling it an accident. He must have told me two or three times, you know, 'this was no accident'. And he said it with his teeth clenched."

They thanked the technician and Tom and headed for the car; the detectives did not stop for another 'usual' at Nick's hands before heading for Harry's home address.

"What are you thinking, partner?" Gene asked. "Do you see a connection between Wilton and the dead guy?"

"Well, a connection, yeah. I think Wilton killed him to get his clothes and get out of the hospital."

"I mean any connection other than that. Even us guys in the cheap seats made that connection."

"I don't know, Gene. What's your sense?"

"I'm kinda thinking there is a connection. The two of them were meeting up in the wee hours, and I don't think that's likely to be random. I bet it was all arranged."

"That sounds believable. And you think it's got something to do with why Wilton was involved in the accident?"

"Sure. I don't really like all those complicated scenarios that run through your head, Walker. I'm going to go with what's right in front of me."

"Let's see what's at his house, and then I'll give you my thoughts."

They pulled into the shaded driveway at Harry's house and noted the absence of any vehicle. They peered into the garage and saw no car there, either. Ron used the keys he found in the jacket to try the front door, and it opened easily.

Inside they found turmoil. Mail on the floor just inside the door, furniture overturned, drawers half-open with contents spilled on the floor, and disarray in every room. The house had been thoroughly searched.

"We're not the first to be here," Gene noted.

"There you go with the B.O., again."

"Someone has to put the Blatantly Obvious into the record. If I didn't do it now, Thor would have been all over it during our report."

Ron nodded in agreement and then spoke.

"And now my opinion is that these things are all connected, Gene. Just like you said, " Ron said, slowly shaking his head.

CHAPTER 27

WEDNESDAY, APRIL 7

"Councilman, you have a call on Line One."

"Who is it?"

"I believe it is Nestor, sir."

"Thank you. I'll take the call."

Greene pondered for a moment. Several days had passed since he sent Nestor and Jorge after Pritchard. He didn't want to have a conversation on that topic on his office phone, but he knew that Nestor would speak only in generalities, so he decided to talk.

"This is Councilman Greene," he answered on Line One, signaling Nestor to be careful about discussing details.

"Colonel, this is Nestor. I believe we located that item you were seeking."

"That's good, Nestor. We can talk about it this evening."

"I thought you might want to know more about it before then."

Greene paused and considered. Nestor was signaling that he needed to discuss something about Pritchard's whereabouts. Perhaps

Nestor had found out that Pritchard was in police custody. That would require some immediate action on his part, and he could not wait until later.

Greene said, "Why don't you check with Charlene for now?"

"Yes, sir. Will do." And the line went dead.

Greene got up from his desk and locked the door to his office. He went back to the chair behind his desk and took out his cell phone. Within five seconds, it rang.

"Greene."

"Yes, sir. I probably should have called the cell phone first."

"What do you have?"

"You know that guy I know in electronics?"

"Yes."

"He found a way to track Pritchard, and we've found his car."

"Lo-Jack, right?"

"What's that, sir?"

"You tracked him through his Lo-Jack thing on his car, right?"

"Uh, no, sir. Lo-Jack is tied to the police reporting system. To use it, we would have to hack into their system or report the car stolen or something like that and . . ."

"All right, you didn't use Lo-Jack. Whatever, where is he?"

"We got his phone turned on and pinged it. Our electronics guy has a very sophisticated GPS tracking system . . ."

"Okay, okay. Enough with the process. Where is Pritchard?"

"Well, we are not exactly sure, but his phone is in his car, and his car is parked at New City Hospital."

"What? Is he a patient there?"

"I don't think so. The car is in the Visitor's Lot."

"That doesn't mean anything. He could still be a patient."

"Sir, that's what we are calling about. I've already called the patient information desk; he is not listed as a patient. What do you want us to do?"

"What do I want? I want you to find him!" Greene's voice was harsh and louder than he realized. He tried to contain his annoyance before blurting out something that could be heard in the outer office.

"Should we go back into the hospital, then?"

"Find that Pritchard guy!"

"Yes, sir." Nestor hung up.

Greene wanted to throw his phone across the room but constrained himself to simply gritting his teeth. What was going on with Pritchard being in the hospital? Why would he have suddenly gotten sick? Maybe he's not sick. Maybe he tried to commit suicide. That would be rich.

First, Wilton was in New City and somehow got away from Nestor and Jorge. Now Pritchard seems to have taken haven there, as well. Do those guys have some connection to the hospital? Or do they know someone in the hospital? Someone who can help them escape from sight? Maybe they are both hiding in the bowels of that hospital, right now.

Greene spun around in his chair to face the front and reached down to open the bottom right-hand drawer of the desk, intending to get himself a drink. Then he remembered the whiskey was in his desk at the law firm, not here in City Hall. Suddenly he wanted a drink even more.

CHAPTER 28

WEDNESDAY, APRIL 7

Harry and Coach Tatterhorn did eat the Chinese food as leftovers for dinner the next night. Jess Tatterhorn cooked a mess of rice, and they spread the remaining entrees over the new rice and divided it in half. They sat at the dinner table and used their choice of eating instruments as before. As Harry began to dig into his food with his chopsticks, Jess asked, "Do you have any word about how the fumigation is going at your house?"

Harry carefully chewed his mouthful of food before answering, "A little, yes. They have removed the tent and will complete checking for pests tomorrow."

"Well, you are welcome to stay here longer if it's necessary."

"Thanks. We'll see."

"Really, it's nice to have dinner supplied."

"Even if it always turns out to be Chinese?"

"Even so."

Later, Jess turned the conversation to local politics, and Harry claimed a degree of ignorance and carefully deflected further discussion to sports. Harry admitted his history of playing football as an offensive lineman in high school. That led to several anecdotes by each man about their time in high school sports. Highlights included a comparison of their most embarrassing moments on the basketball court.

After an hour of laughs at the expense of each other, Jess found some ice cream in the freezer. He covered scoops of vanilla with some chocolate sauce, and they repaired to the table again.

"Harry, one of the teachers told me today that you had been in an accident recently. Are you okay?"

"How'd you hear about that?"

"One of the English teachers is married to a nurse in the Emergency area at New City. She said she thought she saw you in there a couple of nights ago after an automobile accident."

"Huh. Who would think about being recognized in the middle of the night?" Harry spoke as calmly as he could, but he could feel his heart suddenly racing.

"So, you were there?"

"Well, yes, I was, although it's a bit of an exaggeration to say I was in an automobile accident."

"Really, what happened?"

"I was walking to an Uber pick-up point after dinner, and a crazy driver came close to hitting me. I jumped out of the way and cracked a rib on the spare tire case of some SUV. That's all."

"Jackson's wife said she was going to check on you, but she couldn't find your name in the admissions list."

"Clearly not since I wasn't admitted," Harry said, wondering how to get on a different topic. "How did she recognize me, anyway?"

"C'mon, Harry. You're Henry Wilton's father. You were here at every one of his games. Lots of teachers and their spouses know you and the parents of other outstanding students."

"Oh. I didn't realize … Anyway, I didn't spend the night. It hurts a little, but I'm fine."

"Good. I'm glad you're all right."

Later, Jess turned on the evening news, and Harry got uncomfortable when the newscaster turned to a local story about a man found dead in New City Hospital and the difficulty the police were having in identifying him.

Jess said, "Maybe better that you didn't spend the night there, huh?"

Harry made a little laugh and tried to change the subject but Tatterhorn held up his hand indicating he wanted to hear the story on the television. When the story was finished and the station rolled into a commercial, Tatterhorn turned to Harry and asked, "You want some more ice cream?"

Harry was taken slightly aback, expecting questions about the event at the hospital. "Uh, yeah, sure," he managed.

Harry sat and watched the commercial as if he was truly interested in a mattress topper or a 'no cutting' method of improving his urine flow. Jess came back with two bowls of chocolate-covered ice cream, and they ate while catching up on all the national and local sports .scores. When Jess indicated he was ready for bed, Harry offered to do the clean-up. Jess quickly agreed and said good-night. So, Harry took the bowls in the kitchen and rinsed them, before going to his bedroom.

Harry undressed and brushed his teeth before lying on the bed. He turned out the light in the room but found he was not sleepy. After trying several positions without success, Harry pushed himself into a sitting position against the headboard. He knew what was keeping him awake and decided to puzzle his way through it.

The issue was that he had been recognized at the hospital. Someone knew he had not been killed by the hit-and-run attempt. Even though the lack of a death notice would have provided that same information, Harry was concerned that someone in the hospital might know he was at Tatterhorn's house. Who was it again that recognized him? Oh, right, a teacher's wife, a nurse. And a big-mouthed nurse, too, it seemed. Wasn't there some law that said medical personnel shouldn't talk about things like that?

Okay, so, she saw him. That might not be a big deal. But, then she told her husband. Then, the whole topic was discussed at the school. Presumably, by now, everyone at the school knew he had been at the hospital. What if Greene or his thugs go to the school? He had been worried that Greene would be able to figure out which hospital he went to anyway. But being recognized by someone he did not know made Harry very nervous. What if all the teachers at the school are aware of his 'accident'? And what if they all get to talking about it and worrying about his injuries? Then, good old Jess tries to calm fears by saying that Harry is not seriously injured? They would want to know how he was aware of that, wouldn't they? And Jess would have to say, 'Harry's been staying over at my place' or something like that.

And once that information got out, Harry felt that Greene or his henchmen would soon be aware and would come for him. That's why he couldn't sleep. And none of those concerns or circumstances was about to change. Harry decided it was a good thing he could not sleep; he was in danger and needed to flee.

Harry slipped out of bed and dressed. He put his few belongings in his backpack and cautiously made his way into the living room. He found a piece of paper and wrote Jess a note explaining he felt he had to leave and apologized for leaving in the dead of night. He also left Jess one of his burner phones and included instructions on texting Harry's phone 'in case', but he emphasized the use should be minimal explaining, "I might be blowing something up!"

He laid the phone and the note on the breakfast table and let himself out the back door, using the handle to lock it behind him. Then he carefully skirted the house and walked down the alley and two blocks over to where he had left his car. He pulled the cover off and hurriedly folded it before replacing it in the trunk. Then he put his backpack in the front passenger seat, got in, and drove quietly away.

CHAPTER 29

THURSDAY, APRIL 8

Years before, Harry Wilton had come to Cincinnati to work in the construction industry. He brought his wife and son and set up a home. The city of Cincinnati was growing, business was good in the construction portion, particularly for his skill and expertise in demolition. The city seemed determined to rid itself of whatever former style existed and create itself anew. That decision called for the removal of the old, and that usually meant demolition.

Harry was happy to provide his skills to the process and to become part of the 'new Cincinnati'. Partly to be aware of what he was going to be destroying, Harry and his wife engaged in several tours around the city, focusing on the historical. One of those most memorable tours involved the once-a-year ticket to tour Cincinnati's fabled subway system.

The city's abandoned system includes almost three miles of tunnels and platforms just beneath the surface. Absence trains and track, the system is a ghost subway, a tunnel out of sight and generally out of mind. The system route traces an even earlier transportation venue in Cincinnati, the former Miami and Erie Canal.

Early in the Nineteenth Century, the transportation of goods and foodstuffs was best done via water. The western portion of Ohio faced an existential problem of getting their goods to Eastern markets because of the lack of a natural river connecting the county farmlands to either Lake Erie or the Ohio River. Other parts of the country addressed similar problems by constructing canals, a concept endorsed by none other than George Washington. The Ohio legislature authorized the construction of a canal to connect the Ohio River to Lake Erie in 1825.

The completed project was over 550 miles in length and opened at about the same time that the burgeoning railway system connected America from coast to coast. Competition between the two was never on a level playing field; the freezing of the canal during the winter and the slow pace of the transport compared to trains made the canal a disadvantage for passengers and the transport of perishable goods. The city ceased its use of the canal in 1877 and abandoned the waterway.

About that same time, Cincinnati began using electric streetcars for public transportation; this progress created more traffic congestion on the streets between the streetcars, horse-drawn carriages, foot traffic, and the earliest automobiles. Transportation of any sort between downtown and surrounding areas took increasing time.

Americans were interested in rapid transit, and in the late nineteenth century, cities were pushing for subways. Boston and New York pioneered the concept, and Philadelphia was right behind. As early as 1883, Cincinnati newspapers proposed using the canal remnant, dubbed a 'dead old ditch', as the site for a subway system to be capped by a broad boulevard. The public became persuaded and passed a large bond for construction just before America's entry into the war in Europe in early 1917.

After the war, costs had increased, but the city persevered with the digging and construction despite increasing difficulties with right-of-way issues like litigation related to construction-related cracks in foundations of buildings along the route. Finally, by 1927, funds were completely gone, only seven miles of the planned loop had been excavated, and no track had been laid. Sentiment turned against the subway project, and Central Parkway was built on top of the old canal.

Now under Cincinnati streets lies a ghost subway, three miles of empty tunnels, and deserted platforms. Sealed from easy access by heavy manholes and locked steel gates, the subterranean burrow collects dust most of the year. The city maintains the tunnels because of the streets above and the water main and cable lines running through it. And the conventional wisdom, also the official mantra, is that there is no way to gain entrance to the abandoned tunnel. And this is perfectly true unless you know where to go and how to look for a way to get inside.

Harry Wilton took Linn north across Central and turned north on McMicken. He drove carefully, keeping his speed at right at the limit to not attract attention. As he approached the McMillan Street exit at Fairview Park, he heard a siren behind him and looked up to see flashing lights to his left. His heart rate soared to over a hundred as the car in front of him slowed to allow the police car access. Harry was about to bolt from the car when he saw the police car shoot across the Avenue and proceed eastward on McMillan.

He was still breathing quickly when the car in front picked up speed and went through the intersection. Trying to will his heart to slow down and his hands to stop sweating, Harry followed and kept north on McMicken. A few minutes later, he passed the intersection at Marshall and began to look for the familiar landmarks. He took Riddle into the neighborhood and found a parking place where his car would be unnoticed. Harry turned off the ignition, then sat slumped in his seat for more than five minutes until his breathing and heart rate had recovered.

He got out, pulled his sleeping bag and backpack from the backseat, and locked the car. Moving slowly with his head down through the neighborhood, he headed back toward McMicken. He watched the light traffic and chose his moment to dodge across streets to gain his target and then lay quietly in the grass under some shrubs, watching to determine if anyone had followed him. Once convinced he was unobserved, he pushed the backpack and sleeping bag under some bushes and emerged from cover, walking back the way he had come.

He shuffled into the White Castle, keeping the bill of his cap down over his forehead. He ordered several burgers and took his order, and left. He retraced his steps and his traffic dodging to regain his position next to the sleeping bag. He decided to wait to enter his hiding place until the early hours of the morning to reduce the chances of being seen. So, he leaned against the sleeping bag, ate two burgers, and closed his eyes for a short nap.

When he awoke, it was after two in the morning. He stretched carefully and listened to his surroundings but heard only sounds of distant traffic. He picked up his backpack and bag and crept to the sidewall of the old subway tunnel where he had previously loosened an air vent cover. Within 45 seconds, he and his baggage were safely inside. Harry used his torch to locate a relatively clean spot on the platform, not far from the vent. There he opened his sleeping bag. After positioning his remaining goods, he slipped into the bag and finished his nap.

CHAPTER 30

THURSDAY, APRIL 8

Tom and Beverly left the morning meeting, and Tom was agitated.

"I want to see actual data on this," he said.

"You want to tell me what to get or leave it up to me?"

"Your judgment is always pretty spot on, but I do want a couple of specifics."

"Which are?"

"One, she reported that the physicians were not busy in the clinic, so I want to know if they have appointments that are 'no-shows' or were there no appointments for those times."

"I will pull the clinic appointment records for the last three months."

"I also want you to check the names of patients scheduled for end-of-day in those clinics. If we are having enough unused appointments, it's possible we have too many physicians in the clinic. But there may be another, more cunning, explanation."

"That's new. Why?"

"I knew a guy in a dental clinic in the Air Force whose wife called and made the last appointment of the day. Of course, she was a 'no-show', and he knew it, so he left clinic early and was on the golf course by the time the rest of us got to our cars."

"Clever."

"Careful who you choose as a hero, Bev."

"It sounded to me that Alena was saying the clinics don't have enough appointments to be busy."

"I thought she was saying the doctors were lazy."

"Tomato, potato."

"Right, okay. Maybe I do have more sensitivity to her comments than I should. Still, there's a real question here about whether the clinics are under-used."

"I agree. The daily report and the G&L aren't providing information about this. I'll talk with Andy and his guys in Admin about updating the report with better numbers."

"And check into the clinics' income figures, too."

"Of course, boss. I was going to start there."

As they approached the desk of Mary Brighthouse, Tom's secretary, Mary looked up and said, "Dr. Bolling, Lila Ralston wants to see you."

Tom turned to Mary, asking, "When did she ask?"

"Right after you went into the morning meeting," Mary answered.

"Any idea what it's about?"

"No, sir. She said she would come back when you have time."

Tom looked at Beverly, who shrugged, then he turned to Mary and said, "See if she can come down right now." Tom asked Beverly to stick around to see what Lila wanted and they went into his office.

Lila Ralston, RN, got the message from the office of the chief of staff and finished her immediate work on the ward, and headed down to see Tom. Lila, 5'6" at best, always seemed larger in person because of her personality and energy. Her appearance was distinctive, with skin almost alabaster, sprinkled with a decent amount of freckles, and blond hair that appears almost white against her fair skin. She took the stairs rather than the elevator because it was not in Lila's nature to wait if an alternative was available.

She was ushered directly into Tom's office, and he rose to greet her.

"Come in, Lila. What's this all about?"

Lila nodded acknowledgment to Beverly and took the offered chair.

"It's about something that happened on Saturday," she started.

"This past Saturday?" Tom asked, noting that Beverly was already taking notes."

"Yes, sir. Two men came on the ward asking questions about the dead man found last week."

"What! Why wasn't I called?"

Lila held up her hand and tried to calm him down. "I was the only one who knew what they were asking about. I didn't call you then because something seemed fishy about it."

Tom had a high opinion of Lila and thought she was a levelheaded person, so he leaned back in his chair and indicated she should go on.

"These guys were acting like they had badges, but they didn't. They weren't exactly pushy, but they were pretty persistent. They had a picture of our dead guy and wanted to know if anyone had seen him."

"What did people say?"

"Well, they said they had no idea of who he was and that they certainly had not seen him. Of course, they hadn't. The only people who saw that naked man were Johnny, the night aide, the night charge nurse, and the two of us who cleaned him up for the morgue team. I was the only person on days that knew who they were looking for."

"What did they say about him?"

"Oh, they claimed he was a friend they were looking for. They had a really stupid story. I have a teenaged son who can lie better than they did. I thought about calling you but I thought they sounded and looked like they were connected. I thought you shouldn't get involved right then."

"Well, I appreciate your concern, Lila, but you know we are very involved in trying to find out who . . . what do you mean 'connected'?"

"Like Goodfellas, they just had a manner like gangsters."

"Really? What exactly is that like?"

"Well, they both were wearing dark suits that were too large for them. And their attitude was only one step away from threatening. They just looked and acted like something wasn't quite upright about them or their business. And, besides, their story just stunk to high heaven."

"Still, why not call and tell me then?"

"I'm not sure. That was my first thought when I realized who they were talking about. Then, I just decided not to get the hospital involved in any way. Something about these guys made me want them to keep on looking. Now, I think you should know that somebody is missing this guy and is not involving the police."

Beverly asked, "What did they look like?"

"The bigger of the two was probably about five foot nine, black hair and eyes and he moved his hands a lot when he talked. The other guy was pretty quiet. He was shorter, maybe five foot six inches. He was really solid, though, like a weight lifter. He looked like he might be Mexican."

"Could you meet with a sketch artist?"

"Certainly. When?"

Tom looked at Beverly then picked up his phone. "I'll call Detective Looney right now. I'm sure he will want to set something up soon."

CHAPTER 31

THURSDAY, APRIL 8

Ron and Gene entered the café, and Gene waved to Sandy working in the front of the room. She nodded and indicated they should wait while she cleared the booth they usually occupied. While waiting, Gene said, "I still think this dead guy has a connection to the Harry Wilton who went missing."

"I'm not disagreeing with you, Gene."

"Then we agree it goes on the list as a Known."

"I suppose, although we don't really have much on that list, do we?"

Sandy waved them to the booth, and they continued the discussion after giving her their orders.

Gene started, "The list has to start with the dead guy."

"Whose identity is not actually known. No pun intended."

"Someday, we will look back and think that was a clever comment."

"Well, what do you want to list as 'Known' about the naked guy?"

"He was not a patient."

"That's a negative."

"Okay. How about that he came to the hospital as a visitor."

"Do we know that?"

Gene sat up straight and smiled at Sandy as she brought their drinks. "Thanks, honey," he said as she smiled at him and nodded to Ron.

"Okay," Ron agreed after they had watched her walk away, "I guess we can list the very general fact that the dead guy was not part of the hospital activity as a Known. Do you have anything else?"

"Well, we agreed that there is a connection in some way to Harry Wilton."

"That's true. And now we know that some tough guys have been looking for the naked guy, and someone has tossed Wilton's house. Those facts seem to make the connection, too."

"So, how do you see this, so far, partner?"

Ron took a long draught on his iced tea before answering. "Well, now that we feel better about the connection between them, I am even more confident that Wilton killed the guy and took his clothes to get out of the hospital."

"I agree."

"Now that we know some tough guys are probably looking for both of them, I'm guessing they were involved in something dirty."

"I agree again," Gene said, moving some of the silverware around on the table so Sandy could place their orders.

She smiled at them both and inquired about their drinks before moving off. Both men held their conversation to watch her walk to the counter and the rear of the café. Then, they resumed their discussion.

Ron smiled at Gene and said, "Is there anything else you want to add to the Known list?"

"Maybe the Special Operator thing?"

"You mean about the pencil in the ear?"

Gene's answer was a nod as he bit into his sandwich.

"I'll take that as a 'maybe' but not yet a given," Ron said, turning to his own sandwich.

The discussion then waned as they ate and worked on their drinks. Within a few minutes, however, the plates were clean, and both men wiped their mouths. Gene picked up the thread, "And what is the plan for adding to that list?"

"As we agreed, the next step is to talk with co-workers. Finding his wallet and the employee card for ABC Construction tells us where to start with that. The neighbors weren't much help."

"They did tell us about the wife's death and that the boy has gone off to college."

"Yes. But, they didn't know where he went. I take that to indicate a fairly shallow relationship between Harry and his neighbors. Remember, they didn't know where he worked."

"Yeah, that's right. But we do and are going there now."

Following their common practice after lunch at Sandy's café, Ron gave Gene his money for lunch, and slowly went down the block to get the car. Then, he drove around the block to pull up in front about five minutes later. This interlude allowed Gene to spend some additional time talking to Sandy and perhaps making their plans for the evening.

They drove to the current ABC construction site, the downtown bus station, and parked with the workmens' vehicles. As they walked on the site, a foreman stopped them for not having a hard hat. After they explained their business, he arranged for them to meet with some of the crew in a trailer on-site used as a break room.

"Yeah, we heard about Harry having the accident and all. But we expected him to be back here by now," said one of the co-workers.

Others expressed a similar feeling, and many were surprised to hear that he was missing.

"That doesn't sound like Harry," many said, implying that Harry would not easily miss out on being at work.

None of the workers could guess at what Harry's interests were outside of work; most of them were unaware of his wife's recent death and none seemed aware of him having a college-age son except for a construction foreman named Morgan Riley.

"Yeah," Riley said, "Harry's been pretty withdrawn since Carole died. Spent all his time with Henry, the kid. Now that Henry's off at college, I thought he'd have some time to go bowling or something, but it hasn't happened."

Gene asked, "Do you know where he's from? Family and like that?'

"I think he was from Pennsylvania, but I'm not sure. He didn't mention any other family."

"Do you have any idea where he might be?"

"No, I don't. He sent me a text when he left the hospital saying that he wouldn't be in for a day or two. He didn't say where he was or where he was going. We weren't surprised about him not showing up, I mean, we're not ready for his demolition stuff anyway."

"That's his job, then, demolition?"

"Yes. He's our main guy. We're gutting the buildings now to get ready for his work."

"Any idea why he would go missing?"

"None. Harry's a straight shooter. I really don't think he'd be messed up in anything dishonest."

CHAPTER 32

THURSDAY, APRIL 8

Harry sat in the subway tunnel and considered his situation. It was not safe for him to walk around; he had already been identified once by someone he did not know. The discovery that he had been spotted, identified and his presence later discussed with other teachers at Henry's former school was unnerving. It also made Harry leery of getting out and around people. So much so, that he now was missing meals. He knew something had to change.

His decision was straightforward. He could change his appearance to some degree, grow a beard, walk stooped over to hide his height. But that seemed too little; he needed to become someone that was not recognizable, someone who was not Harry Wilton. He spent most of the day considering various disguises and changes to his face and hair before he concluded that he would have a great deal of difficulty altering his height and bulk. So, instead, he decided to become invisible.

There are some people who are not seen by passersby; they are passed with hardly a glance. They may as well be invisible. Eye contact with such people is avoided, and consequently, facial recognition is highly unlikely. Harry determined to become one of those 'invisible' people; he would become a typical homeless beggar on the street.

The plan, simple as it was, required some detail in planning. Harry noted of three areas of his appearance and behavior that would have to change. First was what people could see if they looked. That would include his face and hands. He had already begun to grow the beard and decided to let his face and head hair grow without grooming. For his hands, Harry remembered talking to a homeless man near the construction site one day. That man wore fingerless gloves, and his hands were grimy and dirty. Harry had a good mental picture of that man's appearance and set out to mimic it in detail.

The second area of needed change would be the clothes he wore. His work boots were too new and well kept to be believable, and he thought he could hide his frame with layers of clothing like many men on the street do. If he added a hat that would obscure his features, he felt he could blend in with the street people.

Third, he knew he needed to change his attitude. His tendency had always been to walk upright, braced as the Navy would say. That posture was alien to the dispirited homeless people on the street. Harry knew he would have to be not just bent in posture, but act as if he were bent in spirit, as well. His attitude to whomever he met needed to be subservient and withdrawn; he expected such conduct would keep most people from making eye contact. He also suspected such behavior change might be the most difficult part of his disguise.

He rummaged around through his clothes and found nothing he could adapt to the new planned style of dress. After a bit of thought, he took out his phone and searched for second-hand clothing stores in the area. He located one nearest him and turned his attention to making a list.

Next morning, Harry left the subway, again wearing his raincoat and ball cap with the bill pulled down. He shuffled down the street and circled his parked car twice before going to it and driving off. Harry was assuming that anyone capable of tracking him electronically would know about all his credit cards, so he had taken one of Carole's cards from the house. Trackers might think to check her cards, but maybe not at first. He drove to an ATM near the University of Cincinnati and used the card to withdraw $500 from their joint fund. He knew that if the withdrawal was spotted, the card might also become a liability.

Then he drove south on Clifton past the University and swung eastward on Calhoun until it became William Howard Taft Road. Harry drove past the Thrift Store and went around the block, parking on a side street facing south. He adjusted his ball cap, buttoned the raincoat, got out of the car, and slowly walked over to the thrift store. He entered the two-story building and was immediately disappointed with the array of furniture and knick-knacks that seemed more upscale than he wanted. He walked around a little and found the clothing section and again was dismayed that the items were too clean and fashionable for his purpose.

He stood by the men's trousers section looking but not touching long enough to attract attention from a helpful woman in her fifty's.

"Is there something I could help you with?" she kindly asked.

On the spur of the moment, Harry decided to develop a backstory for his purchases. "Ah, yes, perhaps so. I am actually looking for some clothing not so, shall we say, modern," he replied.

"Anything in particular?" she asked and appeared interested in helping.

"Yes, well, I'm to play a bum in an upcoming amateur vaudeville show and wanted some appropriate garb," he said, looking at her sideways under the cap bill.

"Oh," she said, "You want to look in storage. We get lots of donations that we never put out here." She turned and walked toward the rear, and Harry followed. She took him down some back stairs and into a room filled with boxes and hanging rods of shirts, sweaters, and pants several decades out of style.

"This is the area our theatrical friends come to when a new play is starting up," she said. "I'm surprised no one told you to ask for it."

"Hmmm," Harry said, fingering a thin, ragged sweater. "This will do nicely."

Within a half-hour, Harry had been outfitted with baggy, soiled trousers, too large in the waist but which came with a set of suspenders in garish colors. He also found a large white shirt with yellowed collar and cuffs, a thinning overcoat, and another sweater with what might be food stains on it. His guide then helped him find some very worn tennis shoes, two pairs of woolen socks, and a knit cap large enough to pull down over his face.

He added a plain brown scarf and found the cost of his purchases was very modest. The woman said, "Perhaps you will tell us when the play is to open."

"As soon as I know it myself," Harry allowed himself to smile openly at her, then he took his bundle of purchases and left. He drove back the way he had come until he came to MLK Drive. He continued north, and found his way into Burnet Woods and onto the loop road. He parked on the right side of the road, and sat for several minutes assuring himself he was not observed. When Harry did get out, he went a short way into the woods until he found a spot of wet mud and clay. He scooped up two handfuls and returned to his car, and spent the next fifteen minutes dirtying his license plates and bumper areas. He waited in the car for the mud and clay to dry.

As he sat, Harry returned to a troubling thought. He did not know where the evidence Pritchard had collected was now. Pritchard promised it was 'where no one will ever look', and presumably that meant Harry Wilton, as well. He had driven past Pritchard's apartment before going to Tatterhorn's but did not attempt to gain entry. Pritchard probably wouldn't have left the information lying around his home, anyway. If he hid it, Harry knew Pritchard would have left some clue. But he couldn't get in the man's house to look for one. The best likelihood was that Pritchard put everything in a safety deposit box in a bank somewhere. Now that he was dead, there would be no retrieval of the data, and Harry was missing the leverage he needed for the blackmail.

But, Harry thought, Greene doesn't know that I don't have the information. He probably thinks if he can shut me up, the evidence will stay hidden. And, once Greene finds out that Pritchard is dead, I will be in the bull's eye. He leaned back against the headrest and closed his eyes, feeling safe to do so because of the loneliness of the area. Thirty minutes later, he awoke. After checking the mud drying on the license late, Harry drove back to his subway lair.

CHAPTER 33

THURSDAY, APRIL 8

Anton Greene sat at his desk in his law office and looked at the stacks of hundred dollar bills packaged and bound with small paper slips on his desk. The desktop was covered several stacks deep, but Greene looked at the fortune with no evidence of glee or satisfaction.

He had called in every loan, leveraged every deal, sold every piece of stock he had to amass this pile of currency. But it gave him no pleasure because the councilman was about to arrange to give the pile of money to someone else. At least that's what he was going to pretend to do.

Conor had suggested that Greene not even take the money to an exchange point. "What's the value in that?" he asked.

"He probably will want to see the money before he returns the data file, that's why. If it were me on his end, that's what I would do. Make sure the money is really in the bag before I give up any leverage I have."

"Okay," Conor conceded. "What if he shows up without the goods?"

Greene frowned, "That's not what we agreed to. He gets the money, and we get the information that incriminates me."

"And then you will have him killed and take the money back, right?"

"Right. What's your point?"

Conor hesitated before answering. "Look, sir. Would you take your only point of leverage to a meeting for exchange if you distrusted the other person?"

Greene thought about Conor's point. "Probably not. But I also wouldn't expect to walk away without the money unless I made the trade."

Conor nodded. "Exactly. So, I imagine that this Wilton person is going to not only want to see the money but be able to walk away from the exchange knowing that he still has leverage."

"No file, no money. I'm not letting this rube bankrupt me and get nothing in return."

"Of course not, sir. But let's imagine that he is smart enough to assume that you would prefer to end the exchange with both items, the data file, and the money, in your possession. What would he do to prevent that from happening?"

Green looked at Conor with new-found respect. He had hired Conor as his executive assistant when he first opened the law firm. He chose him because of his interview and the confidence Conor showed then. Greene had not been disappointed to find that Conor had worked with a previous law firm and understood many of the blind spots in the law. Further, and perhaps more importantly for Greene, Conor also showed no compunction about operating in those blind spots. Over the years, Greene had taken Conor into his confidence even more than he did with Quiles and Aramano. That decision had been justified in Greene's eyes on more than one occasion since.

"You really mean, what would I do in that situation, don't you, Conor?"

"Well, sir. Having an idea about the best way to thwart a plan that would leave him with nothing seems like a good place to start."

"And you think I would have the best plan?"

"Certainly, sir."

"When you get right down to it, the only way either individual in such an exchange can walk away at the end feeling like he came out ahead is to approach the deal as if it were a used car sale."

"I don't understand, sir."

"The sale of a used car is considered a good deal on both sides only if each person thinks he got a fair deal from the other guy. The price on the car needs to be high enough for the seller to feel like he got something and still be low enough for the buyer to think he got a good deal."

"I see. And how do we accomplish good feelings on both sides in an exchange like this?"

"I expect it would have to start with clear ground rules and a degree of trust on both sides."

"Do we trust this guy?" Conor asked.

"I'm not sure," Greene said. "But I can certainly imagine that he doesn't trust me. So I need to do something that will let him think he has the upper hand. Make him feel comfortable and more likely to trust whatever is going on."

"And how will you do that, sir?"

"By letting him set the stage for the exchange."

"What do you mean?"

"Simple. I'm going to ask Wilton where to meet for the exchange. If he chooses the field, he will naturally think he has chosen wisely and that he has the advantage. Further, by letting him dictate terms and then showing up with the actual money, I predict he will feel comfortable enough to make the exchange clean and simple. At that point, he will be most interested in getting away with the money."

Conor smiled, "And that's when Jorge and Nestor show up?"

Greene almost laughed at Conor's question. "Oh no, they will be there well ahead of time and ready to take him down as soon as the exchange is complete."

"How can they do that if you let him choose the spot for the exchange?"

"Simple, Conor. That's what these guys do. They get to a place, they assess, they disappear into the woodwork and reappear only at Showtime."

"You seem very certain of that, sir."

"I am, Conor, I am. I watched these men work for several years before I hired them. They are experts at what they do. They were trained by the military, they had more than twenty successful operations in foreign countries, and came home whole. I know they can do what I'm about to ask them. Let's all hope that giving Mr. Wilton the lead makes him comfortable enough to bring the data file."

Green leaned back in his chair with looked at the pile of money once more. Then, shaking his head, he pulled out his cell phone and texted a message to the burner phone Wilton had mentioned in the telegram. The message read: "Got money. Pick a place for exchange. Bring the data."

Greene looked at Conor and hit 'send'.

"Get Nestor and Jorge in here. They will need to move quickly when he answers."

CHAPTER 34

THURSDAY, APRIL 8

Ron had a copy of the sketch artist's drawings of Lila's memory of the two men who came to New City looking for the naked man. He also had a morgue picture of the naked man in the same folder. He and Gene decided to show the likenesses to the men they had interviewed. Then, they intended to walk the site.

None of the men they had already interviewed recognized any of the pictures, so the foreman obtained hard hats for the detectives and escorted them around the site.

"Whatcha guys looking for, anyway?" the foreman asked.

"Harry Wilton is missing, and we think these men might have something to do with that," Ron said and handed him the pictures of the two men from New City.

"Harry messed up in something? That would be news," the man said and indicated he did not recognize either of the pictures. As Ron was about to show him the photograph of the naked man, another worker interrupted.

"Hey, Jake, we've opened up another wall full of asbestos. I need to get some of those special masks for me and the boys."

The foreman excused himself and went off with the worker, leaving the detectives standing in an open area in the middle of the construction. They looked around and saw the interior skeleton of the former bus station, the walls opened unnaturally into the air. The site was not quiet or uninhabited. Workmen were visible at various places all over the building. They moved gingerly toward a group of workers who watched their careful approach with undisguised humor.

"You know," the largest man among them said, "We don't get a lot of guys out here wearing suits." The men around him grinned and chuckled at this witticism.

Ron answered back, "I bet that's right. We don't see many hard hats in our place of business, either."

"And where would that be, your place of business?"

"Downtown, mostly among the suits. I'm Detective Ron Looney and this is Detective Gene Novalchek. Can we ask you a few questions?"

"Sure," the big man said, speaking for the group. "We know you're here about Harry being missing, right? You think something's happened to him?"

"We are not sure and we need some help."

"If we can help, we'll do so."

"Great. Do any of you know where Harry might be if he's not at home?"

The men looked at each other and slowly came to all shake their heads negatively.

"How about these guys? Have you ever seen them before?" Ron asked and handed the sketch drawings around the group. Again, individuals spent a few seconds looking at the drawings before shaking their heads and handing the sheets back to Ron.

"We have some reason to believe that Harry may know this person," Ron said, pulling out the morgue photo. "Is it possible this person works here or has been around the construction site?" He handed the picture to the large man.

In turn, each of the workers took the picture and studied it for several seconds before indicating a lack of knowledge and passing it on. When the picture returned to Ron it was heavily smudged with dirt and soot from the hands of the workers.

"Thanks anyway," Ron said and he and Gene moved off in the direction of another small group of workers unloading items from a truck bed. They seemed agreeable to a halt in their efforts and again offered to help if they could. After expressions of surprise about Harry's absence and the reason for the detectives' inquiries, they, too, studied the sketches and the photo without any sign of recognition.

As the men returned to their work on the truck's contents, Ron said to Gene, "This is not turning out to be helpful."

"Nope. And I'm not at all interested in going any further into the site wearing this suit."

"Are you hot?"

"I'm more interested in keeping the suit in a wearable condition."

"Is it new?"

"No. It's a few months old, but that's not the point."

"I know, Gene. I'm just pulling your leg. My suit is several years old, and I don't want to get it torn or irreparably dirty, either. Let's work our way back to the parking area." They picked their way through the work area and headed for the break trailer again.

Inside, they found the foreman and two other men discussing the asbestos abatement methods they were going to use. The foreman looked up and asked, "Did you find anything to help you?"

Gene said, "Nope, not yet."

"I'm sorry. We like Harry. We'd like to help you guys."

The detectives took off their hard hats and hung them on hooks near the rear of the trailer, and prepared to leave. The foreman stood up and shook their hands as he held the door for them. As Ron was letting the man's hand go from shaking, he remembered he had not shown the foreman the picture of the naked man.

"Last thing," Ron said, as he opened the folder and extracted the morgue photo. "Does this guy look at all familiar?"

"Is he dead?" asked the foreman.

"Yes, he is," Ron answered.

"What's he got to do with Harry?"

"We really are not certain," Ron fudged. "Do you know him?"

"It does look like Tommy Pritchard, I think."

CHAPTER 35

THURSDAY, APRIL 8

"Who is Tommy Pritchard?" Ron asked.

"He's a guy up in Accounting. I've seen him a couple of times when I had to get something approved."

"Where does he work?"

"Is that Tommy?"

"You're the one that thought so. We don't know this man's identity."

"And he's dead, and Harry's missing? What's this all about?"

"You know, we're just beginning to get some useful information. I can't tell you anything more, right now." Where does this Pritchard work?"

"Yeah, yeah, I get it. Pritchard works in the big trailer."

"Where's that?"

"It's on the other side of the construction. Big double wide. Keeps the paperwork on-site and shortens the work processes."

Gene nodded, "That's a smart way to do business, rather than having the paper pushers all downtown, and every time they get involved, it's a day and a half."

"That's right," the foreman said, giving Gene a high five.

Ron looked sideways at his partner. "And this wisdom comes to you from where?"

"I worked construction a while back. I might not have mentioned that to you."

"I certainly did not know that. I could believe you would not tell me you had a sister, but I didn't think you would hide your work history from me."

"You're married. Of course, I would tell you if I had a sister."

Meanwhile, the foreman was edging down the steps of the trailer and pointing across the site. "It's on the corner over there," he said. They decided to walk using the sidewalks and not cut through the construction.

The double-wide was framed in white aluminum and had two entrances. Ron took the first entrance and asked the young lady behind the counter who was in charge.

"Excuse me?" she said.

Gene stepped to the counter and asked, "Is the Site Foreman or Project Manager here?" He looked at Ron and said, "Sometimes you have to use the language they speak."

"Mr. Markham is here," the young woman said. She picked up her phone and dialed an internal number. She spoke quietly into the phone and then looked up at the detectives and said, "He'll be right with you." She went back to her work while Ron and Gene looked around.

Moments later, they were approached by a fiftyish man with graying hair and wide shoulders. He looked like he had a history in the field of construction. "Gene Markham," he said. "Can I help you?"

Ron spoke, "I'm Detective Ron Looney, and this is Detective Gene Novalchek. We'd like to talk to you about Tom Pritchard."

"Thomas? He's not here right now. What is this about?"

"Could we step into your office, please?"

"Certainly. Right this way." He led them down a short corridor to a small paneled office. The office held a walnut desk and an architect's drawing table, and four chairs. He indicated they should take one of the chairs, and he took one himself.

"What about Thomas?" he asked. "Not in trouble, I hope."

Ron took out the morgue photo and asked, "Is this Thomas Pritchard?"

"Oh my God. Yes, that's Thomas. Is he dead?"

"Yes, sir, I'm sorry to say so. He was found dead at New City Hospital a couple of days ago."

"Oh my, that's so sad. I didn't even know Thomas was sick."

"Do you know either of these men?" Ron asked as he showed Markham the sketches from Lila's description.

"Uh, no, I don't think so. What do these guys have to do with Thomas? And why are the police interested in his death?"

"Well, sir, Thomas Pritchard was murdered at New City Hospital. He was not a patient there. Shortly after his death, these two men were asking around the hospital for him.'

"Thomas? These guys? I don't believe it."

"Whether or not you believe it, sir, these are facts. We are here to find out what Thomas was involved in and to determine why these men were looking for him."

"Of course, I just mean, Thomas wouldn't . . . I don't think he was . . ."

"May we see his work area, Mr. Markham?"

"Sure, sure. Right down here."

He led the detectives back down past the entryway and down another corridor to an open area containing six cubicles. Each cubicle was separated from the others by a four-foot-high divider covered in gray cloth. At each corner entry, an attached placeholder stated the cubicle's owner's name. Thomas Pritchard's cubicle was the first on the left.

The desk and cubicle were neat and tidy. The desktop was clean except for a notebook and a small pottery jar. The jar contained several ballpoint pens and two mechanical pencils. A small desktop computer unit rested in a yoke behind the large monitor. On the bottom edge of the monitor was a single sticky note. It held a neatly printed 12-digit entry of alphanumeric symbols and two special characters.

"Probably his password," Gene noted.

Markham said, "I don't think so. First, Thomas would not be that careless, and second, our passwords are only eight digits."

"Well, we'll try it on his personal computer when we find it," Ron said and asked Markham to allow them to search the cubicle.

As the detectives started to search through Pritchard's desk and filing cabinet, the occupants of other cubicles wandered over and stood watching.

Ron addressed them, "Folks, I'm Detective Ron Looney of the Cincinnati Police Department, and this is Detective Gene Novalchek. We are here on police business and would like your cooperation."

They looked at one another and nodded. "Okay then," Looney said, "Go back to your desks, and we will come to interview you shortly."

They stood around for a few seconds, and then, as Ron stood with arms folded watching them, they moved back into their cubicles without comment.

Meanwhile, Gene had tried to open the computer on Pritchard's desk without success. Markham was right about the symbols on the sticky note; it was not a password to Pritchard's work computer. Ron went back to Markham's office to request access to the computer, and Gene began leafing through the notebook. It was a five-year calendar with two years to go and had entries about workload and job requirements listed on every page.

All calendar entries were in the same blue ink, and all entries for previous days were marked with a penciled checkmark in front of them, presumably indicating the task was complete. The desk drawers were similarly neat, all contents arranged and orderly. He noted blank work order forms, boxes of ballpoint pens and mechanical pencils and pencil lead, medium hardness. A bottom drawer held a small traveling shoeshine kit and a catalog for plastic model airplanes and ships. These objects were the only personal items noted.

Ron returned with a password, and Gene opened the computer. Just like the desk, the computer desktop was neatly arranged, with a dozen folders marked with names and numbers of specific accounts. Gene checked the email account and quickly read the correspondence for several days before Pritchard's disappearance. He also reviewed the recently viewed files and all the sent mail. There was no mention of Harry Wilton.

Ron decided they should take the computer to the office for a further forensic examination, so they turned to interview the other employees. They learned that Thomas Pritchard was unmarried, lived alone in an apartment, was well-liked but a quiet individual. He was well respected in the workplace, as evidenced by being chosen to do some cross-over work in Contracting because of his capability. He did not socialize with the others outside of contributing to group gifts for new babies and retirements.

No one knew about Pritchard's family, and only one other person was aware of his interest in model airplanes.

None of them had heard of Harry Wilton, and all were puzzled that Thomas might have enemies.

Armed with his home address and taking the computer with them, the detectives left and headed for Thomas Pritchard's apartment.

CHAPTER 36

THURSDAY, APRIL 8

Later that afternoon, as Harry sat in the subway tunnel sorting his newly purchased clothes, he received a text message on his phone. The message was from the burner phone he gave to Jess Tatterhorn and read, "Two guys at school. FBI (??). They know where Henry is playing."

Harry was disappointed that information of Henry's location had gotten into the wrong hands so quickly. But he was not surprised. He did not believe for a second that the men showing up at the school were actual FBI agents. Greene's men would have dressed in black suits and flashed some sort of badge, but discerning individuals like Tatterhorn would carry sincere doubts about their federal credentials. He was sure that Greene would make some move against Henry if Harry didn't set things up correctly very soon.

Harry wondered why Jess Tatterhorn felt the visit of these men to the school was sufficiently important to use the burner phone. Of course, he had left the phone with Jess hoping he would make use of it to keep him apprised of events at the school, including bad news. If the fake agents were pushing for information about Henry's college, Jess would certainly know that their interest in Harry was less than authentic. In that instance, Harry knew that Greene was ready to close in on him and he needed to be clever about his next step. He also knew he needed to take that step that same day.

Harry put aside the clothes and grabbed something to eat. He sat and leaned against the wall of the subway tunnel. He closed his eyes and pictured a mental image of himself holding a briefcase full of money. He smiled at such an idea and began to work backward from that vision of what he considered a proper and satisfactory outcome to his problem.

Envisioning himself walking down a street with that briefcase full of money, Harry tried to run that filmstrip in reverse. He saw himself picking up the briefcase from the ground, but where was he? In his mind's eye, he began to turn himself three hundred sixty degrees, gazing up at his surroundings. At first, he saw trees closing in on him, then the trees gave way to a street with brick houses on each side. He kept turning because those scenes did not feel safe or correct. When he next turned in his imagination, he found he was in a construction zone. No, not construction but destruction. He saw himself standing in an open area with partially torn-down walls surrounding. The walls were several stories high, and there was rubble and portions of inner walls lying on the ground all around the open area.

He felt a warm glow and realized he had wound the filmstrip back far enough to pinpoint the place where he would pick up the briefcase. He opened his eyes and rubbed his face vigorously. There were a few other points in the filmstrip that he felt he could not see at that moment. He did not see other people and did not observe how the briefcase came to be deposited in the clearing. These were some troubling details to be missing, but he knew how to get them to visualize.

Harry pulled out his phone, turned it on, and found the earlier message from Greene asking where to make the exchange. He nodded to himself and began dressing in his recently purchased clothes.

CHAPTER 37

THURSDAY, APRIL 8

Thomas Pritchard's apartment was a rental in Mt. Auburn. A two-story brownstone with parking in the rear, it was a two-bedroom bachelor's paradise. The apartment was within easy walking distance of several excellent restaurants and green spaces. The detectives had little trouble finding the owner and obtaining entry. There was more difficulty in getting the owner to leave them alone in the property to conduct their search. He unlocked the front door but stood in the way of their entry and made several overtures to accompany them.

"I'll show you around the apartment," he said.

"Sir, we will find our way around inside," Ron assured him.

"But there are some unique features."

"I'm sure there are. We will not disturb anything."

"Why are you looking for Mr. Pritchard, again?"

"It's police business, sir. Please step back and let us do our job."

Once inside, the detectives were immediately aware that they were, once again, entering a space already thoroughly searched. Pictures were off the wall, cushions removed from chairs and sofa, drawers opened, and contents scattered. The refrigerator had been cleaned out, with food containers and ice trays left in the sink. In the upstairs bedroom, they found the closets emptied and contents strewn on the double bed. The bathroom medicine cabinet was open, and its contents emptied into the lavatory.

Ron looked carefully at the rear door and pointed out serious scratches around the lock mechanism indicating someone had picked the lock for entry. Ron started going through the content of the drawers in the kitchen, most of which were scattered on the floor or cabinet top.

Shaking his head, Gene went through the personal papers on the small living room desk, a Governor Winthrop antique. Everything had already been rifled through, and he found nothing of value and no indication of a connection to Harry Wilton. He checked for secret compartments but found none.

"What's the deal, here, partner," he called into the kitchen to Ron. "Why are we behind someone in the search process?"

"Beats me. Given the mess, I believe the searchers didn't find what they were looking for. And we don't even know what we're looking for."

"No wonder we haven't found it, then. I notice the previous searchers are not tearing up walls or flooring, so they are probably looking for something small."

Ron was fiddling with the wireless phone. He put it down and came into the living room, and nodded, "With all the attention to papers and small containers like the ice tray and medicine bottles, I'm thinking they're looking for something small or compact like a computer thumb drive."

"Containing what? Copies of ABC's accounts receivable? Or Wilton's recent movie rentals?"

"Right. I don't know either. But the two searches are pretty good evidence of a connection between Wilton and Pritchard. They either share something these guys are looking for, or one of them has something the other one wants."

"Wait. You think Wilton could be the person who searched here?"

"Could be. He's been in the wind for a couple of days. He had the time. Maybe he and Pritchard were partners, and something went haywire. "

"Like him killing Pritchard, you mean."

"Like that. Sure."

"Then who searched Wilton's house?"

"I don't know, Gene. We don't really know when any of this searching went on, do we? I mean, maybe they each searched the other's home and were unable to find the 'pot of gold', and that led to the fight in the hospital."

"Pot of gold?"

"Analogy, partner. The treasure. Whatever they were looking for."

"Right. Then the two guys at the hospital looking for Pritchard don't have anything to do with this."

"Or they are the ones doing the searching. Searching for the people and searching for the 'pot of gold', too."

Gene leaned back in the chair at the desk, "I like your idea about looking for a computer file or disc or drive."

"Because …?"

"Well there's a internet connection wire here next to the Governor Winthrop and a mouse pad on the desk top."

"But no computer?"

"Exactly. No computer."

"Huh."

Gene said, "I think we need to agree on the Knowns."

Ron walked around the living room, thinking. Finally, he turned to Gene and probed, "Gene, if you were looking for a computer record of some kind, and you broke in here to search for it …"

"I'd start by looking for the computer."

"And if you found the computer, why would you keep looking?"

Gene thought a second and responded, "Because I didn't find what I wanted in the computer."

Ron added, "Or, because you couldn't get the computer open in order to search it."

"The password!"

"So, the searcher continues to look for a drive or a disc but ends up taking the computer somewhere else to try breaking into it."

Ron sat on the couch after moving some debris to make room. "We haven't agreed on much, but we now know that the naked guy is, was, Thomas Pritchard. Further, we have agreed that he was killed in the hospital by Harry Wilton, who took his clothes to escape."

Gene leaned against the wall saying, "I guess we agree that we don't yet have a motive for the murder."

"Right. I agree. But it's beginning to look like they were mixed up in something shady, so I'm guessing they fought over what to do next. And I think that fight had something to do with a kind of computer file that was important to somebody else."

Gene nodded along with Ron's presentation. "And, the searches of their homes indicates that they are connected."

"Perhaps not proved as a Known, but certainly most likely."

They looked at each other, unhappy that their list was so short. Then Gene, preferring to take positive action, asked, "You ready to talk to the neighbors?"

"Of course, and we will have to talk to Mr. Busybody, the landlord."

The landlord provided information on how long Pritchard had lived there and how he made his monthly payments but nothing else. Once he learned that Pritchard was dead, his main interest was to get the apartment on the market. "Will someone come and clean out his belongings?" he asked. "I will have to get the place cleaned and repainted before I can show it."

"Sir, this is a crime scene. You are not to enter this apartment under any circumstances."

"But I need to take steps to make it . . ."

"Crime scene. Do not enter. Got it?"

"Well, yes, but . . ."

"No buts. The department will notify you when you can have possession again."

They left him standing on the top step with a uniformed policeman to watch the site until the Crime Scene investigators had completed their work.

The neighbors on the north side were a retired couple who thought Thomas Pritchard was a wonderful neighbor. They shared recipes at holiday times, and Pritchard was always available to look in on their cat if they were traveling. They knew nothing about the house being searched, but they had noticed that Thomas had not been around the last few days.

The neighbor on the south side was a single woman in her fifties who worked from home in telemarketing. She also thought Thomas was a fine fellow and had no suspicions of any enemies he might have.

"He was so sweet and thoughtful," she noted, dabbing at her eyes.

"Did he have any visitors?" Gene asked

"Not that I noted. I'm home most of the time, but Thomas was working."

"Yes, ma'am. Have you seen anyone around in the last few days?"

"Oh, no. I'm sorry."

"That's all right."

They managed to get a description of his car and when it had last been seen parked in the rear. Gene stepped away from the conversation to set up a BOLO, and Ron was excusing himself from the conversation when the neighbor lady said, "I'm not the best to tell you about Thomas, but did you ask his girlfriend?"

CHAPTER 38

THURSDAY, APRIL 8

"**H**e had a girlfriend?" Gene asked when Ron rejoined him on the street. "How come we always find out these important things at the last minute?"

"We're just lucky, I guess. Remember, Gene, we did find out about her."

"I'm sure you walked out of there with a name and an address."

"Not exactly."

"Telephone number?"

"Nope. But I did come out with an idea."

"Hooray for our team! How are we gonna find this mystery girl, partner? Another séance with J.J. and John?"

Gene referred to his partner's habit of working out problematic issues through 'immersion therapy' in the world of 1950s and 1960s jazz. Ron had discovered this trick of assisting his concentration while stationed with the Air Police at Sembach AFB in Germany in the late 1970s. Unmarried, he spent several nights in an American bar in the small town of Kaiserslautern, where he and another AP rented a room. American airmen frequented the bar, and the band played mostly blues and jazz. Ron came to realize he had unusual clarity about whatever case he was working after spending hours listening to decent renditions of trombone duets of Kai Winding and J.J. Johnson or Miles Davis wannabes wailing on their trumpet into the wee hours. Ron firmly believed in the world of complexity, and, to him, jazz was a complex language that distracted him from linear thought patterns. When he became mired in a case because he couldn't get out of the linear pathway, a night of "J.J. and John" often cleared things up. And it didn't even have to involve J.J. Johnson or John Coltrane.

"Not at this time. I have an idea and came up with this on my own," Ron said as he headed back into Thomas Pritchard's apartment. Gene followed without rolling his eyes, even though he wanted to.

Inside, Ron went directly to the cordless telephone on the kitchen counter. He punched the play button and let Gene hear what he had heard earlier. A woman's voice said, "Hey, it's me. This is going to take longer than anyone expected. I won't get back tonight as I thought. I'll call later with a definite return day. Love you."

Gene stared at Ron and slowly raised his eyebrows, questioning the meaning of Ron playing that message.

"Hang on," Ron said and he hit the button again. The same voice came on, sounding less tired and more upbeat. "Hey, babe. We are going to finish tonight. I'll get an early flight out tomorrow and be there when you get home. You can count on this. Open the Merlot so it can breathe. Love you."

Ron stopped the playback and made a quick nod of his head to Gene. His partner was still puzzled. "I don't get it. Are we gonna check all incoming airlines to identify her?"

"No, Gene. Let's add something to the Known list."

"What? I don't have a name?"

"But, we do have something from this, don't we?"

Gene's shoulders shrugged and slumped. "I don't have the faintest idea what you're talking about. All we know is this girl calls him and leaves messages . . . Oh. I get it."

"Right. I've done this before. I will just change the message and have her call me."

"Isn't there a way to forward calls from that phone to your cell phone?"

"Yes, and I know how to do that, as well. I think the better option here would be for the mystery girl to get a message from me, asking her to call me, rather than have her call Pritchard and have me answer."

"Okay. It's your idea. But, I think you're making it harder than need be."

"You're right, I am using two steps rather than one, but I feel this is better."

"For whom?"

"For her, at least."

Ron picked up the handset and dialed *98, then waited for the system prompts. When asked to record a message, he said, "This is Detective Ron Looney with the Cincinnati Police Department. If you are attempting to reach Thomas Pritchard, please call me at this number." He gave his cell phone number, repeated his name and the number, and hung up.

"Now we wait," Gene said.

"Well, we don't need to be sitting around. We can keep looking for whatever it is that Pritchard got himself involved in. Also, I think it's time we rethink our Knowns."

Gene smiled at Ron and said, "I thought you were going to give her my number."

"Next time partner. Next time."

CHAPTER 39

THURSDAY, APRIL 8

Harry Wilton, dressed in his second-hand clothes and acting like a homeless man, wandered to the backside of the bus station construction site. The street was empty as there were no active businesses there. Harry had heard from Morgan about a carefully hidden breach in the rear chain-link fence, so he paced his movement slowly along the back of the site until he located the cut in the barrier. He knew some workers used this shortcut to get out quickly after work. The fence gap allowed them access to their cars more quickly than walking around the site. Harry sat down on the sidewalk near the access point and waited. Predictably, right at the end of the workday, a few workers pushed through the fence and headed across the street toward the empty lot where they had parked.

The workers paid no attention to Harry, and he did not engage with them. They chatted about whether to go for a beer or to head directly home; the concept involving beer usually won out. Ten minutes or less after the first worker had appeared through the unofficial back gate, all those who had used the exit had reached their cars and driven off. The block was once again empty; the only people visible were several streets away when Harry slithered through the fence and began a quiet and cautious move through the rubble toward the other side of the construction site.

Harry had walked this route around the site a few times during working hours, but the pile of debris, rubble, bricks, concrete and twisted pipe changed almost hourly as the workers stripped the building interior. The hand removal of walls, pipes, lavatories, and granite floors was tedious but required by the contract to save some original materials for use in the new building. When this work was done, Harry's job would be to put the remaining walls into a central pile of rubbish to be hauled away and discarded.

Twice he found his way blocked when following the perimeter of the site. A six-foot-high pile of pipes made him detour into the more central area of the site once, but he soon found a way back to the perimeter. Then, close to his planned destination, he found his way blocked by three large supply lockers. One locker housed the vests, hard hats, and other protective clothing worn by the workers, a second was for pneumatic hammers and jacks, torqueing equipment, generators, and other heavy machinery. The last locker was one Harry knew well. It contained the explosives, fuses, detonators, and safety equipment related to his particular part of the demolition. As he skirted the lockers, Harry touched the key chain on his belt where he kept the key to the last locker.

In the center of the former bus station was a five-story clock tower; this was Harry's destination. Access into the clock tower was not locked but had been barricaded with rubble composed of large concrete blocks, chunks of walls, and floors from above. With little difficulty, Harry climbed on the rubble and entered the clock tower through a break in the wall on the second floor. He ascended the staircase quietly, not expecting anyone to be in the tower but not wanting to call attention to his movement.

On the fourth floor, he found a window that opened toward the center of the site. From there he had a good view of the degree of deconstruction that had occurred to the station. He was able to view the street in front of the site from one angle and, after shifting he could see the open area he remembered in the center of the construction. Harry and Morgan often started their work day standing in that clearing and directing teams toward the work areas visible from that vantage point. He could not see the doublewide trailers on the far side of the site because the remaining portions of the building were still intact.

Satisfied that his presence was undetected, Harry pulled out his phone and texted a message to Councilman Greene. It said, "Clearing at base of clock tower in construction site. Tomorrow night 1930." Then he sat back to wait.

CHAPTER 40

THURSDAY, APRIL 8

Gene sat sipping his coffee and blinking at his partner. They sat at the back table in the small coffee shop down the block from their office. They had been busy all day, re-interviewing the workmen at the construction site and Pritchard's co-workers. Both had taken copious notes, and they were carefully comparing their entries at the end of the day.

Ron noted the odd look from Gene and said, "What's up with you?"

"I'm still not understanding you on this need to fix the 'linear; thing."

"It's not that hard to understand, Gene. Let me recommend a couple of good books on the subject."

"Never mind. That'll be okay. But what I think I need is to understand your perspective."

"Why?"

"'Cause I'm not working with book authors. I'm working with you. I think I understand how you think about most things, and that's why we work well in the partnership. But I get lost on the things when you say we can't be linear."

"And you want me to explain it to you?"

"Yeah, partner. That's exactly what I want."

Ron put his notepad down and sipped on his coffee. He said, "Tell me what you understand about my use of 'linear.' Let's start there."

"Okay. I think you mean things are linear when they occur sequentially in time, and the earlier one causes the later one."

"Really good, Gene. That's exactly right. The two things are connected and related and …"

"But you tell me that doesn't mean they are cause and effect."

"Well, that's right, too. As I have often said, 'correlation does not mean causation.'"

"But it commonly does, right?"

"Yes, and we are responsible for unraveling correlations that are not causation."

"Why not the old, 'If this then that'?" Gene asked.

"Well, that implies causation. Let's do a little thought experiment."

"Do I need more coffee?"

"Maybe before we finish. Let's say there's been an automobile accident, and Driver A drove into an intersection and hit Car B and killed a passenger."

"Well, I don't like this thought at all."

"Stick with me. After you assemble all the interviews and data, it appears that Driver A was speeding and ignored the traffic light. Who is at fault?"

"Is this a trick question?"

"Not yet. Who is at fault?"

"Driver A."

"Agreed. Now, in the same end situation, let's say the data and interviews determine that both drivers were obeying speed limits and that both had a green light to go through the intersection. What then?"

"Wait. That's not possible."

"The data show that the traffic signals were malfunctioning and were stuck on a green light in both directions. Okay, Gene, who is at fault?"

"Uh, the traffic engineer?"

"Well, he was on vacation."

"Then his replacement didn't do his job."

"There was no replacement.'

"That's crazy."

"No, the city council had cut funding to the department because there had been no problems for two years, and now Traffic had a manpower shortage. Who is at fault?"

"Are you telling me it's the City Council?"

"Do you think they will come to that conclusion when they investigate?"

"Of course not. What point are you making here?"

"Only that not every event, good or bad, can be directly traced linearly back to someone's fault."

"That's the old argument about the 'tip of the spear' isn't it?

"Yes. People died on the Titanic because the ship's owner removed the lifeboats to help the ship set a speed record. But everybody blamed the ship's captain because he hit an unreported iceberg."

"Now wait a minute, that's complicated."

"There are actually three stages of difficulty in either performing a task or in assessing the outcome. The first stage is linear. Everything seems rational and Newtonian. If this, then that. Think of things in this category as if you were baking a cake. You have a recipe, and if you follow it, you get a cake, same cake every time. That's linear."

"Okay, I get that one."

"Stage Two involves complicated things. For this example, think about a manned expedition to the moon."

"We actually did that."

"Yes. And it was complicated. But all that means is that many integrated parts were involved, and they were all linear. Calculations of weight, thrust, star mechanics, etc. Those were all linear aspects in a really big complicated endeavor. But basically, linear. If this, then that."

" I feel like we're coming to Stage Three. Do I have time for more coffee?"

"Hang on, Gene. Stage three is the stage of complexity. That means that events are more often unpredictable. 'This' doesn't always lead to 'that'. Timelines are blurred, and one can only deal with such situations with non-linear tools."

"Hold on, partner. I think I've heard this before. You're heading for that old 'butterfly effect' aren't you?"

Ron nodded and took a sip of his coffee. "In a way, that's right. The butterfly effect is an example of how unpredictable certain things are. One day the butterfly flaps its wings and nothing happens, but the next day with the same flapping and a tornado occurs in Kansas as a result. Unpredictable."

"Yeah, I got that," Gene said.

"But the important lesson is that looking backward to see what caused a tornado doesn't always come up with the criminal butterfly. Retrospective analysis of cause is only useful if the events are linear and 'this' always leads to 'that'.

Gene looked steadily at Ron and said, "Now you're making my brain hurt. What's your example of Stage Three? Murder investigations?"

"No. My best example of complexity is raising a child."

Gene stared at his partner. "What?"

"Right. You don't always know what you're gonna get. And when you have something, no one knows for sure why things turned out that way." Gene shook his head and said, "I definitely need more coffee." He headed for the counter just as Ron's phone rang. The caller ID was not familiar, but he answered it anyway.

"This is Detective Looney. May I help you?"

"Detective. My name is Gail Hunicutt. I got your number from Tommy Pritchard's voice mail. What's going on?"

"Where are you Ms. Hunicutt?"

"I'm standing outside my gate at the Las Vegas airport."

"When will you be back in Cincinnati?"

"In about six hours. What is going on?"

"Ms. Hunicutt, I'm sorry to tell you, but Thomas Pritchard has been seriously hurt at New City Hospital. I would like to talk to you as soon as you arrive."

"Oh my God. Is Tommy going to be all right?"

"That's all I can tell you right now. May I have a patrol car pick you up at the airport?"

"Uh, yes. Sure. I was going to take an Uber, but that's fine."

Looney obtained her flight and gate number plus her address and cell phone number and told her someone would be at the gate. When he hung up, he found Gene back at the table, sipping a fresh cup.

"How'd that go?" he inquired.

"Not too bad. She'll be here in six hours."

"Linear discussion?"

"Complicated. I lied to her."

CHAPTER 41

THURSDAY, APRIL 8

Councilman Anton Greene read his text message and felt a rising wave of eagerness in his chest. Over the years, he had been privy to the planning and the post-activity reviews of several operations performed by the SEAL team to which he was the JAG liaison. He was familiar with the basics of such plans. He had always watched with fascination as the team members accepted their roles, each filling in their details only as needed for others to remain out of the line of fire. Greene admired the professionalism of the Special Operators and how they approached every action.

That was a major reason he had recruited Quiles and Aramano to work for him when he retired. Initially, his having bodyguards seemed nonsensical, as his practice was small, and he was not a rich man. In those early years, Greene assigned the Special Operators mundane tasks and allowed them ample free time. By the time their presence around him became expected, his law practice began to produce significant income. That was the same time Anton Greene decided he wanted a less active and busy life during regular work hours so he could spend more time in luxury activities at other hours.

Greene decided to run for public office despite the impact such office holding would have on his law practice. Anton Greene had anticipated all of these occurrences and prepared to manage them to his advantage. First, to belay any concerns about his law practice conflicting with public office, he shifted to a type of law that dealt primarily with wills, trusts, and estates wherein all property management was not in conflict with the City. His campaign projected a civic-minded individual ready for public service. He was elected in his first attempt at office and subsequently re-elected.

He was, by the time he sought the office of Councilman, a wealthy man. He held an impressive stock portfolio, had a sizeable bank account, and his wife had an income of her own. Personal bodyguards then seemed more appropriate than several years before. Quiles and Aramano began to publicly show more of that activity by reviewing security plans before any public event and walking closely with the Councilman on the streets. Again, these attachments became accepted and even expected in the public eye. To a degree, the constant presence of bodyguards suggested to the general public that their Councilman was a man of significance.

Greene read the text message from Harry Wilton again. He was looking forward to the interplay between himself and a contract worker. Greene was confident his Special Operators would out-maneuver the plain man in the hard hat. He was excited to get the setup underway. He called, "Quiles! Aramano!"

The door to the next office opened, and the two men came in. Aramano, the taller and more talkative of the pair asked, "Yes, Colonel?"

Greene said, "I heard back from Wilton. He has set up a meet for tomorrow night."

"Did he give a location?" asked Aramano.

"Yes, he did," Greene said, almost laughing. "He wants to meet at the construction site!"

"At night?" Quiles asked.

"Well, dusk," Greene answered. He went on, "There's a cleared area near the foot of the old clock tower where he wants to meet for the exchange. There should be ample places for you to set up there."

Quiles nodded soberly. He was the more serious of the two men. Jorge tended to think through situations more deeply than Aramano, and he spent less time talking about the process. Jorge Quiles resembled a fireplug on steroids; his bodybuilder frame was often mistaken by opponents as an indication of slowness. He was one of the highest-ranked martial arts practitioners and could be deadly in hand-to-hand combat. But he, like Aramano, had excelled in Special Ops as a sniper, a long-range assassin. Both men had stellar reputations of protecting their force while on Overwatch and in being able to melt into the surroundings at the time of exit. Greene smiled at them, confident they could manage without explicit directions.

Even so, he said, "Don't miss this time."

They nodded and turned for the door. Aramano spun back at the last minute to ask, "You want the setup?"

"NO," Greene answered, "you take care of it. I'll be there at 1930 as he has requested. What you do can be a complete surprise to me."

Both men grinned and left.

Greene knew they would spend the next 24 hours planning the operation. It would go smoothly. The untrained construction worker was out of his league, Greene supposed. It's almost worth the money to see another operation run its course, he thought. Then he corrected himself. No matter how much fun this was, it was not likely to be worth $1 million.

CHAPTER 42

THURSDAY, APRIL 8

Harry pulled a sandwich and a small bottle of water from the pockets of his overcoat. He leaned against the inner wall of the clock tower and ate slowly, thinking and listening. He listened to the sounds of the construction site. Harry was familiar with the daytime hammering and sawing sounds of construction. He also knew the roar of destruction from the crashing, ear-rendering crack of exploding C-4, to the rain of concrete and rock particles following, and the recognition of the slowly lightening of the sound of falling debris as the size of particles decreased. And, he knew the period of silence that came at the end, the complete absence of sound that often was pierced by shouts and applause from onlookers. But he also knew the sounds made by the piles of rubble in the night when no one else was around. Sounds of the shifting of weight, the adjustment of the earth to a new burden, the sliding of a small mound of dirt to a new lower level.

Harry did not have to see the shooters when they arrived, because he heard them. They were quiet but not silent, and their footsteps and the shift of rock and gravel under their feet were clear. Even against the traffic sound of the city only a block away, Harry could discern the shifting of a piece of concrete under the weight of a man and could judge how far away that man was. He looked at his watch; the shooters had made good time; there was more than an hour until the scheduled meeting time. He slowly moved to gain the window vista and was able to see the men determining their best station.

One of the men was directly below Harry and had taken up position on the second floor of the station with the same view of the central area that Harry had. This man laid a strip of insulation on the floor at the edge of the space where a wall had previously been. He bunched the insulation into a brace for his sniper rifle, turned his baseball cap with the bill to the rear, took up a prone position, and sighted into the clearing. The other man was directly across the open area, also on the second floor, was and adjusting his shooting platform for use from a seated position. He also used some torn sheets of insulation to pad an area where he could sight his rifle into the area under the first shooter and also cover the clearing. They took up their positions with minimum effort and settled into a still posture about sixty-five minutes before the meeting time.

Harry shrugged to himself in recognition of the professionalism of the shooters. He also congratulated himself on having predicted their actions. He silently picked up his Gosky monocular spotting scope and slipped his phone into the attached holder. He slowly moved back into the window and sighted on the man across the clearing. For a moment, it was difficult to locate the shooter since he had blended into the rubble. When Harry located him, the man was sitting against some concrete blocks, the rifle balanced with the butt at mid-chest. Harry knew he would be able to bend forward slightly and have the sight on someone with less than a second of warning.

Harry took a picture of the man and his perch. Using his Bluetooth trigger, the camera application on the phone made no noise. Nonetheless, Harry did not move and studied the shooter for a response. When there was none, he shifted slightly and raised his profile in the window to see the man below him.

That man had remained in the prone position and also appeared unmoving. Then, as Harry prepared to take a picture of that second man's position, the man moved his head and twisted his neck to each side. Harry froze, thinking the shooter might have heard him. A few seconds later, however, it became clear the man was only flexing his neck. Harry took the picture and quietly slipped under the window and leaned against the wall.

The three of them remained that way for the next hour. Harry listened carefully to assure himself that the shooters had not moved, and he visually confirmed that every twenty minutes or so. When he heard movement in the central area, everyone was still in position. He peered over the windowsill and saw the Councilman coming toward the clearing from the direction of the back exit. Harry had waited for the Councilman to show for this reason: he needed to know how the man planned to get away once the exchange occurred.

Harry slid down against the wall and texted, "Delayed. Tomorrow. Same Time and Place." Less than a minute later, he heard a foul word from the clearing and caught the sound of the Councilman leaving. He raised his head into the window, and watched the shooters set aside their materials for later use, take their rifles apart, and pack them into their carrying cases. The shooters made their way down from their perches and met at the edge of the clearing. They left, moving to the front of the construction site, away from where the Councilman had been. Harry breathed a deep sigh of relief. So far, the scenario was running according to his expectations.

As the construction site began to seep back into quietude, Harry's phone vibrated. The message was from Greene and was simple: "Better not be playing me or say goodbye to Riley." Harry gritted his teeth. The councilman was insufferable, now threatening his blackmailer. Harry thought about messaging Riley to stay away from work for a few days but couldn't imagine a scenario where he could make such a request believable to Riley. Tomorrow's events would have to follow Harry's planned trajectory, then, and Morgan would be all right. And, so far, the councilman was staying right on script. Harry relaxed and finished the water bottle.

An hour later, Harry emerged from the clock tower and found his way to the explosives locker, and then later around to the perimeter fence. His plan was running true to form so far; tomorrow he would be

back to finish the plot. He knew that the debris piles in this part of the
site were not likely to change in the next day and paid close attention to
potential areas for missteps if he needed to cover this ground in a hurry.

Wondering how the Councilman was privy to the existence of
the entry through the rear chain-link fence, Harry continued his
masquerade as a homeless person, shuffling off away from the site for
several blocks. He initially passed his parked car and circled back to
check about being followed. No one seemed to pay him any attention;
when the street was nearly empty, and no one was watching him,
he quickly slid into his vehicle. Harry slumped in the driver's seat
for several minutes after entering the car, waiting to see if someone
would challenge his presence. When there was no confrontation, he sat
upright, started the engine, pulled away from the curb, and drove back
toward the subway vent.

CHAPTER 43

FRIDAY, APRIL 9

The next morning Ron Looney was sitting at his desk making a few entries in the Murder Book regarding Thomas Pritchard. He looked up and noticed Gene coming from the break room. Gene made a sour face and a motion like washing his hands as he approached.

"Bad, huh?" Ron asked.

"Bad is an inappropriately light-handed adjective for whatever it is brewing in that pot," Gene answered, standing at his chair.

"Is this going to be the dictionary day?"

"I do believe we need more descriptive terms for the foul brew that accumulates in our break room coffee pot. And 'bad' doesn't convey the disgust and inner revulsion I get from smelling that concoction."

"C'mon, man. We don't need to alienate whoever makes a pot. The rules say whoever takes the last cup must make a new pot. You could just throw that last cup away and make a new one yourself."

"This is a new pot, Ron. Whatever malevolent spirit led to its infusion is either from an alien world or straight from the depths of perdition."

"So, dictionary day it is. Do you lay awake nights dreaming of ways to define our break room coffee pot as unpalatable?"

"Unpalatable? That's even less descriptive than 'bad'. You have no imagination, sir." Gene dramatically drew himself up and crossed his arms in mock hauteur.

"Look, spare me the Cyrano soliloquy on all the various ways I should have expressed myself. Let's just go to the coffee shop."

"I thought you would never ask," Gene grinned and grabbed his coat. "What were you putting in the Book?"

"Just catching up on our lack of findings at Pritchard's house. It's all still rather sparse. We don't really know much about the man, do we?"

They walked to the corner of the Dick Pen to take the stairs and passed the open door to Captain Thorason's office. Inside they could see the Captain at his desk, tie loosened, and sleeves rolled up. In front of him was an open file of some considerable thickness. Thor was transfixing the file with what appeared to be the beginnings of The Look. All personnel in Homicide knew to get as far away from the Captain as possible whenever The Look was in play. The detectives quietly slipped past the doorway and into the staircase.

"That was close," Gene said. "He could have looked up and seen us."

"I would have offered to bring him a cup," Ron said. "I've deflected The Look once before by doing that."

"Really? You never told me that story."

"Well, it was a long time ago, and the Look wasn't for me, and I didn't know about it anyway, so it probably doesn't count."

"Still, a thwarted Look. Likely a citation Story if there ever was one."

"Cut the dictionary game."

There was a short line at the coffee shop. They each had a favorite brew from this barista, albeit nothing to compare with what Nick would make for them at New City Hospital. They ordered their drinks, pondered and decided to skip having a pastry, paid their tab and migrated to the end of the counter where their drinks would be placed. Ron checked out the seating and noticed that two men were leaving the table in the rear corner where he and Gene preferred to sit. He signaled to Gene with his eyebrows and Gene was quick to claim the table, using a leftover napkin to clean the top. Ron waited and picked up both drinks as they came available and joined Gene.

They took their respective seats at the table. They particularly liked this table in the rear of the establishment. The table was in a corner and allowed each man to have a wall at his back. This seating arrangement had become routine for them since Ron related the story of how Broken Nose Jack McCall had gotten behind Wild Bill Hickok and shot and killed him. Legend has that the killing occurred on the only instance where Hickok sat with his back to the door of the saloon where he played poker. After relating that story, neither man felt comfortable unless he could watch the door as they sat drinking their coffee.

After the first sip of his coffee, and an approving nod, Gene opened with, "Now that you've updated the Book on Pritchard, tell me what you think about why he got killed."

"Oh, I still think Pritchard was mixed up with Wilton in something. What is not clear is whether they were working together and had a falling out or whether they were at odds on the deal."

Gene took a long swig of his coffee before saying, "I don't think they were initially at odds. If they were, it wouldn't make sense for him to be sneaking into the hospital in the middle of the night to meet with Wilton."

"Unless he wasn't there for a simple meeting. Maybe he was there to take Wilton out of the game."

"Huh, I didn't consider that."

Both men were quiet for a few moments, then Ron noted, "We don't have a good handle on either one of these guys. One is a roughneck construction worker, and the other is a Casper Milquetoast. What do they have in common?"

Gene sat up straight, "Do you mean Casper the Ghost has a last name?"

Ron was accustomed to such sidetracks from Gene who took any instance to make a funny comment. This time, however, the narrowing of Gene's eyebrows as he asked that question led Ron to say, "Gene, did you never read the comics?"

"What do you mean? I read the comics. Garfield is my favorite. And Brewster Rockit."

"A quarter of a century behind, that's you."

"Are you really that much older than me?

"No, I just started reading comics at a very young age. Casper Milquetoast was a comic figure back then. He represented the most timid man you can imagine. Webster even defined him as 'speaks softly and gets hit with a big stick'."

"Now that's funny. Speaks softly and gets hit with a big stick." Then he lifted his cup in a mock toast to his partner. "Never heard of him."

"Well, broaden your horizons, partner. Mr. Pritchard strikes me as a present-day Casper."

"And yet, there he was sneaking into the hospital at night."

"Right. Something doesn't add up."

"Maybe he was Clark Kent and not this Casper guy." Gene smiled at Ron and winked.

"Mild-mannered, for certain. But, somehow, I don't see Clark Kent getting a pencil in his ear and stripped of his clothes. But that's my point exactly. We do not know enough about this guy. We have him dead and possibly - likely - linked to a missing person. He's an all-around nice guy accountant with no record."

"Plus, he was naked," Gene said, smiling more broadly.

"Yeah. Which doesn't help me at all."

"You want me to dig into his background?"

"That's exactly what I want, Gene. You do the Internet thing, and I'll call a couple of people I know, and we'll compare later."

"All right. Back to the sweatshop, then."

CHAPTER 44

FRIDAY, APRIL 9

Ron slid into the booth at the café. "I couldn't find a parking place within two blocks. Do you think the secret is out about this place?"

"Not from me," Gene said, watching Sandy visit other tables. "I don't want any more people in here than now."

Ron sat quietly for a minute or so before commenting, "You know, when I was in school, they used to call that ogling."

"What?"

"What you're doing there. Staring at Sandy and watching everything she does. Ogling. Watching her move from table to table. And that wasn't something that nice boys did."

"I'm not ogling," Gene said, turning to face Ron and look him directly in the eye. Ron smiled, and, when Gene turned back to watching Sandy, he said, "Well, gawking, then. Whatever, it isn't pretty."

"I'm watching her appreciatively. She knows that. She says she likes my attention."

"Attention, eh? Is that what the kids are calling it today? Maybe the old folks called it leering. Yes, that's it, leering. Whatever, it's not nice."

"I don't think I'm going to bring you here for lunch again."

"You are really on the high horse today, aren't you? But you forget the key feature in us coming here. I'm the one driving.

"Yeah, yeah, okay. I know."

"We were going to work on the Knowns List, right? Are you going to help?"

"Of course I am. I just want to be sure Sandy knows we are here."

"Gene, she knows you are here, trust me."

"Alright, then. Known number one: the naked dead man is Thomas Pritchard.

"Agreed."

"Number two is . . . wait, do we agree that Harry Wilton killed him?"

"Not provable, but I agree with listing it as number two."

"Number three, they are in something dirty together, willingly or not."

"I would rather say number three is that someone else is very interested in them or something they have."

Gene thought about Ron's suggestion briefly before agreeing, "Okay, that sounds better."

Sandy arrived to take their orders, and Gene went for the 'usual' again. She paused a moment and then asked him, "Would you like to try the garlic, green beans instead of the potato chips?"

"Uh, that does sound … interesting." Gene's voice inflection and facial expression indicated that he probably would not like food that was 'interesting'.

Ron said, "I'll have the green beans instead of the onion rings today."

Not to be outbid, Gene also chose the green beans.

Sandy checked their sandwich orders against what she thought they wanted: patty melt for Gene and pastrami for Ron, then went to fetch their drinks. They watched her walk away.

"Do we have a number four?" Gene asked without moving his eyes.

"There are some obvious things we probably don't need to number right now."

"Such as?"

"Well, that Harry Wilton is in the wind, for example."

"And that we're waiting to hear from his mystery girlfriend."

They then mulled over some ideas of the next steps in their investigation until Sandy came with their sandwiches. They ate quickly, complimented the chef to Sandy, which made her giggle and finished their iced teas.

Instead of waiting around to talk with Sandy after paying their bill, Gene walked back to the car with Ron. "Should we brief Thor when we get back?" he asked.

"I don't think so. We don't have anything concrete yet. Let's wait and see if he asks."

"What are you going to say when the mystery girl calls?"

"I'm going to get a name and address and then invite her to come downtown to talk to us."

"She's been out of town for days. Do you think she will have any useful information?"

"Maybe not about these last few days but I'm hoping she can tell us a little more about Thomas Pritchard. And maybe about Harry Wilton and what they were doing together."

CHAPTER 45

SATURDAY, APRIL 10

Gail Hunicutt met the plainclothes officer at the airport and allowed him to take her bag and escort her to his vehicle in the emergency-parking zone outside baggage. She sat quietly in the back, after asking the officer what was going on. When he indicated that he was only driving the car, she lapsed into silence for the remainder of the trip.

Hunicutt was dishwater blond, five foot five inches tall and built almost without curves. Her face was attractive, with sparkling black eyes and a broad, smiling mouth. She was dressed sensibly in a dark pink blouse, black slacks and pumps, and a colorful neck scarf. She was carrying an over-the-shoulder leather bag. Despite the distance she had traveled, she appeared ready to tackle any task put before her. And she bore herself with an air of certainty that the task would have an outcome that suited her.

The officer parked in the adjacent parking deck and escorted Hunicutt to an interview room before notifying Looney of her presence. Ron hurried to meet her. She stood as he entered.

"Ms. Hunicutt, I'm Detective Looney. Thank you so much for coming. Please sit down."

"Detective, what exactly is going on? Why aren't we meeting at the hospital? I want to see Tommy."

"Mr. Pritchard is no longer at the hospital. I'm sorry to say, he died."

"Died? From what? And when?"

"Ms. Hunicutt, I'm going to tell you the whole story as we know it. It may take a little time and we need to ask you some serious questions. Would you like some coffee or water?'

"Uh, yes. Coffee, please."

Ron signaled to an officer at the door and took a seat across from Hunicutt. "The fact is, Thomas Pritchard was found dead at New City Hospital several days ago, and …"

"Several days? On the telephone, you said …"

"Yes, I was not completely honest with you about that. I didn't want to give you such news on the telephone."

"You lied."

"Yes, I did. I'm sorry, and I hope you can trust what I have to say from now on." Ron put his hands in his lap and bent his head slightly. Hunicutt fixed him with a steady stare, accusatory but not hostile. Just then, the officer returned with a cup of coffee for each of them. He also laid some packets of sugar and sweetener on the table.

Hunicutt took one of the cups and sipped the black liquid and looked at Looney for several seconds, and then said, "We'll see about trusting you. Perhaps we can start with you answering a few questions. Why was Tommy in New City? You said he was 'found' there, is that right?"

"Yes. The circumstances were very unusual. He was not a patient. His body was found in a unused room on one of the wards. Naked."

"What? Naked? And dead?"

"Yes. We had no way of identifying him for several days."

"Naked? Why was that?"

Ron was impressed with Hunicutt's response and durability. He was unsure of the exact relationship between her and Pritchard; although she referred to Pritchard in a familiar term, Hunicutt persisted in cross-examining Looney about particulars. Ron began to think of her as a prosecuting attorney, undeterred from determining the facts. He decided he needed to direct the interview from that point, so he asked, "What was your relationship with Mr. Pritchard?"

She looked at Looney and cocked her head to one side. "We have been seeing each other for almost a year."

Ron appreciated the lack of tears and wailing and felt more sympathy for her position than he had expected to. He nodded, took a breath and replied, "This may be a little difficult, but let me share with you the particulars. A naked man was found dead on an active ward in New City, and no one in the hospital could identify him. We struggled for a couple of days without identification. Then we discovered that another man had left the hospital against advice and had left his clothes behind."

"You think he …"

"Yes. We determined that man had given a false name on admission but was really a man named Harry Wilton. Do you recognize that name?"

"I don't think so." Ron noted the quick answer.

"We are convinced that this Harry Wilton killed Thomas Pritchard to get his clothes and to leave the hospital."

"How macabre."

"I agree. We searched for Mr. Wilton and learned he was an employee of ABC construction."

"Wait. That's where Tommy worked."

"Yes, we learned that when we went to the construction site and asked around if anyone recognized his picture."

"Did they know each other?"

Ron sat back and took a sip of his coffee. He thought that Hunicutt's reaction to Harry Wilton's name and the fact that he also worked at ABC Construction was without guile. His immediate feeling was this woman had nothing to do with whatever Pritchard was involved in. He knew he could not defend that decision to either Gene or Thor, but he felt it was right. Based on that feeling and decision, Looney decided to give her the full story.

"Yes. We believe they did know each other. We also think they were involved in some illicit scheme that went awry and led to them quarreling in the hospital. That's why Pritchard, ah Tommy, was killed."

"What kind of scheme?" Hunicutt became somewhat defensive of her friend.

"We don't know, and I was hoping you could give us some idea."

She looked steadily across the table at Looney. "How was he killed? Thomas, I mean."

Ron slowly sipped from his cup, recognizing that Hunicutt had not answered his question.

"He died from a mechanical pencil pushed into his ear."

Hunicutt shuddered and looked down at the table. "He always carried a mechanical pencil wherever he went. Was it his?"

"We don't know that for certain, but it was similar to those he kept on his desk at work."

"You've been to his office, then?"

"Yes. Everyone spoke highly of him and gave no indication he might be involved in something shady. "

"I would agree. Thomas was not that kind of guy. More vanilla. I don't see him getting involved in any type of 'scheme'."

Ron sipped from his cup again, taking a few seconds to consider how Hunicutt had come back to his question about Pritchard's involvement. "Was he acting differently in the last few weeks?"

After a bit of reflection, Hunicutt said, "Not so much in his actions. But he did bring up something a couple of times when I thought he was distracted."

"What was that?"

"He said that never again was he going to offer to cover for anybody."

"What does that mean, 'cover for anybody'?" Ron made an entry in his notebook.

Hunicutt shrugged, "I don't know. He didn't explain. He did say it twice, though."

"Was he nervous? Did he imply that he was being pressured in some way?"

"He may have been a little nervous, I don't recall. He definitely did not mention being pressured."

"When you say he seemed distracted, what did that look like? What was going on at the time?"

"Oh, a couple of times I would catch him staring off in space as if he had left the building."

"And he gave no reason for that behavior?"

"Only saying he would never 'cover for anybody' ever again."

Ron held up the conversation for a moment while he looked steadily at Hunicutt. "Are you certain you don't know what he meant by 'cover for someone'?"

She smiled tightly and emphasized, "No, Detective, I didn't ask what that meant, and he didn't tell me. I do know that Tommy was an honest man and not given to lying for any reason. I cannot imagine that he would intentionally provide an alibi for someone that was untrue. Especially if he thought that person was doing anything illegal."

Ron decided to shift his emphasis. "Did he miss any appointments?"

Hunicutt recognized the shift, and her shoulders relaxed, "Not to my knowledge."

"Is there anything else you can tell me?"

"I don't think so. Not right now. What are you doing with Thomas?"

"We are holding his body in the morgue and looking for relatives to notify. Can you help us there?"

"I can. There are no relatives Tommy's parents are dead, and he was an only child."

"I see."

"But I will take responsibility for arrangements if that's all right."

Ron nodded at this statement and said, "I'm sure it will be."

He stood and opened the door to the interview room. Then he turned back to her and stuck out his hand, "Here's my card. If you have forgiven me for not telling you about Mr. Pritchard's death on the telephone, I would appreciate it if you could call me if you think of anything else that might help us."

"Okay. And thank you, detective. For telling me what happened. I forgive you. I believe your intention was from a good heart."

Ron smiled at her and asked, "Why were you out of town, Ms. Hunicutt?"

"It's my business. I train concierge managers for Marriott. I travel every six weeks or so to a city and run a training program for new employees. The session usually runs for five days. We had a training session in Las Vegas. I should have been back home two days ago, but we had reasons to prolong the training."

"I see. Thank you again for coming to the station and providing us with this information. I will get someone to take you home.

"May I see Tommy?"

"Oh, yes, of course. I'll ask one of the officers to escort you to the morgue and then drive you home."

CHAPTER 46

SATURDAY, APRIL 10

Looney arranged for Hunicutt 's admittance to the morgue and went to find Gene. They sat at their desks while Ron briefed his partner on the interview.

"You sound like you believe her story," Gene said.

"I do. It's pretty easy to check out. She gave me the contact information for her supervisor and the hotel in Las Vegas, where she was conducting her training session. I will run that down, but, yes, I believe she had nothing to do with any scheme, and she certainly wasn't around for the death."

"Uh-huh. And she gave you no idea what was going on between him and Wilton either?"

"She says she had not heard Wilton's name before. That's not the exact same thing, but I don't think she was aware of what Pritchard was doing with Wilton. She did say that Pritchard was somewhat distracted recently and said he would never 'cover for anybody' again. Whatever that means."

"And Hunicutt didn't know?"

"She said she had no idea. She also said she did not ask him what he meant. But she was quite clear about her doubts that Pritchard would be involved in anything illegal, with anybody.

Gene said, "Well, I spent the morning running down the other guy in this story. I now have all the references we got on Wilton. He's quite the guy."

Ron leaned back in his chair and said, "Lay it on me, partner."

"Nope. I worked up an appetite going through all this background. I'll tell you over lunch."

"It's too early for lunch."

"See, that's a common misapprehension. There is not a time on the clock that is 'too early' for the next meal. You should know that, partner. In our business, we eat when we can. And right now is when we can."

Ron chuckled at Gene's psudogruff manner, "I know you are mimicking soldiers on the front line of a shooting war. That's not us."

Gene was on his feet and heading for the door, "Could be us. Somebody might want to shoot at us."

Ron casually got to his feet and followed his partner, "I'm coming because I want to hear your story about Wilton. Don't think I'm falling for your nonsense about eating. You think the time to eat is always at hand, so don't act like this is something different."

They continued to talk about the timing of meals and the appropriate time between meals as they went to the car.

Sitting in their accustomed booth at the café where Sandy worked, Gene relaxed a little and started telling Ron a long-winded joke.

"Stop it," Looney said, smiling. "I'm not listening until you talk about Wilton."

Sandy came to the table and took their orders without a lot of fuss, which caused Ron to ask, "Is everything all right in the dating game?"

"What do you mean?"

"Well, Sandy was pretty abrupt with us. She does that to me fairly regularly, but only to spend more time with your order and call you 'honey' and everything. So, what's up here? Am I about to lose out on a great pastrami sandwich place?"

"It's nothing."

"It most certainly is something. What's going on?"

"She suggested we could take a vacation together."

"Ooohh. Going too fast for you, Gene? What's the trouble with that?"

"Nothing really. Except where Sandy wants to go."

"Cleveland?"

"Get serious. She wants to go to Hawai'i. Get a place on Kauai on the North Shore and spend a week."

"Hawai'i?"

"Kauai."

"Listen, buddy, ten other guys in this café right now would jump at that offer. What is wrong with you?"

"Do you know how much that costs? To fly to Hawai'i? Round trip, of course. And Kauai's North Shore is the most expensive place over there."

"Gene, you are not a miserly man. Are you getting cold feet about this girl?"

"Well … I don't think so, but …"

"You've got the money, right?"

"Well … yes, but …"

"No but about it. Today you tell Sandy to pick the date because you are going back to the office to get the tickets."

"C'mon, man, I can't …"

Sandy showed up with their orders just then and smiled sweetly at them both. "Can I get you anything else?" she asked.

"Do you have poi on the menu?" asked Ron. Gene glared at him, and Sandy looked uncertain for a moment before realizing what was going on.

She said, "Not right now. But we can order some for you in the future."

Then she smiled at Gene and left. Both men watched her walk away.

"Okay," Gene said. "Okay, I'll do it."

"Good for you. Now, tell me what you found out about our boy, Wilton."

"Turns out our boy has a military background. He was a frogman for five years stationed out of Virginia Beach …"

"A Seal?"

"Yes, another special operator. We should start a collection."

"Go on."

"He got some injury and transferred to the SeaBees."

"That's the construction battalion."

"Right. Well, he had demolition training in the Seals, so he became a demolition guy for the SeaBees. Traveled overseas a couple of times and retired from the Navy four years ago and immediately got a job in construction as the guy to blow up buildings."

"Cincinnati?"

"Came here less than a year ago to work in demolition for ABC Construction."

"They're big in the area. They've got signs around half the construction sites in the city. What else do you know?"

"Married, wife died a couple of years ago from some blood disorder. One child, a son named Henry who is a freshman at Kenyon playing lacrosse."

"Scholarship?"

"Something like that. What's with this lacrosse fever sweeping the nation? I mean, what happened to good old football and baseball?"

"Can't tell you, man. Debts? Gambling? Drugs? What do we know about this guy?"

"You heard all the guys at work. He's a nice guy, quiet, not a trouble maker. I ran his financials, and he's pretty clean. Got a house mortgage and a car loan and is making payments regularly. No big money flux in his accounts."

"You checked his credit cards?"

"Of course. No activity since he went in the hospital."

"And nothing that Pritchard might have to 'cover' for?"

"I haven't run his phone yet, but I have no indication they knew each other."

They decided to have dessert and coffee to continue their discussion about Pritchard. Ron ate his apple pie in small bites and talked around them, "Maybe he was covering for somebody else?"

"Somebody we don't know."

"Yeah. Could be, I guess, but Wilton's the only other guy we know with a connection. You didn't find anything in Wilton's activity to suggest he needed an alibi or an excuse for missing something, right?"

"I did not."

"Pritchard was an accountant, so maybe his 'cover' would be something to do with his work."

"Like what?"

"I don't know for sure, but maybe he noticed something that didn't get paid and covered it up."

"Or maybe he provided an alibi for whoever failed to make that payment."

"That doesn't sound like anything that would get you killed, does it?"

"No. Unless you tried to blackmail someone with that information."

"Ah-ha, partner, that's a road we haven't been down."

"Maybe we should spend some more time looking in Mr. Pritchard's computer."

"Right. We shall do that this very afternoon. But, a very smart man once told me that I had to take care of something right after lunch. I may be a few minutes," Gene said, finishing his coffee and getting up from the booth.

"Take your time," Ron said, looking at half of his pie still on his plate. "I'm gonna sit here and finish my pie. While you're at it, you could pay for that smart guy's lunch."

CHAPTER 47

SATURDAY, APRIL 10

Ron parked on the side of the construction site near where the double-wide trailer sat. He and Gene approached the building and entered the same door as before. Ron showed his badge to the young woman behind the counter and she immediately dialed a number on her telephone intercom.

Within a few seconds Gene Markham appeared. "Hello, officers, what is it this time?"

"It's detective, Mr. Markham. And we are here for the same reason as before. We would like to talk to Mr. Pritchard's coworkers again and re-examine his computer and work files."

"Right, detective. Sorry. We are still having trouble believing that Thomas is dead. I haven't yet distributed his work to anyone else so it is all still on his desk and computer."

He led the way to the accounting room and alerted the staff that the detectives would like another discussion with them. Initially, both Ron and Gene sat with individuals for discussion but within an hour, Gene decided he would use his time more productively by examining Pritchard's computer.

Markham provided a key for Gene to access the system and said he would be available in his office if needed. He left Gene alone with the keyboard and screen.

Meanwhile Ron talked with individuals who had desks adjacent to Pritchard's

"I know I asked you about such things before but I'd like to once again probe whether you may have seen or heard something that might help us understand what happened," he explained. He had decided to interview folks in pairs this time, hoping that they might help one another remember small details.

The first pair he interviewed were both men and each had an almost freaky similarity in appearance to Pritchard. Ron assumed there must be a 'type' for accountants.

"Would you help me understand just what each of you do?"

"Certainly," one replied. "Each of us in the Accounting Group are assigned several accounts belonging to ABC subcontractors. We work directly with the finance officer and the procurement officer of those subcontractors to approve requests for purchases and to expedite approval of payment on their invoices."

"You make that sound pretty straight-forward."

The other man smiled and let out a little laugh. "And it would be if the world was simpler and everything was linear."

Ron smiled back, "Of course it's not linear. If it was, I would probably be out of a job."

The second man agreed, "And so would we. Truth is, almost everything we do could be computerized and done by robots if it was linear. But we are dealing with people and very few of them ever act in a linear way."

The first man spoke up, "Except for Thomas. He really was kind of linear."

"More OCD, I think," the second man offered.

"Can you tell me about him and his work," Ron asked, putting down his pen and pad.

The story they gave was consistent and detailed. Thomas Pritchard had been with ABC for years and was considered the senior accountant in their group. That title did not come with extra money, however, and Thomas was not one to lord a position over others. He just sat in his cubicle, did his work and answered any and all questions from the rest of the group. They considered him "nice", "quiet" and "very competent". Both men had a story about how Thomas had helped them deal with a subcontractor issue when they ended up getting some praise for the action.

The second set of interviews involved a man and a woman. Ron asked them for stories about Thomas and the man gave a rambling account of some accounting jargon-filled episode that Ron could not understand. The woman said she and Thomas occasionally shared recipes.

Gene stuck his head over the cubicle wall and said, "Hey, I've run down every file and company email with an entry or activity in the last six months. Far as I can tell, it's all clean and above board."

Ron nodded, "Yeah, and it's almost quitting time. Let me talk to these last two folks."

"See if anybody knows about this 12-digit password. There's no hint of it on Pritchard's computer."

Ron went back and asked the people he had interviewed about the strange code; they were certain it was not a password in Accounting and they had no suggestions.

The last pair of the day, a couple of middle-aged women, seemed initially more interested in what Ron could, or would, tell them about Thomas' death.

"Was it just horrible, like everyone says?" asked one.

"You know there are certain things we can't talk about during an investigation, M'am."

"I see. Well, it's very disturbing to me. He was such a nice man."

Ron felt the value of continuing to collect platitudes and praises about Thomas Pritchard was quickly coming to an end. But he turned to the other woman and asked, "Was there anything special about Thomas?"

"Oh yes," she said, without hesitation. "And the supervisors were aware of it, too."

"Can you tell me about that?"

"Well, he was so organized and smart about the business, any of us could go to him and get help with a problem."

"And did you ask him for help at any time?"

"Once or twice. He was very helpful. He was so good there was no question about who would cover for Cindy."

Ron stopped his note taking and looked at the woman. "Who is Cindy?"

"She's one of the young girls over in Contracting, you know. She had a baby back a few months ago and Thomas was asked to go cover for her while she was out. He knew so much about things in the company that the folks over in Contracting said it was almost like Cindy never left."

"Say that again, please."

"The supervisors in Contracting said Thomas did a marvelous job. They couldn't tell that Cindy had even left. And she was gone for six weeks."

"The part about him covering for her."

"That's what he did. Covered for her while she was out on maternity leave."

"He covered for her?"

"Yes, that's right. For about six weeks while she was out on maternity leave."

"What does that mean, he covered for her?"

"Uh, it means he did her job while she was absent. Why do you ask?"

Ignoring the question, Ron called to Gene, "Hey partner, Thomas Pritchard covered for someone named Cindy in Contracting!"

Gene bounced up from the computer and said, "Great, where's Cindy?'

The accountants were puzzled about the sudden interest in Pritchard working in Contracting. Gene Markham was called.

Ron said to him, "You didn't tell me Pritchard covered for someone in Contracting!"

"Uh, no, I didn't think of it. Is it important?"

"It may be very important, Mr. Markham. Show us Contracting."

All the accountants were dismissed and left the building while Markham took Ron and Gene down another hallway to a smaller room with four desks and computers. The Contracting personnel had already left for the day and Markham showed the detectives the desk assigned to Cindy. He explained that her maternity leave had caught the company a little by surprise since she was six weeks early and they had decided that Pritchard could take over her tasks for that time. Markham said Pritchard was pleased to be asked and had done a very satisfactory job while filling in for Cindy.

Gene sat down at Cindy's desk and powered up the computer. When the screen exhibited a sign-in icon Markham entered Cindy's company email address. The screen opened a box for a password and Markham said, "I don't have the passwords for Contracting."

Gene typed in the 12-digit code he had found earlier and watched with no small pleasure as the screen cleared and then opened to Cindy's desktop.

Markham and Ron walked a short distance away to allow Gene freedom to search through the files.

"Tell me the dates that Pritchard was covering for her," Gene asked.

He filled those dates into the search engine and started going through the files. Within twenty minutes he had run a search of files recently reviewed by Thomas Pritchard. The common thread in the files was evident; Gene reached into his coat pocket to get his police thumb drive. He looked up at Ron, smiled and made a flourish of putting the drive into a slot on the computer.

"You got something, partner?" Ron asked, moving over to look over Gene's shoulder.

"Oh, yeah," Gene replied as he began to make copies of the entries. He pointed to various places of the screen and called Ron's attention to the frequent mention of J.Y. Dahgs. "This is something, all right. Just what, I'm not completely sure, right now. We'll take these files and run some other checks when we get back to the station. But it's something, I'm sure of that."

CHAPTER 48

SATURDAY, APRIL 10

Back in his perch in the clock tower, Harry watched with satisfaction as the two shooters returned to their perches. This time they were even earlier, arriving at the site nearly two hours before the scheduled meeting between Harry and Greene. They moved into position almost as soon as the last worker had left the site, quietly reaching their respective shooting platforms and settling in with a minimum of fuss. Harry noted that the two men had changed into clothing that matched their separate sites, effectively camouflaging themselves.

The man prone below the tower was dressed in khaki pants and a gray sweatshirt, blending in with the dusty floor and the concrete blocks. He lay still with the rifle pointing into the clearing and his eye near the rear of the scope, bill of his ball cap turned backward. The man across the clearing was seated in his place and was in a shadowed area; his black pants and shirt blended into the background, his dark complexion making his face also difficult to see.

Harry nodded mentally, all items were settling in as he had anticipated. Given the probable training of the shooters, Harry believed he could anticipate their moves and the positions from which those moves would come. He also felt comfortable about his projected sequence of events and the timing of them. All that remained now was for Greene to show with the money.

So Harry sat in the tower and waited, wondering again where Pritchard could have possibly hidden the data file with all the damning evidence. He knew that Greene would not be pleased when Harry announced he didn't have that data, but that couldn't be helped. The scenario had to play out now before Greene got nervous and decided to go after Henry at college. Harry tried to calm himself into thinking of various ways to make the disclosure that would not cause Greene to lose composure.

He considered one such imaginary conversation so attentively, he almost missed the sounds from outside the tower. He listened carefully and moved cautiously to peek over the windowsill. There was still time before the meeting was to happen, and he wondered what had caused the sounds that disturbed his thoughts. Rats? No, they weren't scurrying sounds, more shuffling. Someone else added to the mix? Possibly. He checked the prone man's position and noted no change. He looked across the clearing to where the sitting man was located but didn't immediately see the figure he had seen before.

With growing concern, Harry put his Gosky scope up to his eye and scanned the area where the second man had set up his platform. There was no one there! Harry paused, wondering could he have slipped off to take a leak? That was not consistent with his understanding of snipers and their setups. Then why move? And to where? Where was number two?

He began to scan the adjacent area with the scope. Not yet nervous about losing sight of one of the shooters, Harry knew the meeting was not for another forty minutes. But, as he scanned the second-floor area without success, he began to think his plan was unraveling. In the back of his mind, Harry began to consider how to back out of another exchange. He feared that to do so would require negotiating skill without endangering Henry and his plan for getting the blackmail money. And then, almost without recognizing it, Harry saw the man's face in the scope.

The second shooter had moved his platform about fifteen feet away from his first position, slightly farther around the edge of the clearing below. Harry felt his heart rate begin to slow once he had located the man, but the new position made a significant alteration of his initial plan necessary. He took careful note of the second man's new position and judged in his mind's eye what field of fire that man now had that was different from before.

As Harry conceived the scene, the new position of the second shooter did not provide a field of fire that would dramatically change the exchange. But it did take the man out of the position Harry had calculated for his dramatic effect; that would mean Harry would have to deal with both Greene on the ground and a shooter on the second floor. Such a change in the threat assessment required some serious adjustments in a counter plan.

CHAPTER 49

SATURDAY, APRIL 10

Half an hour later, Harry was in position. He had left the Tower shortly after locating the second man's shooting platform. He maneuvered down the tower steps quietly. He then found his way, without noise, to a position near the clearing and underneath the overhang where the second shooter was positioned. He managed to stay behind some blocks of rubble and keep out of the sight of the prone shooter until the time of the exchange.

According to Harry's watch, Greene arrived at 1929 hours, one minute early. As before, he appeared on the side of the clearing closest to the rear exit. His approach was not silent, and all players knew his approach was imminent for two minutes before he was visible. He walked a few feet into the clearing and stopped. Greene was wearing a dark suit, white shirt, and gray tie, and he was pulling a wheeled leather backpack. He allowed the backpack to settle on its bottom with the handle jutting into the air. Then, he crossed his hands in front of his stomach and stared across the clearing.

Harry knew he was not visible and that Greene was looking at a point from which he expected Harry to emerge. That point on the edge of the clearing, Harry realized, would have put him in the line of sight of each of the shooters. Harry gave a nod to the planning that had taken place on the opposite team. He took two deep breaths and expelled each slowly before he stepped out of his hiding place. He held his hands at his side, partially concealing the fact that he had his Glock in his right hand. In his left hand was his telephone with a pre-programmed number ready on speed dial. As he stepped into view, Harry felt the hairs on the back of his neck rise.

"Councilman," he said in a clear but not loud voice.

"Mr. Wilton."

"Did you bring the money?"

"I did. And did you bring the data?"

"Well, sir. There's a bit of an issue with the data. My previous partner has a copy, and I don't have it. And never will."

"You don't have the data?"

"That's right, I don't, and no one ever will. But I know where Thomas found the data, and that trove of primary information is what you need to eliminate."

Harry noted that Greene started to make a movement with his right hand but had stopped on mention of the primary data. Harry assumed the gesture was the agreed-upon motion for the shooters to do their job. He knew he needed to get Greene's attention and keep him talking. "You leave the money and walk to your right. I will take a step toward the money with each step you take away. When we are equidistant, I will tell you what you want to know, and you will allow me to take the money."

"And if I don't?" Greene asked with a calm voice.

Harry might have wondered why Greene was so calm if he had not observed the two shooters in place. Harry also knew that his current position kept shooter number two from having a clear view of him, and he was certain that Greene was not aware of that. "I intend to deal with you above board, Councilman. What I will tell you is the truth. I will take the money, and you will never hear of or from me again."

"You expect me to approve of a deal where you walk away with a satchel full of my money in exchange for some vague claim of knowledge about harmful information? You must think I have no sense, Mr. Wilton." Even as he was saying this, Greene was taking the steps Harry described away from the backpack.

Harry matched Greene, step for step. "Yes. I expect you to accept my deal."

"I still have not heard what you would do if I did not accept it."

"We don't need to dally in possibilities. The deal is clear, and you are moving to accept it."

"I am waiting for your answer."

"All right," Harry tightened his grip on the phone and raised his right hand holding the Glock. "If you don't accept my end of the bargain, I'll just take the money anyway. How's that?"

Green had only moved a few steps away from the satchel. He stopped moving, looked at Wilton, and asked, "Is there really no file of incriminating data?"

"It's as I said. My partner hid a file, and I don't have it. But I do know where the original data came from."

"That's hardly what we bargained for, Mr. Wilton. I know where the original data are already. That's not a deal for me to purchase."

"You are purchasing my silence, though, aren't you, Councilman?"

At that point, Green stared at Harry and said, "There are other ways to accomplish that, Mr. Wilton." As he started to move his right hand upward, Harry pressed the speed dial button, and a split second later a loud explosion rocked the scene. The explosion came from the prone man's perch and showered debris and dust over the clearing. Harry was expecting the blast and moved to his right toward the satchel and fired a shot at Greene.

Greene had jumped at the blast and immediately turned to run for the satchel. He heard the gunfire and threw his right arm up, protecting his head and face. He grabbed the handle of the satchel, and ran under the overhang, pulling the cart behind him. He was heading for the rear exit.

The second shooter jumped to his feet when the explosion occurred. He saw his compatriot's position turn into vapor; He gritted his teeth and shifted to his left to bring Harry's position into view. He saw Harry starting toward the satchel and fired a single shot at the weaving runner. Harry then disappeared further under the overhang, and the shooter saw Greene with the satchel heading for the exit. He grabbed his rifle case and ran in the same direction, remaining on the second floor until near the perimeter. He came to a break in the flooring and jumped down on the elevation of rubble below. He arrived at the rear exit almost simultaneously with Greene. The shooter pulled the fencing open for the Councilman and then darted through. They ran the few remaining yards to the Councilman's car, got in, and drove off.

Harry, meanwhile, was forced to take a circuitous course to the exit to stay under the overhang and out of sight of the shooter. When he arrived at the exit, he heard the receding noise of the getaway car. Coming through the fence, he saw the car turning a corner and disappearing. He was crushed; his plan fell apart in so many ways. He ended up without money, only one of the shooters taken out, and the other certain to be looking for revenge. Through the fence, he could hear shouts coming from the site of the shooting, and Harry decided to make his escape. He crossed the street and went a block in the direction the car had disappeared, then sat in a deserted storefront doorway and curled up as if asleep.

CHAPTER 50

SATURDAY, APRIL 10

The explosion was not only heard, but felt in the trailers. The foundation shook, and the pencil holder on top of Pritchard's desk tipped over. Ron felt his feet move under him and grabbed on a cubicle wall to steady himself. Both men looked first at each other, assessed the lack of damage, and turned their eyes toward Gene Markham.

"What the hell was that?" Ron asked.

"I have no idea," Gene answered, puzzlement evident on his face. "We aren't scheduled for any demolition for several days."

"Is that what that was, demolition?"

"Sounded like it, but usually there's a warning siren to get folks out of the area."

"I didn't hear any siren," Gene said, coming to his feet.

"Me either," Ron agreed as they headed for the door.

Once outside the trailer, they turned toward the sound of the explosion and saw a cloud of dust in the site. Without speaking, they both began running toward the front access area. As they ran, they could see the cloud of rising dust off to their right. Once they had turned the corner and got inside the site, they still had to traverse areas of construction, piles of materials, and several large holes in the ground; Gene would later estimate they took between four and five minutes to arrive at the blast site. As they ran, they heard two gunshots spaced a few seconds apart.

Dust was still settling when they arrived, making visibility poor, but both men were certain there was no one visible in the immediate area. Gene thought he heard running footsteps to the left of their position, but the sound faded quickly. He and Ron had each drawn their weapon and stood, somewhat exposed on the edge of a small open area in the construction site, with skeletonized portions of former walls looming above them.

Without speaking, they drifted apart, reconnoitering the open area from its edge, moving in opposite directions. Ron stopped when he was about a third of the way around, and raised his hand. Gene reacted by stopping and scanning the area carefully before crossing to where Ron stood, looking down at something on the ground.

"Is that what I think?" Gene asked.

"It is if you were thinking it's a foot in a work boot."

"That's what I was thinking, all right. And it appears to have been blown off a body."

Both men stood still and nearly back-to-back and closely scanned the immediate area. After that, they began lifting their eyes to search higher and higher in the building remnants. Ron finally pointed to a place on a third-floor segment that was ragged and smoking.

"I think that's where the explosion occurred."

"Where did the gunfire come from?"

"I don't know," Ron admitted.

Gene said, "I think I heard running off to the left, there," he indicated an area under another overhanging remnant of upper stories.

"Check it out. I'm going to see what's up at the point of the explosion."

Gene headed across the open area and under the overhang. As he progressed under the overhang, the lighting was poor, and he had to slow down to keep from running into debris or piles of torn-out materials. Ahead, he thought he heard a car engine start and then fade away. By the time he got to the edge of the construction site, he found himself faced with an eight-foot-high chain-link fence. The street outside was empty of traffic, but he could see a couple of individuals strolling away from the site a block away. There also was a homeless man hunkered in a doorway a block away who looked like he was sleeping. Finding no exit through the fence, Gene turned back and carefully picked his way, returning to the open area.

Gene looked up at the zone where the blast had occurred and saw Ron bent over in the area poking at things with his hand. "Hey, partner, I didn't catch anybody. Looks like it would be hard for anyone to get out over there," Gene called up at Ron.

Ron nodded and said, "I may have found parts of the owner of that foot up here."

Gene nodded and began to move back to where they had found the foot before beginning a more careful sweep of the area. About five minutes later, Ron joined him and noted, "That spot up there looks a lot like a shooting platform. It was all padded and it appears that the explosion was underneath whoever was lying there. We can probably find other body parts around here."

Gene answered, "That agrees with this." He lifted a twisted barrel and the front portion of a rifle stock from the debris. The twisted front portion of the stock had an attachment that partially resembled a mounted bipod. "I think we will find that our body parts belong to a trained sniper."

A few minutes later, they had completed a simple sweep of the immediate area and called for a crime scene team to finish the inspection. As they stood looking around, Ron asked, "What did you think of the gunshots?"

Gene thought a second and said, "I heard two. Different weapons, I think. Separated by a second or so. One was a rifle and the other was a handgun. Can't be sure which was first."

Ron nodded, "My thoughts, too. I think the handgun was first, but I'm not sure either. But regardless, the rifle shot was not from our missing foot guy."

"Right. I agree the explosion took him and his weapon out of the fray first thing. Which means …"

"There were two shooters in here with rifles."

"And whoever they were shooting at was probably armed with a handgun."

"And he took a shot at someone or something."

"You think that was the handgun guy you heard running away?"

"I don't know. Sure could be. But it could be the other sniper, too."

"And who blew up the first sniper? Handgun guy or the other sniper?"

"And, as long as we are constructing a list of important and unanswered questions, what were they all doing here on the construction site?"

The CSI team arrived, and the detectives gave them their impression of events so the team could start looking over the shooting site.

As they watched the team unroll their crime scene tape around the open area, Ron wondered aloud, "Is there any reason we shouldn't shut this whole construction down?"

Gene answered promptly, "I think it would give us some leverage. We have a dead guy associated with the site, a missing guy who is likely a murderer associated with the site, and now what looks like a planned assassination associated with the site. What else would we need?"

"I don't know. It looks clear to me, but I bet the suits on the upper floors at City Hall will have a different take on the whole thing. Come on, let's get home. We've already missed dinner."

CHAPTER 51

MONDAY, APRIL 12

The construction site was not closed; Sunday was not a usual workday on the project and the crime scene investigators had the area to themselves. They combed the area dutifully, collecting specimens from some of the upper floors and many more from the area around the clearing. The supervisor of the crime scene crew told his supervisors that work was likely finished in the construction zone. However, he wanted to leave the crime scene tape in place until the laboratory technicians were satisfied they had everything they needed.

Workers showed up on Monday morning and found themselves confronted with the crime scene tape. Supervisors met with the crews early on to explain what had happened on Saturday night and to prepare work schedules that kept them out of the taped-off area for the day. So, the work of clearing out plumbing, electrical wiring, and solid fixtures went on as much as possible around the cleared area throughout the day.

Material removed from the upper floors could not be cast into the central area and was left on the platform. At one point or another during the day, every worker ended up standing around the taped-off area. They wondered aloud and talked about what had happened. Theories abounded.

Supervisors engaged in providing the crime scene investigators access to the entire site. That access included allowing them to check the inventory in the equipment lockers. Each of the investigators, fitted with a hard hat, was escorted about the construction site by an ABC construction employee, lessening the number engaged in work. By mid-afternoon, all relevant samples, pictures, and information were gathered. Crime scene investigators began to pack up the samples they had collected and their equipment, and leave for the laboratory. Shortly before 4 PM, the last truck of investigators pulled off-site.

Shortly after that, for reasons not clear to anyone, Morgan Riley apparently climbed up in the clock tower and fell from one of the upper windows. He landed in a pile of concrete blocks. Workers nearby hurried to the area and tried to revive him. A rescue team was summoned and assessed the scene; Morgan Riley was pronounced dead on the scene.

CHAPTER 52

TUESDAY, APRIL 13

Sam Mastone entered the conference room for the morning meeting with Holly Ellington close behind him. He took the seat at the head of the table and glanced at the other participants. He nodded to Roslyn Burke, Chief Nurse, on his left, and Tom Bolling, chief of staff, to his right, before quickly looking at the Gains and Losses sheet from the previous twenty-four hours.

"I see nothing major happened during the night. Perhaps this will be a quiet weekend," he opined. Holly nodded vigorously. Roslyn made a brief attempt at a smile in the general direction of the head of the table. Her executive, Alena Preston, did not move. Tom Bolling started to roll his eyes, but his executive assistant, Beverly Hancock, discreetly nudged him with her elbow.

Mastone went on, "Occupancy is high, but the information I got is that the COVID cases are decreasing. Is that still the case, Tom?"

Bolling nodded and offered, "Case rate overall is on a steady downward slope for the past ten days. The decrease in COVID cases has removed the pressure on the bed crunch. You were correctly informed, Sam."

Roslyn spoke up, "Nursing is not facing any further extended shifts, even in the Intensive Care Unit. Their beds are all occupied, however."

Everyone nodded solemnly, recognizing the reality of her assessment and the problem that would arise if another inpatient became too ill to be cared for on the ward and needed transfer to the ICU.

Roslyn went on, "I believe we should consider some recognition for the nurses who worked double shifts and extra time over the last few months because of this pandemic."

Beverly said, "Something in addition to the overtime pay they already received?"

Both Roslyn and Alena stiffened. Roslyn's nostrils may have flared a touch as she countered, "No one was seeking riches. The nurses were responding to a community emergency. Their work should be recognized."

Tom leaned forward and looked directly at Roslyn, "I agree, Roslyn. Everyone who responded so well to the enormous workload should be recognized. However, the organization has already recognized the efforts of all staff with no restrictions on overtime pay. I'm sure that your suggestion of recognition was not to suggest that anyone receive more money."

Roslyn swallowed hard and frowned a little before replying, "No, I am simply suggesting that the nurses, and any others, should be recognized for their efforts."

"Including the doctors and the laboratory technicians and housekeeping, too, I assume," Tom said, with the smallest of grins on his face."

"Well, yes, I suppose so," Roslyn hesitatingly agreed.

Beverly suggested, "Maybe we could have an all-hands meeting soon with coffee and pastries for all staff and publicly recognize the efforts of individuals with very high overtime participation."

Roslyn was taken a bit by surprise and sat immobile, but Alena began nodding and making some notes on her pad. Sam entered the discussion with, "I like that idea very much. Holly, see about finding a good time for everyone to be able to meet in the auditorium. I'll send a note to all department chairs to ask for the names of one or two individuals who stepped up to this crisis. How's that sound?"

Tom and Beverly nodded, as did Alena. After a short interval, Roslyn made a short, quick nod of assent.

Sam moved on, "Tom, I notice you were downtown at the police headquarters yesterday. Are you being arrested?"

Tom ignored Sam's left-footed attempt at humor. He responded, "Yes, I was the guest of the Homicide Division Captain, Thorason. He was holding a briefing about the murder investigation that started here at New City, and he wanted to bring me up to date."

"And, did you get the full story about what went on here?" Sam asked.

"Yes, Well, some of it, anyway."

"What can you tell us about it?"

"First off, they have identified the naked dead man on Ward 4C. His name is Thomas Pritchard. He was an accountant for one of the local construction companies. Apparently, he and our patient Harry Wilton were engaged in a blackmail scheme and somebody found out about it. That somebody is considered responsible for Mr. Wilton's 'accident' that put him in New City. I presume he knew that the 'accident' was an attempt on his life and that's why he was so eager to leave. He had a nighttime meeting with Pritchard, who wanted to call everything off, and he killed him, took his clothes, and left the hospital.

"So, that was Pritchard who was found naked?" asked Roslyn.

Tom went on, "Yes. He was only a visitor when he was killed.

There was a brief moment of silence. Then, Sam said, "Is New City going to be involved in any way with this killing? Are the police thinking that anyone here at the hospital was involved?"

Tom frowned before answering, "I don't think so. But if the case goes to trial, the District Attorney may want our personnel to testify about finding the body."

"Oh, I hope that won't reflect badly on the hospital if that happens."

"I think that's true for all of us, Sam."

Roslyn began bundling the papers in front of her, "Well, I, for one, am certainly glad this whole thing is over."

Tom asked, "Over? You think this is over, Roslyn?"

"Certainly. The police have identified that dead man, as you said. And they do not believe that we, that is, hospital personnel, had anything to do with his death. That is what you said, isn't it?"

Tom's voice took on a slightly more forceful tone, "Oh, yes, they have identified the dead man, and they believe they know who killed him, and they are not considering that New City personnel played any role in his death. But that doesn't close this case for New City, Roslyn."

"Whatever do you mean?"

"The formal police investigation is likely to be concluded soon. The authorities have the murderer, and they believe they know the particulars of why the murder happened."

"Then why isn't the case closed, in your opinion?"

"Because as chief of staff at New City, I want to know why that man, the murderer, with a valid physician order for isolation was allowed to roam the hospital repeatedly. It is a significant question in my mind since that man, the murderer, would not have been able to rendezvous with his partner off the ward if he had been appropriately remanded to isolation. If he had been properly in isolation and was not able to roam the wards, then that man, the murderer, would not have been in a position to murder anyone at all. That's why I don't think this case is closed from my standpoint."

Roslyn stared back at Tom but quickly dropped her eyes to her papers.

"I will not consider this case closed," Tom went on, "until Nursing Service has completed a Root Cause Analysis of why nursing disregarded a valid isolation order and allowed a patient potentially infected with MRSA to roam around the hospital. I will need to share that response from Nursing Service with Joint Commission very soon. The case remains open on my desk until Nursing Service can provide leadership with an answer as to why an established protocol was not followed, and what will be done to prevent such egregious behavior in the future."

Tom allowed his steady gaze to remain of Roslyn for a few seconds. Then, in the silence that extended from the end of his remarks, he turned to Sam and said, "If that's all, Sam, I'll be in my office." He stood and, with Beverly behind him, exited from the conference room.

The silence continued until, thirty seconds later, Sam also stood and commented, "Yes, that's all." He and Holly left the room, leaving Roslyn and Alena sitting in silence at the table.

CHAPTER 53

TUESDAY, APRIL 13

Harry was hanging around a coffee shop collecting a few coins from people who thought he was a beggar. He varied the shops he frequented to prevent familiarity, but he liked this particular shop because the fare included a ham and egg croissant that he thought was delicious. Harry would 'beg' outside for forty minutes or so and then go in and purchase a croissant and coffee, no matter how much money he had collected in donations. Sometimes he would sit at one of the outside café tables to eat, but not when many people were around.

There were few individuals interested in the coffee shop at the moment, and Harry waited only thirty minutes or so before going in. He walked stooped over, eyes cast downward and not making eye contact. The girl at the counter was always polite but distant. She seemed to recognize Harry and said, "Ham and egg croissant with coffee, right?"

He nodded, and she went on, "Would you like cheese on that?"

He nodded again, and she turned to gather the food items. Meanwhile, another server behind the counter heard his drink order, drew up a cup of coffee, and sat it on the counter in front of Harry. He nodded in the general direction of the server and took the cup, and moved toward the register. Harry always carried an assortment of coins to pay for his food and carefully counted out the total when the girl brought him his sandwich.

"Thanks," he mumbled at her.

She smiled briefly and turned back to her work.

She was only being polite; there was no real interest in the homeless bum, Harry thought. I'm beginning to fit too comfortably into this world of no possessions, little money, and no status or power. I need to make things change!

He took his sandwich and coffee outside and saw a table away from the others without a customer. He sat there and used the leftover newspaper to provide a placemat for his food. Harry was not happy about the events of the preceding day. He was trying to create a new scenario in his mind that would end with him having the blackmail money. He was concerned that Greene might now believe that there was no data file to be purchased and would simply send his remaining shooter out to find and kill Harry.

As he replayed the conversation from the construction site in his mind, Harry kept coming back to the feeling that Greene did not sound convinced when told that the data Pritchard had accumulated was missing. If that were true, then Greene would still pay blackmail if he thought he could retrieve the incriminating file. Harry's question centered on whether he could prove that Greene was still concerned about disclosure.

He finished his lunch, crumpled the sandwich wrapper, and put it inside the coffee cup he intended to throw in the trashcan near the doorway to the shop. Consistent with his new persona, Harry also took the newspaper and began to fold it carefully. He stopped as his eye caught a particular two-column headline, "Man Falls to Death at Scene of Explosion". Not wanting to show too much interest in current affairs, Harry did not stop to read the article at that moment. Instead, he tucked the paper under his arm instead of throwing it away and shuffled off down the street. A few blocks away, he took a break in the sidewalk traffic to get in his car and drive away.

An hour later, back in the subway tunnel, he opened the newspaper and read the story. It began below the fold on page one and continued further on page four of the front section. The first paragraph in the story noted that a construction supervisor had fallen to his death from the clock tower at the site the day after an unexplained explosion had occurred there. The account went on to relate that crime scene investigators had been at the site most of the day reconstructing what appeared to have been a fatal explosion and a gun battle. Shortly after the investigators left, the supervisor, now named as Morgan Riley, fell out of the clock tower and was declared dead at the scene. No explanation was known or provided for Riley's presence in the clock tower.

Harry sat back against the wall, a chill coming over him. Greene had warned him that Morgan was at risk, and Harry had not taken precautions to warn Morgan. He felt sick to his stomach. Morgan was totally outside the activity between Harry and Greene, and yet he was the one who ended up in a pile of rocks, dead at the scene. Harry noticed that his hands were hurting and looked down t see that he has clenching his fists and driving his fingernails into his palms. He made himself relax, but the growing fury inside his chest was not responding to his will. In his anger and frustration at the injustice of Morgan's death, Harry lashed out at the subway tunnel wall with both hands, hitting the wall and crying at both the physical and the mental pain it caused.

Later, he slumped and slept, exhausted. When he awoke, most of the afternoon had faded. He grabbed a juice container and left the tunnel. He ambled southward for a few blocks, crossed a major roadway, and headed for a small storefront in a strip mall. As he approached the store, he changed his walk and posture. Standing straight and not wearing his fingerless gloves, he asked the clerk for a mailing envelope, paper and pen. He paid and went down the mall toward a bagel café where sidewalk tables were available. No one was present, and he had his choice of seating. He took out the newspaper from his coat side pocket to check certain details in the story about the explosion at the construction site and then busied himself writing.

CHAPTER 54

TUESDAY, APRIL 13

Two days after the explosion at the bus station, Looney slowly walked into the Dick Pen in mid-afternoon. He was holding a folder with the findings of the CSI team from the bombing site. He had not studied it carefully but the initial and major findings were easily grasped.

"Hey, Gene," he called. His partner was at the copying machine in the corner and answered, "Yo,"

"We need hot coffee and sweet bread."

"Now you're talking my language, partner." He quickly gathered his copies and walked back to his desk. Putting the copies down and grabbing his coat, he first noticed the folder in Ron's hand.

"News?"

"CSI report on the site."

Gene eyed the folder as they headed for the stairs, "Hot off the press?"

"Yeah, and it's got some stuff we have to worry about."

"Like you said, hot coffee and sweet bread."

They did not discuss the folder or its contents while standing in line for their coffee, waiting until they had gotten seated in the rear of the shop with their backs to the walls at their favorite corner table.

Ron handed the folder to Gene and quietly sat sipping his coffee while Gene scanned the summary. "Another C-4 explosive planted?"

Ron nodded, "Which makes me think several things. The snipers were a pair, and whoever blew one of them up was their target."

"And that probably was the handgun guy," Gene offered.

"I expect so. Further, I don't think the C-4 was placed after these guys settled into their shooting platforms."

"Oh no, I'll grant you that," Gene nodded and bit into his scone.

"So, this was not the first scheduled meet. Handgun guy got them to reveal their plans, and he bobby-trapped their positions."

"And we know someone who has the knowledge and the resources to do that, don't we?"

"Yes, sir, we certainly do. It seems highly likely to me that Mr. Harry Wilton is the handgun guy and the explosives guy."

"What about the guy who was blown up?"

"Read a little more in there. The CSI guys found some more body parts and stuff that can give us DNA but nothing that will help make an identification. No teeth, no fingerprints. But they identified the rifle as an Mk11, once a favored military sniper weapon. They think it had a Leupold scope judging by the mount on the barrel."

Gene was quiet for a few moments as he quickly scanned the remainder of the folder's contents. Then he looked up, made a small grimace, and leaned back against the wall.

"I missed the hole in the fence?"

"It was well hidden. And you were not close."

"And that's how Wilton got away."

"Not just him, read again. The crime scene guys found evidence there were four people in that area. Two shooters on platforms on the second and third floor and two people on foot in that little open area. One of those on foot definitely ran straight back into the construction and found his way out that hole in the fence. The other one was on the other side, under the platform of the second shooter. That person ducked back into the construction and circled toward the hole in the fence. They lost his footprints in the construction mess."

"Someone set up a killing field."

"And someone else, probably Wilton, turned the tables on them."

"So who was he there to meet with?"

"I have no idea. But this is pretty strong evidence that we should proceed with that idea about shutting the construction down."

"The shooting site is still marked as a crime scene."

Ron shook his head, "No, I'm thinking this has more to do with the overall construction than just picking the site for an assassination. Wilton and Prichard both worked for ABC Construction. I think we need to move more broadly than just investigate the shooting site."

"Well, I'll certainly vote your way. Let's see if we can convince Thor."

They finished their drinks and headed back to the office, taking the stairs and looking in the Captain's office when they arrived. He was not in the office so they went back to their desks, and began discussing their Knowns as a way of convincing the Captain.

They had only been back for a few minutes when Looney's phone rang.

"Walker."

"Hey Detective, can I get a quote?" came the scratchy voice that Ron remembered from cases past.

"What do you want, Edderman?"

Daniel Edderman was a newspaper reporter with whom Ron had dealings in the past. Edderman's daily column, Daniel's Den, was a first-read for many in the city since it covered local stories in human depth. The column often had some comic relief, but Edderman had already won one regional journalism award for his series about the death of a local youth basketball player from drugs. His persistence on the story led to a police sting operation and the conviction of twelve members of a drug ring. Consequently, Edderman was a bit of a local celebrity. He had covered aspects of cases in the past involving both Looney and Tom Bolling. Edderman had a history of latching on a story and never letting go, often using his biting humor in his column to call attention to slow or inadequate response to issues by authorities. Looney definitely did not want to talk to Daniel Edderman at this point in their investigation.

"Like I said, a quote."

"About what?"

"The killings going on at the bus terminal construction site, that's what. I know you are the lead investigator, so what's going on?"

"What killings?"

"C'mon, detective. Don't be coy with me. You were there for the first one, so I know you know what I'm talking about."

"Listen, Edderman, you know I don't talk about ongoing investigations. Call me in a week."

"What about the other death there today?"

"What are you talking about?"

"Maybe I'm saying too much, detective. Maybe we shouldn't be talking about an ongoing investigation," Edderman's snicker was audible.

"What other death?"

"Some supervisor fell from the top of the old clock tower. Didn't you hear about this?"

"I did not. If it was an industrial accident, it has nothing to do with our investigation."

"Do you know it was an accident, detective? Can I quote you on that?"

Ron stopped talking and took a deep breath. Gene was watching him closely from across the desk. Ron controlled his voice and spoke into the telephone, "I have no information about that occurrence, and I have no comment."

"Okay, detective. I'll call you back in a week, as you asked." The line went dead.

Ron hung up and slumped in his chair. "Edderman says there was another death at the construction site. We may be too late in shutting it down."

CHAPTER 55

TUESDAY, APRIL 13

Gene was pacing around by his desk. "I still say we should go. Show the flag kind of thing. Rocky will understand."

Ron made a snorting noise and said, "I believe that comment might be your best oxymoron this year."

"What? What oxymoron?"

"That Rocky will understand. He is not constructed to be an understanding guy. If ever there was a linear detective on our force, his name is Rocky."

"What are you talking about?"

"Your idea that Rocky would understand and accept our interference in his case. He picked up the falling death at the bus station construction. He will see any involvement by us as trespassing and interference. Just let him do his job. When he gets back here, we can maybe sidle over and share some thoughts. Maybe see if this is anything we should be concerned about."

"We can do that now. By going out to the site and walking in."

"Intrusion. Interference. And then, Rocky will have these high antibody titers, and it will take days to get him off his high horse. Let it be, Gene."

"What did Thor say?"

"What do you mean? Thor hasn't said anything about this. He's been gone all morning. Talking to the chief, calling the mayor, getting an opinion from the DA. He's completely wrapped up in our request to shut the construction site down. He hasn't said anything about Rocky's case."

"Does he even know about it?"

"I'm sure he does, Gene. That's his job."

"Haven't you heard anything from him?"

"No. And we won't for another few hours. Remember, the owner of ABC was a big contributor to the mayor's campaign. Closing down his work on a job this big will have serious financial consequences."

"We made a good case for it."

"I know we did, Gene. Let's let the elephants settle this."

"What if they decide not to close things down?"

"I suspect that Thor will allow us to spend most of our day out there from now until we have a killer in hand. He is trying to do this the right way and not put us in harm's way when stuff hits the fan. Settle down."

"I need coffee to settle down."

"Right, that sounds like a really good idea. Let's go down to the shop and have a cup. Maybe even get you one of those cinnamon rolls, eh?"

Gene cocked his head and squinted at Ron. "Are you trying to pacify me?"

"Placate, more like. I need the coffee, too." They headed for the stairs but were interrupted by an officer entering the area from the elevators and crying, "package for Detective Looney."

Ron stopped short of the doorway and raised his hand, "That's me."

The officer walked over and handed Ron a plain white paper mailing envelope.

Ron asked the officer, "Has this been through the scanner?"

"Oh, yes, sir. We wouldn't have cleared it otherwise."

Okay, thanks," Ron said, taking the package carefully. Noting the absence of an address or postmark and seeing only his name printed with a marker pen on the package, Ron asked, "Where did this come from? It wasn't mailed."

"No, sir. It was hand-delivered this morning."

"By whom?"

"One of those bicycle messengers. I brought it right up."

"Is the messenger still there?"

"Oh no, he was gone by the time we put the package through the scanner."

"Okay, thanks," Ron stood looking at the package. Gene had forgotten the idea of coffee, and nudged him, "Go on. Open it up."

Ron sat at his desk and found his scissors in a drawer. He carefully cut along one edge of the package and spread the paper to peer inside. He reached in drew out a plain, unsealed envelope. He looked at Gene, who shrugged his shoulders.

Ron opened the flap of the envelope and extracted the two pages of handwritten notes. He unfolded them and placed them side-by-side on his desk. Gene maneuvered his position to be able to read over his partner's shoulder. Both men were quiet for the few minutes it took for them to read and digest the contents of the pages.

"Really?" Gene said, having finished first. "A letter from Harry Wilton?"

"Yeah," Ron said slowly. "Explaining what went on yesterday at the construction site. His story fits what we know."

"And adds some other characters and a lot of depth to our case."

"He seems to have left out some things, too. Like what happened at New City Hospital that ended with Thomas Pritchard dead."

"Look, we must get this information into Thor's hands. This ties everything back to ABC and that construction site."

"And a much bigger fish than even we expected."

CHAPTER 56

TUESDAY, APRIL 13

Ron sent an urgent message to Thor but had little hope for a quick response. The Captain was noted for leaving his cell phone on his desk when he went upstairs to meet with the Chief. Ron also called the Chief's secretary and asked her to tell Captain Thorason that he had an important message for him.

While they waited, Ron called the front desk and learned the messenger service that had delivered the package. He called the service and learned the name and cell phone number of the messenger involved. He then called the messenger and got a busy signal; he left a text message asking for a return call.

"We never did get that coffee," Gene said.

"Yeah, and now I've got two calls I'm waiting for," Ron noted.

"You know how to roll your desk phone over to your cell, right?"

Ron grinned and said, "This is why I keep you around. Now and then you get a good idea."

"My partner used to say, 'even a blind hog gets a few acorns'."

"Smart man, your partner. Let's go buy him some coffee."

As they passed the Captain's office, Ron went in and left a note of the center of the desk. Then they hustled down the steps and the block to the coffee shop.

"Good as this stuff is, it doesn't compare to what Nick makes for us," Gene said as they found a seat near the back.

"You know, we could probably get what he fixes for us right here,"

"Is Nick coming here to work?"

"You know what he calls that drink we call a 'usual?'"

"Some fancy Italian name?"

"No, he calls it a 'red eye', And apparently that's a cup of coffee with a shot of espresso."

"He never told me that."

"It's not a secret, Tom told me the name."

"I think that's what some guys call an Americano."

"Whatever. Let's ask for that here, next time. I agree this coffee is good but we need to broaden our horizons, don't you think?"

"Our horizons are gonna be pretty broad when Thor gets a load of that message from Wilton."

"Let's just leave that discussion for the Captain's office, okay," Ron said looking around. No one seemed to be paying them any attention but he still wanted to keep the contents of the message under wraps.

Ron's cell phone buzzed and he answered, "This is detective Looney. May I help you?"

"Yes, uh, hi, detective. This is William Keever, I'm the bike messenger you called."

"Oh, yes, Thanks for calling me back, Mr. Keever. Do you remember bringing a package to the police station addressed to me earlier today?"

"Uh-huh."

"Was that a 'yes?'"

"Oh, yes. Yes, I remember."

"Can you tell me who gave you the package, Mr. Keever?"

"Nope."

"Why not?"

"Never saw him."

"How did you get the package, then?"

"He called the service and asked for someone to come by and pick up a package. He told dispatch to have the messenger call when they arrived. There was no one there when I arrived and I called the number he gave."

"Where was this," Ron interrupted and wrote down the address. "And then what?"

"Well, he answered and said there was a package under the doormat for me plus a twenty-dollar bill. He said just take the package to the police. That's all."

"Did this man have an accent or anything distinctive about his voice?"

"Nah. He just sounded normal."

"All right. Mr. Keever. Thank you for calling me back," Ron was slightly dispirited as he hung up. He turned to Gene and noted, "Didn't see the guy. Talked to him on the phone and he sounded 'normal', whatever that is to a bike messenger."

They sipped their coffee and looked at each other in silence. When Ron's phone buzzed again, Ron looked at the number before answering, "Walker."

"Are you at that coffee shop?" Thor asked without preamble.

"Yes, sir."

"Bring me a cup and get back here."

"Yes, sir."

Gene understood the conversation and stood. Ron indicated they should finish their drinks. "I'm taking a cup to Thor. I think we should have another, too."

"Well, I'm gonna have an Americano!"

CHAPTER 57

TUESDAY, APRIL 13

Councilman Greene was storming around his law office, fuming mad. As he walked and waved his arms over his head, Nestor Aramano sat braced in a straight chair in front of Greene's desk.

"He shot at me, Nestor!" Greene said for at least the tenth time.

"Yes, sir."

"And he blew Jorge up. Blew him up!"

"Yes, sir."

"How the hell did that happen? I thought you had him pinned."

Before Aramano could begin a defense, Greene was off again, "And he expected me to give him that money without providing me the data file they have. Does he think I'm an idiot?"

"Yes, sir."

"What? Do you think I'm an idiot?"

"Sir? No, sir. I can't imagine what he was thinking."

"Then shut up! What I want to know is how did he manage to blow up Jorge and almost kill me and you never even had a shot at him. How did that happen?"

Confused by the conflicting command to stay quiet and the shouted question, Aramano chose to simply shrug his shoulders. He had an idea that Wilton had tricked them into revealing their shooting platform placement but he knew such comment would only fuel Greene's anger further.

"Well, I'm not an idiot. I know for certain that he and his partner, that weasel Pritchard, have a data file that will send us all to jail for many years. He's got it and I have got to get it back!"

Still not prepared to answer out loud, Aramano nodded vigorously.

"And, speaking of Pritchard, where is he?"

"No idea, sir. His car was at the New City Hospital and we looked for him there but he wasn't ever a patient. He may have just left his car there and run."

"What? What makes you think that?" Greene's voice fell a full register and came out sounding reasonable.

"Well, you know how some people hide their car at the airport in the long-term parking? He might have been doing the same thing here, just using the hospital parking lot."

"You think he scooted?"

"He hasn't been to work. He's not been back to his apartment. And we never would have found his car if he hadn't left his phone in it. Yes, sir, I think he scooted."

"And left his partner here to collect."

"Yes, sir. It seems so."

"So, the picture is that the weasel is sitting somewhere safe, like maybe Park City while Wilton gets the cash. Pritchard has and keeps the data file for future use and Wilton tries to con us into thinking there is no file."

"That's good, sir."

"And you've tried everything to find the weasel?"

"Yes, sir. Our guy checked all the bus, train and airline passenger lists. If he left using anyone of those, it was using a fake name. We'll never figure that out."

"Could he still be here in Cincinnati?"

"Sure. Hiding out. But I'm betting he left. He's got Wilton to handle this end. He must trust him."

"And where is he, Wilton, I mean?" Greene was ramping up his anger again.

"I don't know, sir."

"Doesn't he have a kid?"

"Yes, sir," Aramano was not happy about this turn of the conversation. He didn't mind going after anybody as part of the job. He had not complained or balked at the requirement that he push Morgan Riley off the clock tower. After all, Greene had warned Wilton about that. But, Aramano did not want to be going after someone's child. Children were off-limits as far as he was concerned and his voice and body language signaled that to Greene.

"Cut it out, Nestor," he said, "I'm not going after the kid. But maybe if he thinks we are, Wilton will come out of hiding."

"Yes, sir."

"Where is the kid, again? You said he went off to college somewhere. Is it near?"

Aramano pulled out a flip-top notebook from his hip pocket and consulted his notes from the visit he and Jorge made to the school. "He went to Kenyon to play lacrosse."

"Athlete, huh? Dad may be interested in following his kid's games. Where is this Kenyon?"

"Somewhere east of here, I think."

"After what happened to Jorge, I don't need you thinking anymore. Go back to that school and find out about his kid. You do know how to do that, don't you?"

"Yes, sir."

"Then get going. Call me as soon as you learn anything."

CHAPTER 58

TUESDAY, APRIL 13

Historians believe the game of stickball as played by the Algonquian tribe in the St. Lawrence River Valley was the forerunner of the game known as lacrosse or lax. Whether the initial purpose was for athletic training or only for recreation is unclear, but the popularity of the activity throughout the area is an integral part of the local saga. Missionaries described the endeavor as involving no set number of participants or boundaries.

In the middle of the 19th century, the activity took on an interest in Canada and developed rules and improved sticks. A touring team from Canada introduced the sport to the world, and the Summer Olympics in the early 20th century featured the game. American colleges, especially in the Northeast, adopted the game for intercollegiate competition beginning shortly before the Civil War. "National" championships were awarded on a points basis for most of the 20th century. In 1971 the NCAA began sponsoring a playoff system for major, Division I schools, and several years later, similar playoffs were conducted for Division II and III teams.

Most colleges and universities with a lacrosse program play in Division III: virtually all of those 230 plus schools are located in the Northeastern part of the United States. Kenyon College lacrosse began in the middle of the 20th century and by the beginning of the

21st century had been ranked nationally and appeared in the national tournament several times. Kenyon coaches recruit nationally and Henry Wilton was excited to have been offered the support of the coaching staff for his academic application to Kenyon in the absence of an athletic scholarship.

Nonetheless, Harry Wilton faced a significant financial outlay to send Henry to Kenyon. Henry applied for and received a partial, need-based academic scholarship, but that still left Harry with more potential cost than he had put aside for Henry's education. Harry was a supportive father, attending all of Henry's games in high school, even though he knew nothing about the game of lacrosse. Father and son spent many evenings talking strategy and play with the son being the teacher and the father the student of the game. Harry missed having Henry around and would have moved himself closer to Gambier, Ohio, when Henry matriculated had he not needed the employment with ABC in Cincinnati.

Father and son maintained a line of communication after Henry's move to Gambier. After his mother died, Henry had developed a habit of contacting his father at least daily. At first, this was easy as they lived together and shared a meal at night. Over time, that contact was more often by texting as each of the men developed other interests - Harry with his job and Henry with some friends. But the daily texts continued even after Henry left for Kenyon.

Texts were often terse and devoid of solid information from Henry's side, due to involvement in lacrosse practice, college course work, and other things. Harry always took the time to make his end of the texts contain some news of the day and to ask for a comment. Since his move into the subway tunnel, Harry's texts had grown a little longer, and he became more interested in hearing his son's voice. Harry was aware of the Kenyon schedule and knew that they would play in Wilmington soon. He decided to talk with Henry.

CHAPTER 59

TUESDAY, APRIL 13

Looney rubbed his eyes and his head with both hands and took a deep breath. He and Gene had been in the Captain's office for almost three hours talking and theorizing about the contents of Harry Wilton's note. They spent what Ron thought was an unnecessary amount of time considering whether the author was Harry Wilton or not before moving on to consider the implications.

Their consensus, after more than an hour, was that the message conveyed four new attestations. They felt challenged to consider and prove each of them. First, there was the allegation that a skimming operation involving ABC Corporation was present and had been in operation for years. The message stated this as a fact and mentioned where corroboration might be found but provided no data in itself. The discussion at that point mostly was between Gene and Thor. Gene had just tumbled to the J.Y. Dahgs files as part of Thomas Pritchard's search in the Contracting employee's computer when the explosion occurred, and his search ended. Gene wanted a warrant to seize the contents of that computer immediately for further forensic investigation. Ron and the Captain were hesitant to take such a public step at this point, especially in light of other allegations in the message.

Second, Harry Wilton's note accused a sitting City Councilman, Aton Greene, of being the benefactor of the skimming project. Again, no clear factual documentation of this assertion was in the message, at least there was nothing that would stand up in court. However, the note implied hard evidence of this allegation was in Harry's possession. The three men had a substantive discussion on this point before finally deciding that the best and most clear step to take was a frank discussion with the chairman of the City Council. Thor indicated he would make that arrangement the next morning.

Third, and most descriptively, Harry's message laid out the persons involved and the sequence of events that culminated in the explosion and gunfire at the construction site two days before. After briefly touching on the matter of blackmail, Harry explained the reason for the meeting, the cancellation of the first meeting as he watched the snipers set up their positions, his wiring the shooting platforms with remote phone detonators, and rescheduling the meeting. He told how he saw the snipers get into position for the second meeting and his dismay when one chose a different spot from before. The message then described the arrival of Councilman Greene in the open area on the ground and how Harry had entered that area from a position that allowed him to detonate one shooting platform while remaining out of sight of the other. His description of the events following the explosion fit well with the CSI rationalization of their findings.

However, it was the fourth accusation in the message that troubled the detectives the most. Harry claimed that Councilman Greene had warned him before the second meeting that any outcome Greene did not like would create "goodbye to Morgan". Harry said he had a text message from Greene confirming that threat and continued saying that Morgan's death was the reason he was contacting the police. He accused Councilman Greene of murder.

The Captain looked at Ron and said, "Huh."

Ron nodded and said, "I know. He's been out there a long time. I'll go see what's going on." He went to the door and looked toward his partner's desk but did not see Gene. Ron walked into the Dick Pen and called out, "Hey, Gene, where are you?"

"Back here," came a voice from the break area.

Ron walked into the area and saw Gene at the coffee pot. "What's up?"

"I decided we needed to have fresh coffee."

"You made a pot?"

"More than that. I cleaned the pot of what likely was about three years of grime and scab. I also found a bottle of vinegar under the sink and rinsed the machine innards twice with that and flushed it several times before making this good smelling brew right here," he said, pointing at a pot of freshly brewed coffee.

"Wait, who are you, and what did you do with my partner?"

"Well, we couldn't run down the block in the middle of that conversation, could we?"

"Gene, you were supposed to be researching on J.Y. Dahgs, not playing Martha Stewart in the break room."

"Oh, I got all that. Kinda interesting, up to a point."

"Well, let's go talk to Thor."

"Sure. Grab a cup, and I'll get one for the Captain."

The Captain was surprised at being given a cup of fresh smelling coffee. He was more surprised when he took a sip and found it tasting as good as it smelled. "Huh," he said and put the cup in front of him.

Gene took the hint and said, "J.Y. Dahgs stands for an incorporated business called Junk Yard Dahgs. It is incorporated in the State of Ohio and has no business elsewhere, nor is it listed with a DUNS number."

"Huh?"

"A DUNS number is given to any business entity that wants to be listed by Dun & Bradstreet and have their financial health available to investors or customers."

"So, the absence of this D-number means …"

"It means a company is not interested in being open and transparent about its business dealings."

Ron said, "Very interesting."

Gene went on, "That's not all. The State of Ohio does have incorporation papers for the business, and there are only three people in the corporation." He gave the names and received blank stares from the Captain and Ron.

Gene said, "Yeah, I felt that way, too. Until I did a little look-up on these people. The lawyer retired within a month of incorporation and now lives in Florida. The woman is the mother of the third guy. And she's actually been known in these parts."

The puzzled looks did not fade, so Gene continued, "You may recall that a certain prominent lawyer decided to run for public office a few years ago, and his wife was not using his name. That caused a little stir. She was not a professional with a degree in her maiden name, she simply didn't want to be known as Mrs. Someone. So, she kept her maiden name, and that's it on the corporation papers. She's the wife of Councilman Anton Greene."

Ron was the first to speak, "That clears up the question of why the councilman was meeting with Wilton in some blackmail payoff."

"Huh," said the Captain. "Get all this stuff together. We'll meet with the council chairman in the morning."

CHAPTER 60

WEDNESDAY, APRIL 14

Harry sat in the subway tunnel and thought about his future. Greene knew his name, and now he knew his face. There would be little chance of escaping his revenge if Harry stayed in Cincinnati. The house Harry was renting could be let go; there were no significant items left behind other than clothes, and those were replaceable. If he were on his own, Harry knew he could just hop a freight train and be gone. But that would mean leaving Henry unprotected, and that was not ever going to be a viable option.

As he considered his situation, Harry's first thoughts turned to how he could safely remain a part of the Cincinnati construction scene, keep his job and his home and push circumstances back to 'normal', whatever that might be. He knew he could not stay in the city and be visible if Councilman Greene remained at large; that realization had led him to notify the police about Greene's profit skimming operation. The newspaper article about Morgan Riley's death mentioned that the area around the explosion was considered a crime scene and was under active investigation. The detective in charge of that investigation was Ron Looney.

Harry's immediate reaction to Morgan's death was to attempt revenge; that emotion led him to write to Detective Looney about the councilman's involvement in fraud and to implicate him in Morgan's death. Now that the heat of that emotion had cooled, Harry saw that his decision to notify the authorities about Greene might have a personal reward, as well. Even if the police are slow in responding to fraud allegations, any implication of the councilman's involvement in a murder should draw sustained attention, Harry thought. Such close attention might well push the envelope around the councilman sufficiently to bring some of the shady business operations to light.

But, Harry thought, such attention and investigation might well take weeks or months to bring sufficient pressure to bear that Harry could live in the city without fear that Greene would be looking to have him killed. Such consideration led to the inevitable conclusion that Cincinnati was not a safe environment for the Wilton family, probably not for several months.

Once Harry began to think of how to leave Cincinnati without a trace, and carry on a life elsewhere, his primary concern became Henry. Despite their closeness, Harry knew his son would not easily give up his own new life as a college student and lacrosse player to start dodging police and hit men throughout the country. Henry would have to be persuaded to think of the time away from college as a sabbatical. So Harry began to plan how best to present his situation to his son in a manner that would persuade him to accompany his father in exile, at least for a few months.

Harry also gave serious thought to the question of the blackmail money. Greene became aware that he, Harry, had no 'smoking gun' to turn over in return for the money. At least, Harry knew that his statements were the truth about the absence of those incriminating data in his possession. He was uncertain whether Greene believed him. The more he thought about the events at the construction site, the more Harry began to question the probability that he could ever leverage money out of Greene. The man had prepared to have him killed at the point of exchange. As he considered the meaning of the attempt on his life, Harry became convinced that Greene held off on signaling for the shooters to kill Harry because he was uncertain whether he would then be able to close the door to future blackmail.

The most reasonable explanation, Harry supposed, for Greene's behavior was that he, Greene, must have believed that the data file implicating him in fraud was hidden somewhere, and that the blackmailers were planning on future efforts to get money from him. Harry thought he had heard of blackmailers not handing over their leverage at the time of any money exchange for one of two reasons. The first, as Greene may have suspected, was for future use. The second reason was for fear that the person being extorted would kill the blackmailer once the evidence was safely out of their hands.

Of course, that created a conundrum for both parties. How can we make an exchange without risk to one or both? Importantly, how can either of us trust the other? Harry began to understand why Greene would have been skeptical about the lack of a data file for exchange and why he might very well believe that Harry was lying when he said the file did not exist. Harry had been truthful about such a file not existing in Harry's hands. As he came to that conclusion, Harry sat bolt upright. The idea came that Greene still believed he, Harry, had the data. He also likely was unaware that Pritchard was dead. And those concepts allowed Harry to think anew about a scenario where he would get his money.

He pulled out his phone and carefully crafted another telegram.

Councilman Greene stared at the telegram. He lifted his eyes and snarled at Conor, "I knew that SOB was lying to me. I knew it." He tried to throw the telegram at Conor, but it fluttered to the floor.

Conor picked up the piece of paper and read it carefully before engaging in the conversation. While Conor read, Greene opened the bottom drawer of his desk and took out a bottle of whiskey, and poured a drink. He did not offer one to Conor.

"So, what do you think of his new demand?" Greene asked.

Conor looked up and said, "Well, he's very clear about not trusting you."

"Yes, yes, I know that. What about his demand?"

"Well, in light of the, ah, unfortunate way the last exchange was handled …"

"Unfortunate? The SOB blew one of my men up!"

"Yes. Well, sir, in honesty, that man was going to kill the SOB."

"Yeah. That was the plan. SOB!"

"It seems he has struck a bit of a deal with you in this latest telegram, sir."

"Explain."

"Well, he was asking for two million dollars, as I recall, and this request is now only for $1 million."

"Still too much."

"Certainly, sir. But it does seem that he is saying he can't trust a face-to-face exchange again but is willing to take a smaller payoff for a different arrangement."

"Is that the way you see it?"

"Yes, sir. He is offering a distant exchange, based on some trust on both sides, and a lower figure to start the negotiation."

"How do you get that from that piece of paper?"

"It reads, 'DISTRUST FACE-TO-FACE STOP SEND $1MIL BOX 2020, LAS VEGAS BY 1500 TOMORROW FOR FILES STOP FAIL AND PAPERS GET FILES. SEND TRACKING INFO'. And, of course, there is no signature."

"So, you think he's going to send me the files if we pay?"

"He says so, sir. The clear implication is, the money will buy you the files. He does not specify how they will be returned, but that's the clear implication."

"He still wants $1 million!"

"Yes, sir. But that is half what he asked for last time."

"Why Las Vegas?"

"I presume he has left the city, sir. You did make a concerted effort to have him killed."

"I get the idea you are recommending I send him the money."

"I am, sir. I also recommend that you send me to collect him when he appears to claim the money. He has not seen me."

"Huh, that's very clever, Conor. Very clever. Yes. Well, make the arrangements. He wants the tracking information so he knows when it will arrive, I guess."

"That's my guess, too, sir. I will see to it that the money is sent. And I will be on the next flight to Las Vegas." Conor turned to leave.

Greene stopped him, "Conor, Insure the package."

"Yes, sir."

CHAPTER 61

WEDNESDAY, APRIL 14

Council Chairman James Allegarten leaned back in his chair and placed both hands on the table. He took his time before speaking to Captain Thorason and his two detectives sitting across the table from him.

"I share your concern here, gentlemen. Now that we have closely examined the minutes of our meetings for the past several years, as well as supporting correspondence, I agree that Councilman Greene's support for the ABC Construction company bids for city business is uniform, vigorous without being blatant, and supportive even when ABC was not the lowest bidder. It is surprising to me that none of us on the Council have been aware of this trend."

The Captain nodded, "ABC is a respected company and has always done a good job on the projects it wins in bidding. There's no obvious reason to be suspicious. Plus, they didn't win all the bids, so nothing existed to cause you or any other person to become skeptical of the award system."

Ron interjected, "We do not want any suspicions raised at this point. No leaks to the press or allowing Mr. Greene any possibility of starting to clean up his operation."

Allegarten frowned and said, "I certainly was not about to call a press conference …"

"Not what I was implying, sir. I mean that we need to keep our current suspicions limited to the people in this room. Councilman Greene may have individuals in his pay on various city rolls just watching for any indication of concern about his business dealings."

The Captain noted, "I believe we may well have a police department mole and we are keeping our apprehensions on this matter tightly contained."

The chairman relaxed, "I understand, then. I shall not speak of this issue or any doubt we might have about the Councilman's honesty until you have had time to bolster your case."

Ron agreed, "Thank you, sir. As we discussed earlier, this review has provided us with some weight for our opinion, but not sufficient information to take to the District Attorney."

"Huh," said the Captain.

"Right," Ron agreed, "We do have enough for a warrant to obtain additional information, however. That will be our next step."

"Is there anything I should be doing from the standpoint of the Council," asked Allegarten.

All three of the others shook their heads. Gene spoke, "There's nothing to be done at this point without tipping him off. We ask that you put this information into a small little box in the back of your mind and try to keep the box closed."

"That is much more easily described than accomplished, detective."

"Yes, sir. I am aware. We needed to have your assistance in obtaining this information. and we realize that we have made you a bit of a conspirator along with us. Our intention is not to rattle Mr. Greene's cage at present. Perhaps all you have to do is not talk with him or have any personal meetings for a while."

"There is not a Council meeting scheduled for a couple of weeks and Anton does not call upon me for individual meetings, so perhaps I shall be able to meet your request."

"We thank you, sir." Ron went on, "And we would also like to know if the Councilman tries to meet with you."

"Why would he do that? As I said, that has not been his practice so far."

"Exactly, sir. If he changes his practice, it may indicate he has become suspicious of his under-handed practices becoming known."

"Oh, I see."

"Furthermore, you have my word that we will notify you when our case is about to break. We don't want you reading about it first in the newspaper."

"That would be very much appreciated. I thank you, gentlemen, for bringing this to my attention and helping to keep the city out of the newspaper."

"Oh, I daresay this activity, and its financial impact will all be in the newspaper at some point. We will do everything we can to show the city as a victim and not as a part of the plot."

"Well, I certainly will applaud that effort."

"Good day, Mr. Allegarten."

"Good day, officers."

Later they sat in the Captain's office. Gene accepted the role of writing the case for a warrant to place a wiretap on the telephones of Councilman Greene. They intended to listen to conversations on his law office and city office telephones plus his cellular phone.

The first three attempts Gene made were determined to be lacking in strength by both Ron and the Captain. They discussed his fourth attempt as very strong but potentially not sufficient to overcome a judge's concern that listening on the law firm telephone might endanger lawyer-client confidentiality.

Ron suggested they could tell the judge they would not keep any recordings that dealt with a legal case handled by Greene's law firm. He thought that was clean and completely aboveboard.

When the Captain opined, "Huh," Gene immediately saw the fallacy in the argument. "And how will we know whether a conversation is related to one of the legal cases unless we listen to it?" Ron nodded and agreed his idea would not appease the judge.

Gene countered with a different approach, "Why don't we ask for the first two for now; let's get what we can from the cell phone and the council phone. That's where we think he's likely to be doing his illegal business anyway, isn't it? Even if we leave the problem of the lawyer-client question off the table, we will still have to assure the court that we will not be listening to legal cases, right?"

"Huh."

"Good idea, Gene. Rewrite the request without mentioning the law office and get it over to the ADA."

CHAPTER 62

THURSDAY, APRIL 15

Nestor parked just outside the school grounds and walked to the main door. He remembered that Jorge had been with him when they visited the school before, and his jaw tightened a little as he remembered how his friend had died. Students were milling about in the hallways, but they paid little attention to the tall man in the black suit. Aramano went directly to the Principal's office.

The secretary recognized him when he entered, and he did not have to show his fake credentials again. She indicated he should wait while she notified the principal of his presence. Just moments later, the principal came out of his office and said, "Back again, agent? I hope there's not more difficulty."

"No, sir, I don't think so. Just a few details to be cleared up."

The principal gestured for him to come to the office, and Aramano went through the gate in the counter. He sat without being asked and smiled at the principal, who inquired, "And what can we do to help out today?"

Aramano kept smiling, "As I said, just some details. You recall that our reason for interviews had to do with federal clearance for the father of one of your students, Mr. Harry Wilton."

"Yes, I remember. His son, Henry graduated last year. A former student."

"Right. A former student. To complete our investigation for a Level Two clearance for Mr. Wilton, we need to talk with individuals who also knew his family members."

Aramano reached into his jacket pocket and withdrew a small black notebook. He thumbed through the pages as if looking for a particular entry. He appeared to find what he was looking for and said, "Mr. Wilton's wife died and cannot be directly interviewed, but we would like to talk to individuals who knew the son."

"Well, as I said, he graduated last year, as did most of his friends and mates. I think you have already talked to some of his teachers on your last visit."

Aramano thought there was a bit of resistance to his visit developing and tried to calm any fears by saying, "Yes, sir. We were speaking to them mostly about Mr. Wilton at the time. I would like to ask them about the son."

"Well, All of those teachers and here today if you must question them again."

"Perhaps, since we are more interested in the son right now, there may be a different one or more of the staff that could answer those questions?"

The principal thought for a moment, "Yes, there are a couple. His Home Room teacher and the Yearbook sponsor would have very good information about Henry. And, of course, there's always Coach Tatterhorn."

Aramano stood and nodded at the principal's suggestion. "Yes. We have already met with the Coach. Could you introduce me to the Home Room teacher and this other person?" Indicating with a nod of his head that Aramano should follow him, the principal left the office and headed down the hall. There were no students around this time. The principal did not seem interested in creating additional conversation until they came to a classroom door in the second hallway. At the door, he peeked through the glass window and said, "It's quiet right now." He knocked gently to attract the teacher's attention. When she opened the door, the principal explained the reason for the interruption and Introduced 'agent' Aramano.

"Ma'am," he said.

"What is it you want to know?" she asked, keeping her foot in the door to prop it open slightly so she could hear what transpired in the classroom.

"Just a few questions about Henry Wilton, that's all. Have you any reason to suspect his allegiance?"

"Really? No, not at all. What's this about?"

"It's part of a security clearance for his father, ma'am. As a legal adult in his household, we are obligated to look into his background as well."

"Huh. Well, Henry was Grade A American. No questions."

"Have you heard from him after he left school?"

"No. I didn't expect to."

"All right, then. I appreciate your time. Thank you very much."

The teacher opened the door and returned to her class without looking back. Aramano dutifully made a few entries in his small notebook, then looked at the principal. He shrugged and turned to walk further down the hall. Aramano followed until they came to a door without a window. Both men stopped, and the principal knocked just below the sign reading "Yearbook Staff Only".

A moment later, the door opened to reveal a man in his thirties in shirtsleeves. "Yes, sir?" he addressed the principal.

"Gordon, this agent would like to ask a few questions about Henry Wilton. Would you show him out when he's finished?"

Aramano looked at the principal with a question in his eyes. The principal said, "I have some other duties right now. I hope this is the last time you need to come here."

"Yes, sir," Aramano said deferentially. "I'm sure this will provide us all we need for clearance."

The principal nodded and walked away, heading back to his office.

The man in the yearbook office stuck out his hand, "I'm Gordon. How can I help you?"

Aramano shook the offered hand, "I'm Jim," he said. "I just have a few questions about Henry Wilton as part of a security clearance for his father, Harry."

"Security clearance, eh? Big stuff. Okay, what do you need to know?"

"Have you any reason to suspect the allegiance to the United States by Henry Wilton?"

"Absolutely not. Henry was a red-blooded patriot. I knew him fairly well, working together on the last yearbook. Why ask about him if you're vetting the father?"

"He's an adult in the household."

"Ah."

"Have you heard from him since he left school?"

"You mean after he graduated? No. I haven't. But that may change."

Aramano perked up at this and followed with, "Can you explain that?"

Gordon shrugged and said, "It's not really my news to tell, but Betty Oberlin said she had a text from Henry that he might be back in town later this week."

"Who is Betty Oberlin?" Aramano scribbled in his notebook.

"She and Henry were pretty tight all last year, and I guess he may be coming home to visit her."

"Is it possible for me to speak to her?"

"Sure. I guess. She's in here working on the yearbook. Come in."

Betty turned out to be a nice-looking brunette about five-foot-four inches with a turned-up nose and a bright smile. She seemed willing to talk about Henry. When asked about the possibility of a visit to Cincinnati, she said, "Well, he's at Kenyon, you know, and they're playing at Wilmington this Friday. So, anyway, Henry said, you know, that his dad is going up to watch the game, and Henry thought he could ride back with his dad and spend some time here. With me, you know."

"That's interesting, Ms. Oberlin. Can you tell me if Henry has a strong allegiance to the United States?"

"What? Oh, you bet. I mean, you know, he always makes us all stand up and cover our heart for the national anthem, and like that."

"All right, then. Thank you," Aramano dismissed her and turned to Gordon, "And, thank you for arranging that discussion. Can you show me the way out, as the principal said?"

As soon as he got back in his car, Aramano pulled out his cell phone and called Greene.

This is the recording of the wiretapped conversation on Greene's telephone:

GREENE: Green.

NESTOR: Colonel, I just talked to the Wilton kid's girlfriend. She says he may be coming home for the weekend.

GREENE: How's that help us?

NESTOR: She says he gonna ride back from a lacrosse game with his dad.

GREENE: What game?

NESTOR: In Wilmington on Friday. She says the kid said his dad was going to be at the game, and will give him a ride back to Cincinnati after.

GREENE: Wilton's going to be at the game?

NESTOR: That's what she said.

GREENE: That's good news. We can take him out there. It's away from the city and got no link to us.

NESTOR: Anything else you need me to find out?

GREENE: No. Just get on back here. We need to plan this out.

NESTOR: Roger, that.

The line went dead.

Looney took off his earphones and looked at his partner, eyebrows raised. Gene nodded solemnly and noted, "I believe we have just heard a plan to kill Harry Wilton."

Ron replied with equal gravity, "And we know who will make that attempt and when and where he will do so."

"Lucky us."

CHAPTER 63

THURSDAY, APRIL 15

The Las Vegas Post Office experienced a steady flow of patrons purchasing stamps, arranging to ship packages all over the country, and obtaining money orders. Conor MacCarter lounged at the writing desk and conscientiously filled out form after form, waving others to pass by him in line. He had been in place at the desk beginning shortly after 1:30 that afternoon. He reckoned that gave him 90 minutes before Wilton would arrive for his package, scheduled to be at 1500 hours or 3:00 PM.

Conor's back ached, and he periodically stretched and moved his arms into different positions instead of the hunched-over posture he took in his writing. He maintained his line of sight with the desk clerk and overheard most of every conversation the man held with customers.

Conor had left Cincinnati early that morning on a flight to Las Vegas. He flew first to Chicago Midway and experienced an hour layover before finally getting on the plane that would take him to the Las Vegas McCarron Airport. His economy seat was slightly smaller than he liked; Conor was unable to nap on the flight. He arrived late that morning with an aching back, thirsty and hungry. On departing the plane he had an initial impression that he had landed inside one of the renowned casinos. Slot machines were lining the walkway from his gate to the main terminal and every machine hosted an eager player.

Since he had brought no baggage, Conor allowed himself to sit in one of the fast-food franchises and enjoy a breakfast sandwich and a cup of coffee before he made his way down to the baggage area to hail a cab. His breakfast thoughts turned back to the problem of how he was to handle Wilton once he apprehended him. Conor had bought a handgun, a nickel-finish Colt .38 revolver online before leaving Cincinnati and had arranged to pick it up before going to the post office. But he still had no concrete plan for handling the man Wilton and the package of money from 1500 hours until he could get a plane out of Las Vegas at 2230 hours, 10:30 PM.

Conor had spent his hours on the plane wondering about this issue and had decided that he would need some additional manpower. He left the breakfast kiosk and found a traditional telephone booth complete with a telephone book and Yellow Pages. He searched in the Private Investigator section of the Yellow Pages and started making calls. The third man he contacted indicated he would be available for a flight out of Las Vegas to assist in transporting a fugitive with a guaranteed return flight and a large retainer. Conor told him to be prepared to take his call in the mid-afternoon and to come to assist with the transfer.

Conor then left the airport, caught a cab downtown, and walked several blocks to the pawnshop to pick up the handgun he had purchased. The walk helped to stretch his back and settle his stomach. He entered the pawnshop and asked for the manager. From the back room, a man came to the counter and said, "Greene?"

Conor answered, "Yeah."

The man indicated that Conor should follow him behind the counter and into the back room. There, he laid the polished and shiny handgun on the corner of his desk and looked at Conor.

"What?" Conor asked.

"Do you know how to use this?"

"Of course," Conor said, as he picked up the weapon, opened the cylinder, and spun it, then closed it with a flick of his wrist. He twirled the handgun on his finger, reversing the handle and grabbing the barrel. He then offered the handle to the owner and said, "I will need some ammunition, as well."

The man did not take the weapon but turned and opened a drawer on the desk and set a box of .38 copper-tipped bullets on the desktop. "That's extra," he said without a smile. Conor looked at the container; Winchester, round nose, 50 rounds.

"I don't need that many rounds," he said.

"Never know 'til you're in the gunfight," came the answer coupled to a lack of movement to exchange the box.

"All I need is six for the chambers."

"I don't sell singles. You buy ammo by the box."

"You got any boxes with less than 50 rounds?" Conor felt he was losing this argument.

"Nope. This one is $50."

"Right. Well, I can't very well accomplish my task with empty chambers. Give me the box."

Conor pulled out his wallet and withdrew a $50, and laid it on the desk. Then he opened the box of ammunition and loaded each of the six cylinders in the revolver. He closed the cylinder, looked at the owner, then put the gun in his waistband behind his back. Then Conor turned, and walked out of the office, leaving the rest of the ammunition sitting on the desk.

Conor had caught a cab and gone directly to the post office and taken up his stance, pretending he was filling out forms as he watched the hands on the wall clock creep slowly to the appointed hour.

At exactly 1500 hours, Conor willed himself more alert, checking every customer closely. He had a picture of Harry Wilton from his employment data file with ABC but Conor thought it very possible that Wilton would wear a disguise. So every person, male or female who entered the post office after 1450 hours was scrutinized in depth.

Conor also knew Wilton might send someone else to collect the money, so he remained close to the desk where he could hear every request of the clerk.

By 1520 hours, Conor was beginning to tire of his tension and knew he needed to remain alert. He took some deep, controlled breaths after checking the latest customer entry. Then he squeezed his fists tightly enough to cause pain that helped him to be more alert. He wondered why Wilton would have specified the package must arrive by 1500 unless he intended to retrieve it and head somewhere else on a tight timetable. Conor played the airline schedules back in his mind, but he couldn't recall any outgoing flights from Las Vegas before 10:00 PM. If there had been an earlier flight, he would have booked their return on it.

When the clock moved around to 1545, Conor began to worry that Wilton had somehow come earlier and collected the money. Then he recalled that when he had made the shipment, the initial tracking information indicated the package would arrive in Las Vegas no earlier than 1:30 PM that day by air. Arrival at the addressee post office by 3:00 PM was cutting things a little close; there was no chance the package had been here earlier and that Wilton was now in the wind.

Then Conor thought, is it possible he was able to intercept it someway at the airport? Could Wilton have sidetracked the package during its transit from the airplane to the truck? Might he have already gotten on a different airplane, and headed for Hawai'i? Conor realized he was getting a headache. He needed to resolve the issue of why Wilton had not shown to pick up the money.

At 1550, there was no other person in line, and Conor stepped up to the window.

"Yes, sir?" asked the clerk.

"I was asked to pick up a package here this afternoon and I wonder if you could check when it will arrive," Conor said, making up a story.

"Certainly, sir. Do you have the tracking number?"

"Yes, I do," Conor said while pushing a piece of paper with the number on it to the clerk. He stood and watched the clerk open a form on his computer screen and begin to painfully and slowly enter the multi-digit number. When the clerk made a mistake and had to back up and start entry again, Conor almost yelled at him. But the clerk was oblivious to Conor as he painstakingly entered the number and hit the return key. The screen wiped off to be replaced by another screen. The clerk read that screen and scratched his head and came back to the window,

"Are you sure you were supposed to pick that package up here?" he asked. Conor stared at him and said, "Of course," but his mouth was suddenly quite dry.

"Well," the clerk said in a good ole boy drawl, "that package was re-routed to Seattle. It'll be there in a couple of hours."

"Seattle?"

"Yes, sir. That's in Washington. State."

"I know where Seattle is," Conor fumed and walked away from the counter and out to the parking lot. He had spent the day traveling, eating cheap food, paying an exorbitant price for a weapon and ammunition, and now had no need for any of it. Wilton had tricked them. That's why he had asked for the tracking number. Conor walked down the sidewalk to a seating area outside a coffee shop and took a seat. He pulled out his phone and, with more than a little hesitation, called the councilman.

This is the recording of the wiretapped conversation on Greene's telephone:

GREENE: Greene

CONOR: It's Conor, sir.

GREENE: I've been waiting for almost an hour. Did you get the money? And where's Wilton?

CONOR: I don't have either one, sir. He tricked us.

GREENE: What?

CONOR: The money never came here, sir. He had the tracking number and re-routed it to Seattle.

GREENE: Preposterous!

CONOR: No, sir. He's pretty smart. He was never in Las Vegas, and neither was the money. Do you want me to try to get to Seattle?

GREENE: (after a pause) No. If he can send that money to Seattle, he could have sent it anywhere. My guess is he'll keep it close by once he does get it. And we have some new information about where he's going to be.

CONOR: Really? What's that?

GREENE: Never mind. Just get back here as quick as you can. We have some serious planning to do. I know where Wilton will be on Friday night, and I think he'll have the money with him. And I'm going to see to it that he won't get to enjoy a moment of it

CONOR: On my way.

The line went dead.

CHAPTER 64

THURSDAY, APRIL 15

"Are you sure we are putting this together, right?" Gene asked.

Ron was leaning back in his chair with his feet on his desk, eating a KitKat. He nodded and said, "Don't you? I mean, look, the wiretap caught somebody we think is Nestor calling Greene on his cell phone. This Nestor person said Wilton is likely to attend his son's lacrosse game when Kenyon visits Wilmington and you heard Greene say, "We'll take care of him there. You heard all that, didn't you?"

"Yeah."

"Are you now thinking that Greene is going to sidle up to Wilton on the sidelines and hand him a bag of money to "take care of him'? Or do you have another idea?"

"No, I don't have another idea. And, yes, I heard all that and agree with our general conclusions about it."

"But …?"

"Well, not 'but' exactly. It seems we are taking a big chance here thinking that Greene is going to go out to Wilmington to kill Wilton."

"Whoa, hold on, partner. I do not think that at all. Greene is not likely to be anywhere near an assassination attempt."

"But you seem to be banking on him saying "we can take care of him there" and I assumed the 'we' meant that he would be there, too."

"Not my thought on this, Gene. I'm glad you probed on that. My thinking here is that Greene is using a royal 'we' and he means that someone else from his operation will be "taking care' of Wilton at that game."

"That makes sense to me. So why aren't we flooding the zone with cops to stop any attempts to kill Wilton?"

Ron put his feet down and swung around to face his partner. "Look, Gene, let me walk you through my thinking on this. I appreciate you questioning the setup. But, here's the way I put it together. Greene may know by now that Pritchard is dead. He certainly knows that whatever Pritchard had on him is not in his house."

"Unless it was in the missing computer."

"And if that's the case, then he isn't afraid that Wilton will release anything to the press. I believe he thinks that Wilton has the goods, probably hidden away someplace and not likely to surface. I think Greene wants to take Wilton out, kill him, and deal with whatever surfaces after that."

"I'm mostly with you on that concern."

"And what have we seen as Greene's method of killing someone?"

"Sniper."

"Absolutely. I've looked at Google Earth of the campus where this game will be held, and there are only three decent sniper posts within four hundred yards of the field. We don't need a battalion of cops to cover the risk. We need three.

"You seem pretty certain that Greene is ready to shoot someone publicly."

"And I could be wrong. Greene may arrange for someone to bump Wilton on the sidelines and inject poison, or he might try to create a fatal car accident on the return trip. But I am convinced he will try to eliminate Wilton in this setting."

"But …"

"And I am convinced he will most likely attempt it from long range. I think he does not care if the death is ultimately ruled a homicide, Greene is in a position to color the character of Wilton to make this look like a mob-related hit. His concern will be that Wilton may have left the information about the skimming activity somewhere to be made public in case of his death."

"That would be clever."

"Actually, such planning is clever only if it works to deter anyone from trying to kill the holder of the information."

"Well, yeah."

"And the deterrence is known to the potential killer."

"Of course."

"And yet, when told where Wilton will be, Greene's immediate response is "we can take care of him there", not "wait, let's find where he hid the information.""

Gene hesitated for a moment. "So, you think Wilton has hidden the information, and it would die with him."

"I do. And I think Greene is thinking that, as well. That leads me to infer that he will likely make an attempt of Wilton and will do so in the same manner as he tried once before."

"Are you sure that Wilton is going to be at the game?"

"We only know what this Nestor guy said on the wiretap. Wilton may be there to watch his son play, but he will likely be in a disguise of some sort.

"I plan to be there well enough ahead of time to cover the three shooting platforms and capture whoever sets up to make that shot."

"And the game is tomorrow?"

"Yep, and you and Chet and I will be in those platforms before sunup."

"That's pretty early."

"Right. As my favorite western hero, Walt Longmire used to say. That's an OIT."

"OIT? What's that?"

"Old Indian Trick. Get to a meeting you're worried about before the other guy does."

CHAPTER 65

THURSDAY, APRIL 15

They parked in different places around the campus and met in the stadium near the south end zone shortly after dark. Chet Simmons had agreed to join this plan to foil a long-range assassination. Chet was one of the smallest men on the Cincinnati Police Force at five foot four inches. Ron thought Chet's lack of bulk would help him hide in a tight spot if that became necessary when they surveyed the various shooting platforms. No one was concerned about Chet becoming involved in a personal fight with a shooter since he was the department champion both in judo and karate.

Ron's assessment of the circumstances on the ground seemed well aligned with the information he had gleaned from Google Earth. The men stood at the south end of the playing field and could look directly westward through the opening in the stands at that point to see the southern end of the administration building. The two-story building extended a block further north, and Ron initially thought the rooftop might provide a shooting platform. Now, as they assessed the reality all three men agreed the sidelines were not visible from the rooftop of the administration building. They agreed that a shooter up there would have no line of sight to where the suspected target, Harry Wilton, was likely to be.

To the south of their position, however, was the old-fashioned scoreboard. It was a large flat structure with internal walkways accessing the various lighted panels. Chet opined that such a platform would have an advantageous line of sight no matter which sideline the target was on. So the three of them climbed the railing and the supporting ladder to examine the interior space and potential for a sniper.

"You know," Chet said, "This is really tight in here. There's barely thirty inches of clearance between the walls. I don't think this is the best place for a sniper to set up."

"Explain," Gene asked.

"Snipers usually want to have plenty of room to be able to set their long gun up without it sticking out in the open. Anyone setting up in here would leave at least a foot or more of the barrel jutting out one of these openings. Too easy to spot."

"Maybe if we were securing this field for the President, but who is going to be checking the perimeter throughout the game looking for rifle barrels?"

"Good point," Chet conceded. "The other thing a sniper will want is a quick, unobtrusive exit. From here it looks like someone could make a shot, run to the end of the scoreboard, slide down that ladder, run less than fifty yards to a parked car at the curb, and be moving away in 15-20 seconds. That's actually not bad."

Ron thought for a moment and then asked, "Is there a place in here for you?"

"Sure. Look up."

Ron did and noted that the open space went up the full extent of the scoreboard height, giving Chet, or anyone else ample space to set up well above the lower walkway. "You want to take this one?"

"Seems probably best."

They left the scoreboard and walked to the east side of the field. Chet checked angles from the various scoreboard openings and noted that the field of fire was wide open for a sniper from that vantage point. The three then walked up the steps in the east stands to the small three-person booth at the pinnacle. They each stood in front of the booth and scanned the open playing field and sidelines.

"Can't be much more open than this," Gene said.

Ron and Chet agreed but also went to the heavy glass front of the booth and cupped their hands against the glass, peering inside. Ron quickly assessed the situation, "No place in there to hide. And there's no opening in this glass."

Chet added, "Any exit would have to be down these steps and through the crowd of spectators here. I don't think this is a good platform."

Gene asked, "What about the roof of the booth? Flat place to lie, good angle, maybe jump down the back to get away?"

Chet leaned over the back wall of the stands. "No place to go down there. Some kind of construction going on, and there's a big hole with fencing all around. You may be right about the roof but there's no good escape line."

Ron added, "Plus, anybody that wanted to get up there would have to do so tonight. There's enough activity around here that he'd be seen anytime after dawn."

Gene nodded, "Okay. Not a good platform. What's next?"

Ron pointed to the north, through the open end of the stadium. His interest was a solitary church tower two hundred yards away. "From the internet perspective, it appeared that anyone in that tower could see both sidelines cleanly. We need to check the access and all, but an exit strategy from there would be simple. And there's a parking lot immediately adjacent."

They continued to talk about possibilities as they walked to the church; by the time they arrived the group had decided there were only two platforms they needed to cover with personnel. They accessed the church bell tower and walked up the three flights of steps, noting the curvature of the staircase and the wedge shape to each step.

When they gained the top platform, Ron's first question was to Chet, "What do you think of those stairs as an easy get away?"

"Not good. Running down those steps will likely cause a misstep and a fall. And that's a long way down."

Gene said, "I had a little trouble walking up those steps."

But when they looked out the view from the tower room, all three were impressed with the wide vista. Ron pulled out his 10x scope and checked the stadium sidelines. "This is like shooting fish in a barrel. I think this is the best location."

Chet looked through the scope and agreed. Gene asked, "Me or you?"

Ron smiled and said, "Right to the heart of the matter, partner. I think it should be me up here, and my reason is to have you on the sideline in case we are all wrong about this being a long-range setup."

Gene nodded before saying, "Just make sure this guy doesn't decide to shoot me, okay?"

Ron nodded grimly, "We don't want him shooting anybody, Gene. Certainly not you."

CHAPTER 66

THURSDAY, APRIL 15

The detectives had discussed their needs for the remainder of the time they would be hidden. Each of them carried a bottle of water and a juice container and an empty plastic bottle to pee in. Their plan involved being hidden and immobile for the rest of the night and most of the following day since the lacrosse game was a late afternoon start. Each man carried his favorite sidearm in addition to a stun gun. If they were correct about Greene's intent and method, they would be dealing with a sniper in close quarters.

Gene was allowed to sleep in his car with instructions to get to the playing field the next afternoon as soon as anyone else showed up. Chet hiked himself back into the scoreboard. Ron had reviewed the various options and suggested that a sniper would like to seat himself close to the end of the scoreboard where the ladder was positioned to make the fastest exit. Chet thought that was also likely so he found his perch immediately above the exit path. Before settling down, however, Chet found a canvas bag of gears and numbered slates used by a former scoreboard operator. He positioned the bag directly over the ladder and tied it in place with a slip knot he could quickly release if the sniper beat him to the ladder. When that was done, Chet draped himself in a black hanging cloth and lay down on the second level of the wire footing.

Ron closely examined the bell chamber at the top of the tower. The overall space was 12 feet square with a sizeable portion of that area taken up by the large bell hanging in the center. The platform was open in the middle and skirted the circumference of the room except for the section where the staircase ascended. Ron found there was no hiding place on the staircase so he could not risk waiting where he would be seen by the sniper coming up the stairs. The circumferential walkway was only four feet wide and offered no hiding place. Ron looked up and appreciated there was space above the dome of the bell on the suspension rafters.

He used the open window and the ends of the suspension beams to pull himself into the space. Once in place, he realized his only way down quickly would be to jump from the ten-foot height. With that idea in mind, he shifted his position to be directly over the spot from which he imagined the sniper would be shooting. In that position, he sat on a crossbeam with his feet on the suspension rafters. He could lean back against the top of the bell at its shoulder. The bell normally would be rung using a pull rope, which was threaded over a wheel on the side of the suspension beams. Ron situated his feet and body to avoid touching the wheel, fearing that might cause enough movement in the bell to cause noise.

Once in position, Ron activated his earpiece and said quietly, "Three, in position."

He heard Chet answer, "One, in position."

After a few moments of silence, Gene's somewhat muffled voice said, "Two, in position. Sorry, had my mouth full."

Ron silently shook his head and took stock of the situation. It was more than an hour to midnight and the team was in place. Uncomfortably in place, but ready for Greene's next move. He tried to stretch his back muscles without moving his body significantly and then settled into waiting, Ron had done such waiting many times before, he realized. There were deer stands in his teens and stakeouts in the Air Force, so he was familiar with the tedium, and the need to remain still and quiet. An hour later, he began to consider that all of those previous stakeouts had occurred when he was much younger and less liable to get stiff by remaining motionless for hours.

He considered allowing himself a light nap, presuming that he would be able to awaken when the sniper made his entrance. Ron thought there was very little chance the sniper would make it up three flights of stairs without making a sound. But he didn't sleep, mostly because he was too uncomfortable. Twice he sat more upright, taking his weight off the bell and allowing his back muscles to stretch. The second time, as he leaned back against the bell, he heard a metallic clanking sound underneath him followed by a metallic skritching sound that ended with a loud click.

He checked his watch. 0215 hours. He listened carefully for the sound of footsteps on the stairs and heard nothing. Then, distantly at first, but slowly gathering amplitude, Ron heard more scratching and episodic breathing. He closed his eyes to enhance his focus on the sounds. As they continued to increase, he began to see a mental Rembrandt of the cause. Finally, just as the sniper pulled himself through the rear window, Ron grasped what was going on. The sniper had thrown a grappling hook through the window and ascended the back wall of the bell tower on a rope. Ron was impressed. Three floors in the dark of night and done quietly. He listened as the climber removed his gear and hoisted a pack he had left on the ground.

Listening still with his eyes closed, Ron could imagine the sniper bringing the sniper rifle up the side of the tower and into the bell room. He heard the man open a zippered case and then caught the distinctive sounds of rifle assembly. Willing himself to breathe lightly, Ron strained to catch the sounds from just a few feet below his perch. He heard the case being closed and re-zippered, and then some shuffling steps moving from the back window toward the front. Looking down, Ron faintly perceived a dark form huddling under the window and then become still.

Ron continued to sit silently and unmoving as he wondered, did the shooter go to sleep? In their previous discussions, he and Gene decided that they probably would not get far with the shooter if they arrested him on arrival. They knew they needed better evidence of his intent to kill someone for a case against him to hold together. For that reason, they had decided to allow the shooter access to his perch, and to use their phone to record movements of loading the weapon and using the scope to survey the field before making an arrest. As Ron thought back on that decision, he knew his back would be hurting several more hours before it got relief.

Ron decided to distract himself from his discomfort by thinking through the steps he would take to capture the shooter. He rejected the idea of just announcing his presence and ordering the man to lay down the weapon. That course would undoubtedly lead to an exchange of gunfire. The only other possibility meant he would have to come down from the rafters. That left the question of whether he should try that before any announcement or at the same time. He replayed in his head the struggle he had had getting into the rafters and came back to the original conclusion: he was going to have to jump.

Since he had taken pains to situate himself directly over the front window opening, Ron realized that his jump would be relatively easy. Pull the legs from the side rests and push himself off the crossbeam. He would land directly on top of anyone poised at the front window. That decision made, Ron decided he would have to try some other distraction since his back was starting to cramp. Then he heard the soft sound of snoring coming from the shadow on the floor beneath him and realized he could move around and stretch a little bit without the likelihood of being detected.

CHAPTER 67

FRIDAY, APRIL 16

Ron heard the shooter beneath him begin to stir, and he checked his watch again. 1042. Mid-morning and still almost six hours to wait. As the man on the platform began to rustle around and open his kit, Ron allowed himself a deep breath and a final shoulder-hunching attempt to relieve his aching back muscles. He bent forward slightly and saw the top of the shooter's head as the man peered out the window toward the ball field. Ron had prepared for this opening during the dark hours and had his phone ready to record now that there was sufficient light. Ron saw the man's hand come to his face holding a package and initially thought the shooter was raising binoculars. When the man tipped his head and took a bite of the package, however, he realized the fellow was eating breakfast.

With that realization, Ron felt the pangs of hunger himself and became concerned that his stomach would soon make noise enough to reveal his presence. He quietly slipped his hand into his shirt pocket and retrieved a piece of hard candy, one of three he had put there for just this reason. Ron slipped the candy in his mouth and let the saliva flow. But he remained in a forward position to watch the movements of the shooter below.

When the shooter had finished his breakfast and taken several large swallows from a water bottle, he moved away from the window and out of Ron's line of vision. Then came the sounds of rifle disassembly and reassembly again. Three times the man took his rifle apart and restored it to a functional status before he was satisfied. All these actions, however, took place outside of Ron's line of sight and were not recorded. Almost thirty minutes elapsed before the man reappeared, this time standing and positioned just to the right of the open window. And this time he did hold a pair of binoculars to his face. He surveyed the area with a patterned sweep of the glasses, taking almost two minutes before finishing. Ron was able to capture that action on the phone.

The man was dark-haired and dressed in denim jeans and a dark shirt. Ron could not see his face directly and caught only an occasional shot of the side during the binocular sweep. He knew that would be a problem for a court case if he could not get a definite identification on the camera, but he did not want to move or cause the man to look up in his direction just yet.

At 1337 hours, the man laid down under the window and curled up, placing his head on his crooked arm, and went back to sleep. Ron grasped the importance of the opportunity and turned his phone camera back on. When the man's breathing became regular and deep, Ron took the chance of making a sound that might awaken the sleeper by inching forward and leaning down with his hand holding the telephone extended to better capture the shooter's facial image.

From what Ron could see, the man seemed to be tall, maybe six feet, and thin. The man's face had a dark complexion, and the slicked-back hair appeared black. The face was unfamiliar, but it was recorded on the phone for posterity. The movement to obtain a good likeness with the camera had allowed Ron to further stretch his aching back. He maintained the position for several minutes before settling back against the shoulder of the bell. He reviewed the footage he had captured so far and decided he had sufficient imagery for positive identification. He was ready for this stakeout to end.

Ron leaned back and allowed his head to fall on his chest. He closed his eyes and rested, confident that he would not snore even if he did fall asleep. After stretching his back and shaking his shoulders, he felt comfortable enough to allow himself to drift. Then, suddenly, Gene was talking in his ear. "I hope you're still up there, partner. People are starting to arrive for the game, and Chet says his platform is clean."

Ron jerked and realized he had fallen asleep. He quickly checked his watch. 1810 hours. Less than an hour before the game would start. He looked down and noticed that the shooter was also awake, sitting on the platform under the window and peering over the bottom sill. Ron knew he could not risk answering Gene audibly, so he used his phone to message him: 'Shooter here. Chet to base.'

Everything went quiet, and Ron wondered if Gene had decided to stop his voice messaging. He sat quietly watching the shooter, recording his actions when the man was visible. He caught the man to the side of the window doing some stretching exercises and later kneeling just under the window checking the rifle assembly and loading a magazine. He heard the game opening whistle.

CHAPTER 68

FRIDAY, APRIL 16

Harry Wilton waited in the parking lot until a crowd of several people passed his car on their way to the field. He quickly slid out of his car and joined them, everyone wearing a bright purple sweater indicating their attachment to the Kenyon Lords. Harry struck up a conversation with the man in the rear of the group. They all passed into the stadium with Harry as one of the group, not as a single man. His method of hiding in plain sight was successful as Gene's attention did not linger on the group, looking instead for a single individual probably looking guilty about something.

As was common for spectators at lacrosse games, the seating was not particularly close to the field. However, entry to the seating area involved walking a short distance along the sidelines. The teams were still in their pre-game warm-up routines; the sidelines were inhabited only by coaching staff. Harry stopped walking when he got to the bottom of the stairs up to the seating area and allowed the rest of the group to proceed without him. No one paid any particular attention to him, and he waited for the teams to come back to the sidelines. Standing in the coaching area, clad in a purple sweater similar to the ones worn by the coaching staff, Harry did not attract attention.

Five minutes before the scheduled starting time, the players left the field and clustered around the coach for last-minute encouragement and reminders. Harry was able to catch Henry's eye as he joined this group, and when the coach dismissed the team, and the starters took the field, Henry moved over to speak with his father.

"Hey, Dad. I didn't expect you to be on the field."

"Well, it's just to give you this," Harry said, handing Henry a burner phone.

"What's this for?"

"I have come into a lot of money, Henry. Now, some people want to take it away from me. I'm afraid they have my phone and yours tapped. I'll send you messages by text to this phone, okay?"

"What do you mean, a lot of money?"

"I mean a lot of money, Henry. But it probably means I have to go away and into hiding."

"What for? Is the money dirty?"

"No, nothing like that. It's just that other people wanted the money, and when I ended up with it, they want to take it away from me."

"Is this something dangerous, dad?"

"Somewhat. I'll tell you more after the game. You coming back to Cincinnati with me?"

"Yeah, I told the coach I wouldn't be on the bus and he said that's okay, as long as I'm back for classes on Monday."

"That shouldn't be a problem," Harry said, suddenly realizing that he could not take his son back to their home without serious risk to them both. "We'll make a weekend of it."

A whistle from the field indicated the beginning of the game, and Henry's attention became divided between talking to this father and watching what was happening on the field. Harry recognized the dilemma and said, "Go on. I'll see you right after the game."

Henry said, "Okay," even as he was turning away and walking toward the sideline.

Harry stood quiet for a short time, also watching the game with only mild interest. Henry was still on the sideline, and Harry didn't completely understand the intricacies of lacrosse. He walked along the stadium wall, remaining on the sideline, trying to get to a position with better visibility of the field. He found himself near mid-field, situated between the two benches and with an open view of the field and the action. He knelt on one knee and was about to relax when the loud crack of a high-powered rifle split the air.

CHAPTER 69

FRIDAY, APRIL 16

When the shooter sat up and knelt beneath the window and extended the rifle, Ron tensed. He saw the shooter sweeping the scope from side to side, obviously seeking a target. His tightness and readiness to jump almost caused him to fall when Gene again appeared in his ear: "Holy crap, Ron. Harry Wilton is walking down the sideline!"

At almost the same moment, the shooter raised up into a firing position and put his eye to the scope. Ron recognized the risk of waiting; he could not allow the sniper to make a shot. He lifted his feet and pushed himself forward as he had planned and went directly down on top of the shooter's position.

The man was not where he had been, however. His reflexes responded to the sound of Ron's jump, and he twisted to the side, rolling with the rifle. Ron landed hard on the platform, but his left foot hit the shooter's arm and loosened his grip on the rifle. Ron fell backward on landing and tried to roll to the side where the shooter was lying. The man rolled, too, and they ended up perilously close to the center edge of the platform with a three-story drop yawning at them.

Both men pushed away from the edge and tried to stand; the shooter tried to get the rifle to swing into position to fire at Ron.

Grasping the obvious that a rifle was not the best weapon for close infighting, Ron ducked and lunged at the shooter's feet. They again tumbled around on the platform with their feet dangling over the edge. Ron's hands and arms were engaged with the shooter's legs and feet, leaving the man's hands free. He swung the butt of the rifle at Ron and connected on his shoulder that caused Ron to let go for an instant. At that moment, the man kicked his legs free, scooted backward, and used the butt of the gun again, this time striking Ron a glancing blow to the right side of his face.

As Ron slumped to the platform from this blow, the man jumped up and turned to look out the window, thinking Ron was unconscious. The shooter took a step toward the window, raising the rifle into position. Ron groggy and wobbly, jumped from his position into the back of the man's legs, causing him to lose balance, fire the weapon aimlessly in the air, and lose his grip on the rifle at the same time. The rifle fell from his hands, hit the window sill, teetered for a moment, and then fell out, three stories to the ground.

The shooter jerked free of Ron's grasp and kicked him in the head before racing to the back window. Still not unconscious but stunned and momentarily immobile, Ron saw the man had affixed a cable to the bell struts and was fastening his chest harness carabiner to the rope and clambering out the window. Then he disappeared out the window in the next second and Ron stumbled to his feet and around the bell to the back window. He looked down to see the man rappelling rapidly down the wall. Ron turned to look at the attachment of the rope to the strut and saw an odd knot. He blinked and stared before recognizing he was not looking at a knot around the strut, the rope was simply looped around and back against itself. Ron dimly understood what he was seeing, then grabbed at the free end sticking out. He pulled as hard as he could but felt little give. He pulled again, and this time the knot gave way suddenly. The rope snapped in the air and disappeared out the window accompanied by a stifled yell and followed by a squishy-sounding thump. Ron wobbled back to the window and looked down.

The shooter was lying at the foot of the bell tower on his back, the rope strewn around the area. The man was not moving. Ron could hear some voice that seemed a long way off yelling, "I got him," just before he slumped against the wall and slid to a sitting position. That was how Gene found him ten minutes later after running up the stairs.

"You alright, partner?"

"I certainly am not. My head hurts, there's a loud ringing in my ears, and I have the worst headache ever. But mostly, I'm hungry and sleepy."

CHAPTER 70

FRIDAY, APRIL 16

Harry reacted immediately by moving quickly back to the wall and starting to walk in the direction of the gate and the parking lot. He noticed that almost everyone else had halted their activity and were staring around attempting to locate the source of the sound. Suddenly, he felt his purple sweater made an excellent target, even with all the others up in the stands and coaches on the sidelines. He moved next to a group of Kenyon players near their bench and knelt again. He slipped the sweater off and put it on the bench, leaving himself only wearing the white polo shirt he had underneath the sweater.

Harry realized that the white shirt would also provide a good target; he looked around for something to cover himself. He noticed a jacket lying on the other end of the bench and he scurried there, grabbed the jacket, and pulled it over his shoulders. Then he stood up and again started walking toward the gate. Behind him, the momentary pause in the game lapsed, and once again, the field echoed with players' calls and crowd noise.

At the end of the stands, Harry turned the corner and put his arms into the jacket. He realized he had taken a Barbour jacket and thought, 'at least I got a good one.' Without hurrying, he moved on to the parking lot, got in his car, and drove out the gate. He turned left, toward the body of the campus and saw in his rearview mirror a police car come from the opposite direction, and pull into the gate area he had just left. The police car slewed to one side, blocking the exit, and turned on the flashers. Harry realized he had just escaped being blocked in the lot.

He drove slowly and cautiously back to the highway and then to the Interstate. He took the first exit off the Interstate to a mega filling station and food store. He parked in the area away from the pumps and pulled out his phone. He selected the number of the burner phone he had given to Henry and typed, "Had to leave. You are in danger. Don't go back. Get a bus to Aunt Lily's. I'll see you there.' He hit 'send' and sat back in his seat.

Somebody knew he was going to be at that game. That somebody had to be Greene. And Greene must have sent his remaining shooter. The puzzle was why the shooter had missed. Harry knew that at the moment he heard the shot, he had been very exposed on the sideline. He was kneeling down and virtually a sitting target. Harry could not explain the shooter's failure but was not about to second-guess or hang around. Certainly not when he had a windfall to collect.

CHAPTER 71

FRIDAY, APRIL 16

The game was over, and spectators had long ago left the area. Ron Looney was sitting on the tailgate of the local ambulance holding an ice pack to the right side of his face. The EMT completed her brief exam and asked, "Are you sure you never lost consciousness, sir?"

"I'm pretty sure. I can remember almost all of it. Especially that part where he swiped me in the head with that rifle butt."

"I don't think anything's broken there," the EMT said, again probing with her fingers over the bones surrounding the eye. "And your vision is intact, and there's no sign of intracranial bleeding."

Gene offered from his bystander position, "Does that confirm the hard-headedness we have all witnessed?"

Quick on the uptake, the EMT responded, "At least harder than a gun butt."

Ron carefully took a bite of the candy bar Gene had given him and grimaced at his partner. "So, what do we know?"

"You want the good news or the bad news."

"I would prefer there not be any bad news."

"We have some anyway. Wilton got away. Probably broke for his car when he heard the gunshot. Anyway, by the time we all figured out where the shot came from and organized a response, the guy I asked to block off the parking area went somewhere else, and later we realized Wilton was gone."

"That was a good idea, though. Blocking the exit."

"Like the old barn door story, it doesn't work if the horse is already out."

"Is there good news?' Ron asked, leaning against the doorframe of the ambulance.

Gene danced a step and said, "You bet there is. Largely due to your efforts, I might add."

"Whee. Good for me," Ron said without enthusiasm.

"The shooter fell about fifteen feet or more after you cut that rope. Dislocated his shoulder by landing flat on his backpack. Knocked him out, too."

"So we got him?"

"Of course. Chet got your message and was just arriving at the bell tower when he fell. Cuffed him up, EMT there put his shoulder back right, and he's on his way to the lock-up."

"Who is he?"

"ID says he's Nestor Aramano, and he has a calling card listing him as a member of Anton Greene's security detail."

"Greene has a security detail? Paid by the city?"

"I don't know. Probably private."

"Is this Nestor guy talking?"

"Of course not. Asked for pain medication and a lawyer. Not sure which was most important to him."

"But Wilton got away?"

"Yes. Leave that alone for a minute. We will get you to give us the story in your report, but I want to know how did you cut that rope?"

"What?'

"I know you Arkansas guys always carry a knife, but I've seen yours. It's that little Swiss thing on your key chain. Good for opening letters and packages but nothing you'd take to a knife fight."

"What are you talking about?" Ron asked, moving to feel in his pocket to confirm that his keys and knife were still there.

"So, how did you cut that rope?"

"I didn't. I untied it."

"How? With that guy climbing down and hanging on it?"

Ron shook his head and removed the ice pack. He touched his cheek gingerly and grimaced a bit, then smiled a Gene. "He used a kind of slip knot I have seen in the past."

"Explain, please."

Ron sat up straighter and rotated his shoulders. He put the ice pack down and tried to demonstrate with his hands. "I did some climbing in the woods in Arkansas. We didn't have money for fancy metal hooks and things, so we had to learn how to use just the rope to get up and down, and take the rope with us. There's a kinda knot where you really wind the rope around something and pull it over itself. As long as you keep weight on the rope on the climb down, everything's okay. Once you release the weight and flip the rope, the upper end goes loose, and you can pull the rope down. I don't know if he wanted to take the rope or he was more interested in not leaving it for me."

"What?"

"All I had to do was pull on the free end of the rope where he wrapped it around the stud. Then he wasn't tied to anything."

"Another old Arkansas trick, eh?"

"Something like." Ron turned to the EMT, who industriously was closing up her bag and equipment. "Hey doc, can I go now? I just want to get home and get some sleep."

She looked up and then stared at Gene. He nodded, and she turned back to Ron, "Yes, you can go as long as you promise not to drive. And go see somebody if your headache persists."

"Okay, I promise," Ron said as he stood up and showed Gene his left hand with the crossed fingers as he reached for his keys.

CHAPTER 72

SATURDAY, APRIL 17

Harry sat in his car a block away from the branch post office in Cincinnati. He had a breakfast sandwich and a cup of coffee from a drive-thru. He watched the front door of the post office for an hour before he felt certain that it was not surveilled. He had considered hiring someone else to pick up the package for him but decided against it at the last moment. There was no need for involving any additional people.

Harry looked at his watch for the twentieth time and then rechecked the application on his phone. The package he had re-routed from Las Vegas to Seattle and then to Cincinnati had been logged in by bar code as delivered. Even knowing that, he did not yet feel the elation that he expected from having a million dollars. Of course, it was still sitting in the post office and not actually in his hands, but still …

He got out of the car and opened the trunk. Inside, he located the folding luggage cart he had purchased at the AAA store the day before. He also grabbed the pack of bungee cords and headed for the post office. Once inside, he found a short line waiting for service. Harry kept his eyes down, and the ball cap on his head pulled low on his forehead, but no one seemed to pay him any particular attention.

When he stepped up to the counter, Harry told the clerk he had come for the package in the box he had rented a week before. The clerk left the counter and returned a few minutes later to say, "This is a big, heavy package, bud. How you gonna carry it?"

"I have a carrier," Harry explained.

The clerk looked over the counter at the luggage cart and said, "Okay, Let me have it." He opened a gate at the end of the counter, and Harry handed him the cart.

Several minutes passed before the man reappeared with the cart loaded with a medium-sized box. Harry was pleased to see that the container was larger than the wheeled knapsack that Greene had brought to the construction site. At least he wasn't faking the size and weight of the package.

Harry signed the receipt for the box, noting that it was insured for $5000, the maximum allowed by the Post Office.

"What's so important that it gets that much insurance?" asked the clerk.

"Books," Harry answered. "Antiques and rare books."

"Huh. And I see these books went all over the place, too."

"Yep. I thought we had buyers for them, but no one turned up."

"People are not considerate at times."

"No. They're not," Harry said, offering the clerk a small smile as he handed him back the pen used to sign the forms.

There were two women in line behind him by this time, and Harry did not linger. He took the handle, turned the cart, and headed for the door as the clerk said, "Next."

At the door, Harry met two men in long overcoats coming in. He stopped in alarm and caught his breath as they entered. One of the men smiled at him, turned to the other man, and began talking as they passed Harry on their way to the counter. Harry waited until they had passed before resuming breathing and then moved toward the exit. He slowly walked to the car, opened the trunk, and lifted the heavy box inside. After he had folded the cart, and placed it in the trunk he took out a small knife and cut through the heavy tape securing the flaps of the the box.

The contents were enclosed in several layers of polyethylene wrap, but he could see the color and form of currency bills through the covering. He became more excited as he loosened the plastic covering and pulled out the first wad of bills. Looking around to assure that no one was paying attention, Harry quickly then glanced through the few bills he had pulled from the interior of the box. All of them were 100 dollar bills.

Harry knew from his research that $1 million in hundred dollar bills should weigh around 22 pounds. He thought that was very close to the weight of the box he had just lifted into the trunk of his car. He looked back at the bills in his hand and noted that the serial numbers were not sequential. Another good sign, probably indicating that banks did not have the numbers to check against any incoming hundreds in the future.

He closed the trunk and put the handful of bills in his pocket. He got back in the car and waited until his pulse had fallen below 90 beats a minute before starting the engine and driving away. All that remained for a successful getaway was a drive to his sister's to pick up Henry.

CHAPTER 73

MONDAY, APRIL 19

When Ron and Gene made it to the luncheon café on Monday, they had already completed their reports of the school shooting and a two-hour unproductive meeting with Nestor Aramano. Ron's face was dark blue from mid-cheek to his hairline on the right side, and he took his usual seat facing the door with his left side to the café seating area.

Sandy met them at the table and expressed some dismay at Ron's bruise. "Are you sure you shouldn't be home?"

"Yes, Sandy, I am sure. This looks bad, and yet it is not painful. I plan to use the image to terrify criminals for the next day or so."

Gene nodded, "Better use of the hard head than when you try to make decisions."

Sandy looked at Gene and said, "Shush, now. What do y'all want for lunch?"

Gene smiled at her and noted, "I'll have the usual."

"With the green beans or the fries?"

"Ah, back to the fries, please."

"Okay, honey. And for you?" she asked, turning to Ron.

"I think I will have a big bowl of the clam chowder and lemonade to drink."

"Okay, I'll be right back."

They both watched her walk to the kitchen in the rear of the café. Gene commented, "So, chewing is a problem, then?"

"Maybe I just want to have soup."

"That is one possibility, of course. But, remember, I am a detective, and I'm trained to notice little things like that when they are out of the ordinary. You have never had soup in this café before."

"Okay, it does hurt a little to chew. No need to make things worse. And I happen to like soup, and clam chowder in particular."

"Point taken. More to the bigger point, did you get anything from Aramano's reaction today?"

"You mean his sitting like a wooden statue and saying only one word, "Counsel"?"

"Yeah. I noticed that you did your trick of talking to him without asking questions, looking for some reaction, like when you told him we knew he was there when his buddy got blown up."

"His pupils dilated at that, did you see?"

"No. His eyes are too dark for me to see that. You also told him you knew that Councilman Greene was present at that time, too. I didn't see much reaction then, either."

"I thought he blinked."

"Well then, we got him. I'm sure those observations will stand scrutiny in court."

"I didn't think he would spill the beans. I was letting him know how bad it was for his boss."

"Why?"

"I hope that will weaken his reliance on Greene getting him out of trouble. Maybe he'll think differently about his chances when he sees that Greene is going down, too."

"Ah. Gotcha."

Sandy arrived with Ron's soup and their drinks and told Gene his patty melt would be 'right up'. They watched her walk away again. Ron started on his soup.

Gene went on, "But at the moment, we have only circumstantial evidence, and we are the responsible officers for at least two, maybe three deaths in this stinking case."

"You're counting Riley Morgan, aren't you?"

"Absolutely. That was what fired Wilton up enough to write to us."

"I think you're right about that. I believe it was Nestor who shoved him off the high beam."

"Why?"

"Mostly because Greene doesn't do those things himself."

"Still, the guy responsible for the other two murders got away. I mean, he was less than ten yards from me when I warned you. I should have grabbed him right then. I was moving around behind him when the shot occurred, and everything went haywire for twenty or thirty seconds. Then he was gone."

"Well, if I had jumped a little more accurately, there would not have been a shot, so that isn't your fault."

"Still seems like it."

Sandy brought Gene's sandwich and fries and created another mild interruption in their discussion until she had completed her walk away from them.

"We'll get him, Gene. We are certain he is on the hook for Thomas Pritchard. And, even though he said it was necessary, he admitted killing the other sniper in the construction site that day."

"Oh yeah," Gene said around a large bite of food. "There's something else I learned this morning. I called the school where Wilton's kid attends to try to set up a conversation with him. The coach said he didn't return on the bus with the others. The kid said he was coming into Cincinnati with his dad for the evening and would be back on campus the next morning."

"I think I hear a 'but' in there," Ron commented as he pushed his empty bowl away.

"But he didn't show. No idea where he is."

"Curiouser and curiouser."

"you know those aren't real words."

"Lewis Carroll thought they were. Anyway, we need some leads on where Wilton might have run to. Sounds like he's trying to take his son with him."

Gene answered, "And we have no one who knows anything more about …" He stopped in mid-sentence as Looney's phone rang. Ron pulled it from his pocket and answered, "Walker."

"Detective, this is Gale Hunicutt."

"Yes, Ms. Hunicutt, how can I help you?"

"I think I'm going to be helping you, detective."

"How's that?"

"I just got a package in the mail. From Thomas. I think it's what you were looking for at his house. Want to come see?"

CHAPTER 74

MONDAY, APRIL 19

Gene wanted to take his remaining French fries to eat in the car, but Ron wouldn't allow it. His rule of no eating in the car dated back to when his children were small, and Ron had maintained that rule with each succeeding new car. Gene objected several times a week, claiming he was being treated like a pre-school child, but Ron held firm. He even insisted they finish any coffee before getting in.

Gene's question was not about food, this time, however. "What was that you said about things being odd?"

"Curiouser and curiouser."

"That's it. That's what this pack thing sounds like. What does Hunicutt mean, she got a package from Pritchard?"

"I'm not sure, Gene. That's why we are going to her house."

"But is she telling us that our naked guy is not Thomas Pritchard?"

" I don't think that's what she's saying at all."

"Did you get her to make a positive ID? I mean, she was there with the body, right?"

Ron paused a moment before answering. "No, I didn't go with her to see the body. I arranged for that. But I'm pretty sure she would have made a case if that wasn't him in the morgue."

"Well, then how could he be sending her a package now?"

"Work it out, Gene."

"And what did he send? I mean, is it something from the grave?"

"Get serious, Gene. It's something that he mailed before he was killed, and she just got it. That's how he kept it from being discovered in his house."

"Oh. Hey, that makes sense."

"But he must have mailed it over two weeks ago. What I don't understand is why it is only being delivered now."

Gale was waiting for them. She lived near Pritchard's apartment in a small single-family home with a small fenced front yard. Ron parked at the curb, and the porch light immediately came on. Gale opened the front door as they walked up the sidewalk. "Detective. Is this your partner?"

"Gale Hunicutt, this is Gene Novalchek."

"Welcome, Detective. Please come in. See what turned up in my mail this morning."

They sat on the couch in her living room, and she handed them a small package about the size of a postcard, but thick with padding. The typed, front label was to "G. Honeycut" at a post office box in Sitka, Alaska. The package was unopened.

Ron looked quizzically at Gale, "Have you not opened it?"

"Oh, no. Once I figured out what it was, I knew it belonged to you."

Ron looked back at the innocent-looking package before asking, "And how did you figure it out?"

"Check the return address," she said.

They carefully looked at the label again, paying close attention to the return portion. The address given was where they were sitting at the moment, Gale Hunicutt's house. The name on the return, however, was "P. Richard, c/o Gale Hunicutt."

Gene asked, "Do you know this Richard guy?"

Gale said calmly, "Of course. It's Thomas. 'P. Richard' is Pritchard."

The detectives nodded.

She went on, "Notice this is a piece of registered mail. That means someone would have to sign a receipt for it to be delivered, or it would be returned to its sender."

Ron nodded and said, "And there's no 'G. Honeycut' in Sitka, Alaska."

She nodded and said, "I guess not. So, this package probably sat in the 'to be claimed' area of the Sitka post office for a couple of weeks and then was sent back here. Tommy put my address as the return so it would not go back to his house. I'm assuming this package is something he was hiding. And I remember, Detective," she said, looking at Ron, "you told me you thought Tommy might have been involved in some kind of scheme."

"Yes, I did. We have more reason now to think that was the case."

"Well, if he was involved in something like that, Tommy would have documented everything."

"We searched his work computer, but someone stole his home computer," Gene noted.

"He wouldn't have left anything on either of those machines," Gale said, grinning at the detectives. "He would have put everything in a transportable file, wiped any copies he might have made, and then he would hide the file where no one would ever find it."

"Like in the U.S. Post Office," Ron stated.

"Exactly," Gale said, leaning forward and touching the package. "This is precisely what he would have done. Mail it somewhere no one would think to look and use a misleading return address."

"Clever," Gene said, reaching for the package.

"Absolutely," Ron agreed, handing Gene his keychain knife to open the package.

Inside they found a small thumb drive marked '2GB'. There was no accompanying note. Gene held up the small drive and said, "I guess you're right. This has likely got what we are looking for."

She nodded and asked, "Want to see?"

After a brief second's pause before he understood, Gene replied, "Sure. If you don't mind."

She stood and said, "Not at all. I put my laptop on the dining room table. Can I get you guys some coffee?"

Forty-five minutes later, Gene leaned back in his chair and picked up his third cup of coffee. "That's it. This file has everything we would ever want. It has all the fake contracts with J.Y. Dahgs, copies of all the invoices from back five years or more, Contact with the waste management sites indicating they have never heard of Dahgs, everything." He sipped his cup. "And this is really good coffee Ms. Hunicutt. What is your secret?"

She tipped her cup in his direction and said, "No secret that I'm aware of. It's Folger's. The blend is called Black Silk. I keep the can in the refrigerator."

"It's gotta be something more than that, what did you add?"

"Nothing, I promise. I just made a regular pot."

"How?"

"In my Mr. Coffee brewer. Had that thing forever."

Ron interrupted, "Excuse me for wanting to focus on the reason we are here, but what about showing the Councilman's connection to everything?"

Gene put his cup down and turned back to the screen as he answered, "Well, our boy, Tommy put the information in here like I got from the Ohio Department of State showing the incorporation papers for Dahgs, so we have his wife and son connected. Also, we have that information about the company not having a DUNS number. But we don't have the actual smoking gun in Greene's hand."

"Anything in there tying Greene to Nestor?"

"Didn't see anything. But we can get that from other sources. The guy was known to be one of Greene's 'bodyguards'." He emphasized the last by making air quotes with his hands. "And he wasn't the only one."

"Then we still have a way to go in all this, partner," Ron said as he rose from his chair. "I have to agree about the coffee, Ms. Hunicutt. It was wonderful."

CHAPTER 75

TUESDAY, APRIL 20

"Are you ready for this?" Gene asked as he sat down at the rear table in the coffee shop. Ron scooted into the chair opposite Gene while holding a cup of coffee and a cinnamon bun. He smiled at his partner and brushed his hands, "Of course, I am," he replied. "You and the financial guys have boxed this case up. All I have to do is ask some questions. If he admits guilt, case done. If he denies the truth, we go the lockup and trial route."

"I know all that. You have literally said that fifteen times this morning. And that big grin on your face is another tipoff. But I'm asking are you, Ron Looney, ready to go in the ring with a City Councilman and accuse him of several heinous crimes?"

Ron took a bite of his bun and a sip of coffee before answering, "Yup. And I'll be even more ready in twenty minutes."

"What happens then?"

"We will be fortified with hot coffee and sweet bread."

"Oh, yeah. There's always that."

"Look, you did a great job leading the financial guys through Greene's accounts. You have put together the factual case that we all suspected from the circumstantial evidence. This isn't completely a slam-dunk but it's close. What are you worried about?"

"Maybe I'm worried you're gonna overplay the hand and he's gonna wriggle out on some technicality."

"Right. I've done that so many times before. How many exactly? None, that's how many. What's really up, bud?"

"I'm just nervous when someone else is on the free-throw line."

"You are going to be right there with me, remember?"

"Yeah, I do. And I'm nervous as a cat in a room of rocking chairs so I think you should be, too."

"Maybe I should have put more Xanax in your coffee this morning."

"We'll be fine, won't we?" Gene gulped his coffee.

Ron looked sympathetically at his partner. Gene always could imagine how a criminal would twist circumstances and squirm through an evanescent window in the evidence to escape. Initially, Gene's overweening concern in this regard had annoyed him. He interpreted the angst as a lack of confidence in the people on their side of the law. Over the years, he came to appreciate Gene's concern about the intricate fibers of their cases and how meticulous he was at crafting the net that prevented those they had apprehended from getting loose. He decided Gene's apprehension was similar to an actor's opening night jitters. Ron didn't have any such angst. Gene had built an incredibly tight case.

They finished their coffee and strolled the block back to the office, this time entering the main building and riding the elevator to the fourth floor. As they entered the Dick Pen, they felt the tension rise; everyone turned to look at them, and the sergeant said, perhaps more loudly than necessary, "Your guests are in the Interrogation Room."

Ron went to his desk and gathered the small pile of folders he and Gene had worked days to create. Then he followed Gene down the hall to Interrogation. Ron opened the door and let Gene pass him on entrance and then closed the door behind himself. He turned to see the Councilman standing across from the two-way mirror, arms crossed and a look of fury on his face. "Are you the one responsible for this?" he hurled at Gene.

Ron waved his hand and drew the attention of the Councilman. "No, he's not, Mr. Greene, that would be me. My name is Detective Ron Looney. Please be seated."

Instead of complying, the Councilman drew himself up and said, "I demand to see the Chief. This is an outrage. Collected from my office like a common criminal."

Ron remained standing and waited until the Councilman had finished, then said in a firm tone, "You will have every opportunity to see the Chief when we finish our discussion. Now, sit down." Gone was the pleasant tone and the polite 'please'. The Councilman looked at his counsel sitting at the table and complied, scooting the chair around several times to indicate his displeasure.

Ron sat across from the Councilman and said, "We have a few questions, sir." He placed the folders on the tabletop, closed.

"Aren't you supposed to read me my rights?"

"We always read the rights to an accused person, Councilman. You are not being accused of anything, as of yet."

The Councilman's counsel spoke up, "If there are no charges against my client, why are we here being treated like criminals?"

Ron's voice was calm and measured as he answered, "Well, counselor, this is exactly how we treat suspects. And that's what your client is at this moment, a suspect. If he can answer a few questions and explain some facts we have come to know, then he will no longer be a suspect."

The lawyer looked at Greene and nodded. Greene made a move of assent with his head.

Ron opened the first folder and read from the top sheet, "Mr. Greene, do you know Mr. Nestor Aramano?"

Greene sat back in his chair, and his eyes darted around the room. Finally, he said, "Yes. He's one of my ..." He was interrupted by his lawyer saying, "Yes or no will suffice, Anton."

Ron went on, "Do you know a Mr. Jorge Quiles?"

Another short pause, then, "Yes."

"What do these men do for you, Mr. Greene?"

A longer pause and a look to his lawyer preceded Greene's answer, "They were my bodyguards?"

"Were?"

"I haven't seen them for several days. I suppose they quit."

"And if I told you they had tried to kill someone, would you be surprised?"

Greene tried to look insulted but failed, "Of course I would. Although they were both killers in the Corps."

"You knew them in the Corps?"

"Well, yes. Both men were in the division where I was the JAG."

"And you hired them to be your bodyguards?"

Another long pause and a furrowed brow from the lawyer before Greene said, "Yes."

"Did these men do any other jobs or tasks for you other than guarding?"

"I don't know what you mean?"

"Would they, at any time and for any reason, have set out to kill someone for you?"

Greene jumped to his feet shouting, "No!" The lawyer also stood and said, "What are you suggesting?" Ron remained calm and turned an inquiring face to each of them. "Sit down, both of you," he said.

Nostrils flared, Greene complied, as did counsel. The lawyer asked, "What are you implying, Detective?"

"Pay attention, counselor. I was not implying anything. I asked a direct question. And I will now ask it again." Turning back to Greene, Ron asked, "Did you, at any time, ask one or both of these men to kill someone for you?"

"I resent your implication! I have never advocated any such thing!"

"Calm down, Councilor. Where were you at seven-thirty in the evening nine days ago?"

"How can you expect me to remember where I was?"

"I would imagine you could remember watching your bodyguard blown up in front of you."

"What are you talking about?"

"Were you at the bus construction site at seven-thirty in the evening nine days ago?"

Greene gritted his teeth and spit out the answer, "No, I was not."

Ron looked at Greene's lawyer and said, "Counselor, I recommend you remind your client not to lie to the police."

Greene yelled, "I am not lying!" and started to get out of his seat again. Ron stopped that notion with a look. After Greene returned to a seated position, Ron asked, "Did you send Nestor Aramano to Wilmington four days ago to shoot and kill Harry Wilton?"

Greene exploded to his feet. "This is insane! I did not do such things. I don't even know who these people are!"

"Really, Councilman? Who is it you do not know? You admitted that Quiles and Aramano worked for you."

"I, uh, I don't know that other guy you said."

"Harry Wilton? You are saying that you don't know Harry Wilton?"

"Yes. That's right. I don't know him."

"Then perhaps your lawyer can help you to explain why you recently sent a package to Harry Wilton in Las Vegas and insured it for $5000. I certainly have difficulty understanding why you would send a package worth at least that much to a person you do not know. Can you tell me why?"

The room became quiet. Greene resumed his seat and stopped talking, but his face was red with anger, and his eyes flashed at Ron. Greene's lawyer leaned over to him and whispered in his ear.

Ron watched the two of them for a moment and then asked, "If you're not ready to tell me about the package you sent to someone you claim not to know, how about telling me what you know about a company called …" he referred to his notes, "Junk Yard Dahgs?"

Greene's face got even more flushed, and his lips started moving without saying anything. Ron persisted, "Do you know about the company Junk Yard Dahgs?"

"No," came Greene's answer through gritted teeth.

The lawyer said, "Enough, Detective. Your line of questioning is bordering on abusive. My client has said he knows nothing about these people and events, and entities. We are leaving now." He stood, but before Greene could join him, Ron asked, "Do you recognize this woman's name?" and he pushed across the table a copy of the incorporation documents for J.Y. Dahgs with Greene's wife's name prominently displayed. The lawyer looked at the document, and sat down. Greene glowered at Ron.

Ron let a minute pass without speaking and then said in a firm voice, "Here's what we know, Councilman. First, we know there was a money skimming operation between ABC Construction and J.Y. Dahgs that has been in operation for more than five years. We know that you have lobbied in the city council for ABC to get construction projects awarded to them. We know that J.Y. Dahgs is a front, owned and operated by your wife without assets, making considerable money for you and her from city contracts.

Second, we know that your operation was discovered by Harry Wilton and Thomas Pritchard, and that they tried to blackmail you. Pritchard is now dead, and Wilton is in the wind. But, before he disappeared, he had an agreement to meet with you for a payoff at the bus station construction site nine days ago at seven-thirty in the evening. We know that at that meeting you had your two bodyguards set up as snipers to kill Harry Wilton when he appeared, but he turned the tables and blew up Jorge Quiles.

Third, we believe you had Aramano kill Morgan Riley in retaliation for Quiles's death.

Fourth, we believe Wilton made another attempt to blackmail you via the U.S. Postal Service. And we believe that relates to the package you sent to him in Las Vegas. We also know that you were aware he would be at his son's lacrosse game in Wilmington, and you sent Aramano there to kill Wilton. Mr. Aramano is in our custody and has confirmed this." Ron paused and noted that Greene was staring at his lawyer.

The lawyer made an effort, "This is ridiculous! You have no proof for any of these allegations. We are leaving!' He stood up but made no motion toward the door. Greene half-heartedly rose from his chair. Ron nodded to Gene, who stepped behind Councilman Greene and said, "Anton Greene, you are under arrest for complicity in murder, attempted murder, grand theft, wire fraud, and lying to the police," Gene pulled Greene's hands behind his back and handcuffed him. "You have the right to remain silent. Anything you say can and will be used against you in a court of law. You have the right to an attorney. If you cannot afford an attorney, one will be provided for you. Do you understand what I said?"

Greene nodded dispiritedly. Gene said, "Please indicate you have understood your rights by saying, Yes, I understand."

"Yes, I understand."

Gene then maneuvered the handcuffed prisoner to the doorway and released him to a uniformed officer who would take him to the cells. Greene's lawyer stared at the two detectives like they were lizards. "You will not be able to make this stick, you know," he spit at them.

Ron shrugged, "The D.A. seems to think it's open and shut. We have paperwork spanning five years and an inner circle witness ready to testify for a lighter sentence of his own."

The lawyer made a huffing sound and left. Gene winked at Ron, "That was mighty good, partner. You even pulled some tricks I didn't know about."

"Yeah, well, I'm glad I wasn't under oath. Let's take this recording down and play it for Aramano. I think he'll be more interested in making a deal once he hears how his boss has thrown him under the bus."

CHAPTER 76

WEDNESDAY, APRIL 21

Harry and Henry Wilton were enjoying their dinner. They had walked from Lillian and Lars Olafsson's house to the restaurant on the Red River for a leisurely meal and the necessary discussion about their future.

"Who would've thought we could have this good a steak at someplace called the Toasted Frog," Harry said as he finished the last of his New York Strip.

Henry, who had already finished his, agreed, "This was wonderful. Wait till I tell the guys that to get a really good steak, you should go to Grand Forks!"

"Well, that's something we still need to settle, isn't it?"

"What's that?"

"You going back and talking to the guys," Harry said, signaling the waiter they were ready for dessert.

"That's what I want to do, Dad."

"Henry, I explained that my windfall of money came with some risk. Some people want that money, and they are not nice people. We cannot have any kind of a public presence, or they will come after us. Or after you to get to me."

"What did you do to get his money, Dad?"

"I applied some of my skills, that's all. But I can't have you staying at Kenyon and playing lacrosse where they can find you."

"They can probably find me, or us, where ever we go, Dad."

"Not if we change our names."

"What? Is this a witness protection program you're talking about?'

"Well, maybe something a little like that."

The waiter took their order for dessert. They had decided to split a baked brie with coffee. When the waiter had left, Henry picked up the conversation again, "Did you get involved with some gangsters or something dirty, Dad?"

"Well, I said they were not nice people, and yes, they were doing something illegal."

"And what did you do?"

"I stopped them and turned them in to the police."

"Then why do we have to run away?"

"Because the police don't have them in custody. That shooting at the lacrosse game was aimed at me. But it could have been aimed at you."

"I know you said that. But how do you know? A little something was going on a couple of blocks off-campus but nothing around the playing field. Why are you so sure that someone was shooting at you?"

"Mostly because they have tried it before and …"

"What? You've been shot at? When?"

"Calm down, Henry. Clearly, I was not shot. That happened a week or so ago and was the reason I finally got the police involved."

"What was going on, Dad? How did you get involved?"

The waiter arrived with their dessert and placed cups in front of each of them. He then poured their coffee from a small carafe arching the stream into each cup from a maximum of two feet away. He then left the carafe on the table and left.

"Did you see that control when he poured the coffee?" Henry asked.

"Yeah. I've seen that before. Professionals say that puts some air back into the liquid and makes the coffee smell and taste better."

"I bet you have to practice a lot of coffee pouring to get that skill."

"Like most things, practice improves performance."

"Speaking of that, I still want to play lacrosse. I'm getting some excellent coaching at Kenyon, and I'm enjoying it there."

"Mmm," Harry said, with a mouthful of brie. He swallowed and said, "I know, son, but surely you can play somewhere else."

"But why? Why not stay where they know me?"

"Mostly because the guys who are after me also know you're there. That's why they came to the game, knowing I'd be there. If they can't find me, they will go after you. It's a lot of money."

The conversation continued throughout the remainder of the brie and beyond the second cup of coffee. Harry paid for the dinner with cash, leaving a substantial tip for the waiter. He was continuing to avoid the use of a credit card for fear the transaction would be traced.

The two Wiltons left the restaurant and walked back west toward Lillian's house, continuing their discussion. Henry continued to press the issue of his returning to Kenyon. "If you've turned these guys in, Dad, won't I be safe back at school?"

"I don't know that. Remember the shooting during the game. These guys know where you are."

"But it looked like whoever was doing that shooting; got caught."

"What do you mean?" Harry stopped walking and faced his son.

Henry shrugged and said, "Maybe you had already left; there were all kinds of flashing lights and police checking the parking lot at the end of the game. The word was, the police arrested somebody for firing a rifle. So, if they have been arrested, why can't I go back?"

"I didn't know anyone was arrested. But that's still just one person. And the guy behind it all is still on the loose. I don't want you back there at risk."

They walked on for more than a block without talking. Finally. Henry said, "I don't want to go on the run and change my name. I have a reputation with this name, and it's a good one. I certainly don't want to start over. I want to go back."

Harry realized he had lost the battle for complete relocation and new identities, but he persisted on one point. "Okay. I understand. But maybe we can agree on this: let's wait until I am certain that the men who want to hurt me are in custody and won't be coming after you. Can you give me that?"

"How long do you think that's going to be?"

"I'm not sure. Maybe a week, possibly less."

Henry thought about a week away from campus and classes. That wouldn't be too bad. Aunt Lillian and Uncle Lars seemed happy to have him stay with them, and he didn't want to go completely against his father's concerns. He said, "Okay. But just a week. I can tell Coach I got sick and ask him to tell my teachers why I'd be missing class."

"That's a good plan," Harry said, smiling.

"But just a week."

"Just a week," Harry agreed, thinking to himself about how to get more incriminating information to the Cincinnati police to get Greene and his men off the street.

They were approaching Lars and Lillian's house, and Henry said, "Look, Uncle Lars is sitting on the porch waiting for us."

"He's got some buddies with him," Harry noted. "This is the social network in Grand Forks. Sitting on the porch after supper with friends."

They turned onto the Olafsson's front walk, and Lars said, "Here they come. And well-fed, it appears."

"That was some good food, Uncle Lars," Henry noted.

As they reached the stairs to the porch, Lars said, "Harry, here are some friends of yours, come to visit." He indicated the two men sitting with him on the porch. Harry had the faintest glimmer of anxiety when the two men stood and started toward him.

The older of the two visitors said, "Harry Wilton?"

"Yes."

"I'm Detective Ron Looney of the Cincinnati Police Department. You are under arrest for the murder of Thomas Pritchard."

Stunned, Harry did not move as Ron descended the stairs and stepped behind him, placing handcuffs on his wrists.

Henry backed up a step and asked, "Dad, is this true? Is this how you got the money?"

Harry dropped his head and said nothing. Henry looked at his uncle, who nodded and put out his arms for Henry to come to him. Ron said, "You have the right to remain silent. Anything you say can and will be used against you in a court of law. You have a right to an attorney. If you cannot afford an attorney, one will be provided for you. Do you understand what I said?"

Harry croaked, "Yes."

Gene came down from the porch and frisked Harry; he found a roll of 100 dollar bills and a set of car keys. He held up the car keys and raised his eyebrows toward Lars.

"Parked around back," Lars said. Gene went to investigate. Ron started walking Harry to the police car at the curb and Harry asked, "Can I say goodbye to my son?"

"Sure," Ron answered, "through the car window." He put his hand on Harry's head and guided him into the back seat, then indicated to Henry that he could approach the car.

Harry looked up with tears in his eye, "I'm sorry, son. It all just got away from me."

"Are these the bad guys you were afraid of? Police from Cincinnati?"

"No, I'm still worried about gangsters."

Ron interrupted, "Greene is in jail facing serious charges, and Nestor Aramano is charged with attempted murder."

Harry took a deep breath and said to Henry, "Go on back to school. No one will be looking for you now."

Gene came around the corner of the house carrying a large backpack. "I found the money," he said. "I think we have everything."

CHAPTER 77

THURSDAY, APRIL 22

They met in Captain Thorason's office. Ron and Gene made a quick trip to the coffee shop beforehand, and everyone was fortified for the discussion. The Captain sat behind his desk, Ron and Gene in front and their special guest, Tom Bolling, in another armchair added for the event.

Ron had asked that Tom be allowed to hear the briefing since the cascade of events began with the finding of Thomas Pritchard's naked body at New City Hospital. The Captain had agreed; the meeting time was set convenient for both the Captain and the guest.

The small talk finished, Ron opened the presentation by noting that as he and Gene would relate events, each would maintain chronology as much as possible. He also noted that some aspects of the case would be well-known but needed inclusion for the sake of completeness.

"Our involvement in the case," he opened, 'began with a call from Dr. Bolling asking for the department to take the lead in investigating a murder on one of their wards."

"Huh," said Thor.

"Well, yes," Ron noted, "Dr. Bolling knew that the department would naturally be involved and was asking if Gene and I could take the lead."

Tom sipped from his cup, Thor nodded; Ron went on.

"What we found is now familiar, the naked body of a man, identity unknown, murdered using a mechanical pencil thrust into his right ear and his brain."

Gene spoke up, "Identification was immediately lacking because the man was neither a patient at New City nor an employee. We were puzzled for a day or so about how he came to be undressed until a second visit to the hospital uncovered a seemingly unrelated event, a missing patient from a different ward."

"When we learned that the missing patient had left his clothes, we were able to identify him as Harry Wilton, a construction worker for ABC Construction, engaged in the building of the new bus station."

Ron took the storyline again, "We went to Wilton's home and found it had been searched. We decided that most likely Wilton and the naked man were connected, and our next step was to seek an identity for the other man at ABC Construction."

"In the meantime, one of the nurses at New City notified Dr. Bolling that two men had been walking the halls at New City, asking personnel about their 'friend', the dead man. She provided us with sketches of these men, and we took those sketches and a morgue photograph of the dead man to the construction site. We canvassed many of the hard hat workers without success but finally found a supervisor, Morgan Riley, who identified our dead man as Thomas Pritchard."

Thor sat up a little straighter and said, "Huh."

"Yes, sir. That's the same Morgan Riley who later was killed at the construction site," Ron noted.

Gene picked up at that point, "Thomas Pritchard was an accountant for ABC who never went on the construction site. That's why no one out there knew him. Apparently, Riley had met him during some approval process. His work site was in a double-wide trailer on the other side of the site. We talked with his manager and co-workers and found nothing at his desk, so we went to his house. And found someone had preceded us who searched the premises and took Pritchard's laptop computer."

Ron wanted to explain the next set of events and said, "We discovered that Pritchard had a girlfriend, and she had left messages on his phone indicating she was out of town but returning soon. I changed his message and asked her to call me. When she did, I made an appointment for her to come to the station for an interview."

Thor sat back in his chair and said, "Huh."

Ron did not address Thor's comment and instead said, "Gail Hunicutt, Pritchard's girlfriend was not immediately helpful but did tell us that Pritchard had been distracted, in her words, recently. She said he repeated that he would 'never cover for anyone again'. She couldn't explain what that meant."

"So, we went back to the ABC trailer and re-interviewed Pritchard's co-workers. One of them mentioned that Pritchard had been asked to 'cover' for someone in Contracting a few months back while this person had a baby. I asked Gene to look into this person's computer; everyone had gone home by then." Ron leaned back in his chair and nodded at Gene.

Gene sat forward and explained, "Earlier, we had found a twelve-digit number on a sticky on Pritchard's desk, and that turned out to be the password to open the Contracting computer. I found the files of recently opened materials and searched on the dates that Pritchard was 'covering' for the pregnancy. I identified several files from ABC and several files he had downloaded from the Internet and was copying them to a flash drive to bring back to the office when a bomb went off."

Tom Bolling did not know about this part of the story. He reacted by almost spilling the last of his coffee. "What's that?" he asked.

Ron held up his hands and said, "It was a little bomb, Tom. It went off in the construction area, and Gene and I ran over there, going around the block to get there. As we ran, we heard shots but when we arrived there was no one there. We searched the area and found a shooter platform, a sniper nest, blown up by C-4. It killed the sniper.

We turned the site over to the crime scene folks; they found another sniper nest also booby-trapped with C-4. They also determined there were four people in the site, two snipers and two other men at ground level who ran and exited the construction site through a hole in the barrier fence."

Ron paused at that point, and everyone sat back in their chair and sipped on their coffee. He said, "We considered closing the site, but the politics were against us." Thor said nothing.

Gene said, "And, the following Monday, Morgan Riley 'fell' from the old clock tower and was killed. There was no reason for him to be up there." Again, this statement was followed by several moments of silence.

Ron said, "Two days later, I received a note delivered by bike messenger from Harry Wilton. He said that he arranged for the booby-trap and was there to get a blackmail payoff from City Councilman Anton Greene. He said the snipers were Greene's men and that Greene killed Riley in retaliation. He said that the Councilman was dirty, and he had proof."

Tom asked, "Did he say anything about killing Pritchard at New City?"

"Nope. The note was light on specifics but definitely turned us on to the trail of Councilman Greene."

Gene explained, "We had all the data in the files I pulled off the Contracting computer, but we didn't understand them at first. The Captain and Ron and I poured over the files for hours …"

Ron interrupted, "Until some smart-aleck pulled additional data off the Internet and discovered what the blackmailers had discovered."

Gene jumped back in, "Apparently, several years ago, Green created a dummy company, J.Y. Dahgs, incorporated in the names of his wife, his son, and a dirty lawyer. Then he brought pressure to bear on the owners of ABC Construction to skim off some small sums from city contracts and pay them to Dahgs. It looks like he contracted with one of the office support systems to send a monthly invoice to ABC from Dahgs for 'waste removal' as the explanation for regular payment. A couple of years after this process began, the lawyer retired to Florida; he's still getting his cut."

"Huh," said Thor setting his cup down on the desk.

"Right," Ron noted. "This was all hidden in plain sight because the incorporation papers for Dahgs used the wife's maiden name. When Gene dug that information out of the Internet, we had the picture, plain and simple."

"The chairman of the city council confirmed that Greene had been lobbying, softly but effectively, for ABC to get city construction contracts, and that convinced Judge Satler to give us wiretap authority on all of the Councilman's telephones."

"With those wiretaps in place, we heard the Councilman make plans to kill Wilton. We were able to disrupt those plans and capture the remaining sniper, but he refused to cooperate."

Ron picked things up, "So, we questioned Mr. Greene and caught him in several lies, including that the sniper was acting rogue and not under his orders. That taped conversation was enough to tip the sniper into confessing that Greene had ordered him to kill Riley."

Tom was nodding at all this but asked, "And the blackmail?"

"Well, you might think Wilton lost out on all that with blowing up the sniper," Gene said. "But not so. Somehow he convinced Greene to send $1 million via overnight mail to a post office in Las Vegas. He knew the tracking number and re-routed the package, first to Seattle and then back to Cincinnati. He got the money, and Greene got nada for it."

Tom persisted, "But you have Wilton in custody now, right?"

Gene nodded and explained, "When he disappeared from the attempt on his life, we had no idea where he went. But my partner noted that the son also did not go back to school. That made him think the two were meeting up somewhere, so he went looking for family connections. He pulled Wilton's entry application for the Navy and found he came from eastern North Dakota, and we were able to find a sister who still lives there, in Grand Forks."

Ron said, "Sure enough, we found the sister and the brother-in-law, and they were hosting the runaways. Smooth arrest, no running or fighting, and Gene found the money in the trunk of Wilton's car."

"Another day, and he would have been gone," Gene added.

"Huh."

"So, the bottom line is, we have the man who murdered someone in your hospital, and there's no connection to your operation in any way," Ron recognized Tom's major interest in the outcome.

Gene added, "And we have the sniper, Nestor Aramano, on charges of murder for hire and attempted murder and the Councilman for murder for hire and fraud."

Tom put his cup down on the Captain's desk and stood. "Thank you, Captain, for allowing me to hear this story to its fullest. I've been worried since we found that body that something was going to snap back on me and the hospital."

"Huh."

"And," he said, turning to the detectives, "thanks to both of you for clearing things up so quickly." He stuck out his hand, and they shook. "And, I have to say, it's no wonder you want to get up to New City as often as you do." They looked at him, puzzled.

"Well, if this is the coffee you have to drink around here, it's clear why you prefer Nick's."

As they both nodded, Thor stood and said, "Nick?"

"The barista at New City, Captain. Come over sometime, and I'll treat you to some marvelous Italian coffee. These guys are there so often, Nick has a 'usual' for them."

"Huh."

Other Books by G.L. Barbour

Fiction

Ron Looney Mystery Series

Death Unexpected

One, Two, Three Times a Murder

A Twisted Death

A Researched Death

Alibi for Death

Montana in the Rearview Mirror

Non-Fiction

Redefining a Public Health System

Quality in the Veterans Health Administration

"Acknowledgements"

I want to thank my wife and children for their encouragement during this writing process. Their feedback, support, and encouragement were positive factors in me finishing the original manuscript.

I also want to recognize Elle Murray for her faithful and frequent efforts to clean up the manuscript and to assist me in getting to the right place in decisions about format, artistry, and pagination.

Any errors that escaped these screening activities are mine alone.

Galen Barbour

Alexandria, Virginia

January 2023

Interested in another G.L. Barbour
Medical Murder Mystery?

When a major medical researcher is found murdered in a locked building, the arrest of the only other person in the building seems straight-forward to most people - but not to Tom Bolling, chief of Staff of the building in question. He puts his reputation on the line for Ron Looney to discover the truth about the locked building. That turns out to be the easiest part of the murder investigation for Ron.

Excerpt

Hector Richmond was a happy man. His wife had packed him a wonderful meal for his midnight lunch break. Her meatloaf sandwich on Italian bread with mayonnaise and onion was all a man could hope for - well, after a strong cup of coffee and a smoke, anyway. Hector's meal break came at eleven pm, a third of the way through his twelve-hour shift as a night watchman at the Railway Building. Hector intended to save the apple turnover and the Butterfinger candy bar to snack on later. He had another break in the early hours of the morning; but he couldn't wait to get at the meatloaf sandwich, his mouth began watering before he had it unwrapped.

Hector had been doing the night watchman shift at the Railway Building in Cincinnati for more than a year. He knew every hallway and office owner in the building like the proverbial back of his hand. And he knew his 'rounds' of the building well enough to complete them blindfolded, as he liked to say. Hector clock in time was seven PM on the weekends; he chose the weekends because of the extra pay, although the work was the same as during the week. Weekend nighttime watch tours meant an empty building most of the time. This night, however, he was scheduled for Thursday night in a swap he made so Andy could spend the weekend in Cleveland celebrating his daughter's marriage. The schedule change meant little to Hector; the job requirements were the same every night of the week. He would patrol the five stories of South Railway, clocking in once on every floor and then doing it again and again. His simple responsibilities were to assure that the unoccupied offices and labs were locked and that anyone working late had protection.

Hector had often told his wife he didn't know what he was protecting anyone from since the access to the building was tightly controlled with keycards restricted to physicians working in the adjacent New City Hospital. At least that was true for the south end of the building where he patrolled. The north end held professional offices and medically related activities such as the dialysis unit of New City. The north end was not his responsibility, though.

Hector finished the sandwich and got up for his post-meal walk. When he resumed his seat in the small break room on the third floor, he poured a second cup of coffee from the thermos, and checked his watch. Eleven-twenty; he had another twenty minutes on this break. Hector reached into his bag and pulled out the Zane Grey novel he was currently reading. He leaned up against the wall and found the dog-eared page where he had ended last time. He began reading, moving his lips just a little with the words as he enjoyed the mental picture of the western United States decades earlier. Hector wanted to visit those areas someday. A nice vacation for him and his wife. He liked thinking about that.

At eleven-forty-five, Hector picked up his book, carefully turning down the corner of a page to mark his progress. He packed the paperback and the remainder of his lunch in his carryall bag and put the apple turnover on top where he could easily find it at the next break. He stood and stretched then carried his bag over to the small counter and put it in the corner. Then he adjusted his belt and headed for the toilet. Minutes later, he was on his way to the elevator bank to start his next round of patrolling. In the elevator, he hit the button for the fifth floor, and cracked his knuckles as the elevator silently and smoothly rose to the top of the building.

He was on the fourth floor checking that doors were locked and secure when his Motorola two-way radio came on with a buzzing sound and one of the hospital guard's voice said, "Hector, this is Jack. Come in."

Hector pushed the response button. "Hey, Jack. This is Hector. What's up?"

"Everything all right over there?"

"Man, the building is sound asleep. Why?"

"I just got a call from Mrs. Abbate. The cancer doctor's wife."

"Yeah?" Hector remembered Dr. Abbate's office on the third floor.

"She says he's late coming home."

Hector nodded. "Well, I know he's been here. I saw him in his office right after I got here and the light was still on last time I went by there."

"She wants him to call her. She says he's not answering his phone, office, or mobile." Jack said, with a little tinge of annoyance in his voice.

"Yeah, that's odd. I'll go check. That's down one. I'll find him and tell him to call her."

"Okay. Thanks, man. Over."

"Roger. Over." Hector took his finger off the response button and shook his head.

Hector went back to the elevator bank and summoned a car. He didn't use the stairs even on his rounds because of pain in his knees. Besides, there weren't any doors on the stairwells to check. He went down one floor and headed in the direction of Dr. Abbate's office. Hector knew that the doctor spent Thursday evenings in his office almost every week doing something. On the other times Hector had worked a Thursday night Abbate was usually finished and gone by the time Hector started his rounds after his first break, though, so this call was definitely different.

He found the office door locked, as it had been earlier. Through the glass portion, he could see the doctor's desk, well lit by a small LED lamp. Hector could not see the doctor in the room. He knocked on the door and got no response. Knocking more loudly was no better. Hector pulled out his master key ring and unlocked the door. He opened it and called into the room, "Doctor, are you in here?" He waited for a response.

There was no answer. Hector decided to look around and entered the room, and walked toward the desk, again calling out, "Hey doc, are you here?" As he approached the desk, he saw the doctor, lying on the floor behind the desk, screened from view by a low credenza at the right end of the desk. Abbate was sprawled on the floor on his back; his head turned to the left and bathed in blood and gore. His sightless eyes stared off into the distance. Hector stood transfixed for several seconds before he was able to react. He had never seen a dead person before, let alone one that had been killed like that. For a few moments he felt numb, then he noticed his legs were trembling and he had forgotten to breathe.

Hector took several deep breaths and swallowed the bile rising in his throat, willing himself not to vomit. He recognized the area as a crime scene and carefully retraced his steps back to the doorway. He pulled out his two-way and engaged it, saying, "Jack. Jack, We gotta call the cops."

Jack came on immediately, "What's that, Hector?"

"He's dead, Jack. Call the cops."

"Are you sure, Hector?" Jack said, with a trace of doubt in his voice.

"Oh man, I am very sure. Somebody beat him to death."

"Hold on. You mean somebody killed Dr. Abbate?"

"He sure didn't do this to himself, Jack. Call the cops."

"Okay. Gotcha. Are you all right?"

"Hell, no, Jack. I'm about to puke. Get the cops."

"Right. I gotta call the Director and then …"

Hector yelled into his two-way, "Call the cops right now! Over." He jerked his finger off the talk button and stood frozen in place for a few seconds. He dropped his two-way trying to reattach it to his belt. He leaned against the doorframe and slowly sank to a sitting position in the doorway still willing himself not to vomit. That's where he was when the other security officers and police found him when they arrived at the Railway building twenty minutes later.